MY BIG FAT FABULOUS FLING

Eight concerts. Eight cities. Eight chances to fall in love with a man I'm supposed to hate.

LYNDSEY GALLAGHER

PROLOGUE

Jayden

Nine years earlier...

Desolate sleeping bodies lie strewn across the floor. The stench of stale sweat and desperation lingers in the air, stains my hair and permanently resides in my nostrils. The homeless shelter is nothing more than a run-down local community hall with draughty single-glazed windows but it's a shell over our heads, for the night at least.

My brother, Ryan, dozes at my feet. We take turns at keeping watch. The shelters can be every bit as rough as the harsh, dark streets of LA.

A fight breaks out somewhere along the corridor and the increased pounding of my own ragged heartbeat reverberates through my skull.

Fighting's common around here. People fight over nothing. They're frustrated. Angry at the world, with nothing to lose, bar the shabby clothes on their backs.

Sofia stirs, adjusting her cheek which rests awkwardly on my shoulder. She's the reason we've made it this far. She might be small, but she's savvier than Ryan and I ever were. She had to be to make it across the border from Mexico.

Her olive skin is flawless, apart from the dark circles beneath her enormous oval eyes. Long, jet black hair's secured in a loose ponytail which extends halfway down her back.

Homeless or not, there's no denying her beauty.

We met a few months ago, bonding instantly through similar forlorn circumstances. Sofia has a teenage sibling she's determined to keep safe, too. No mean feat while trying to claw our way from the streets to a better life. And Lula doesn't make it easy on her, rebelling at every opportunity.

They fled here from horror. We fled here in hope. Although, so far, we haven't found a sliver of it. Ryan busks the sidewalks daily, hoping one day someone will spot his talent, offer him a gig, and us a way out of here.

The nights Sofia and I end up in the same shelter are a small solace in my otherwise dismal existence. To escape reality in my darker moments, I imagine a different life. One where we'd have met in happier circumstances. I'd have asked her out. She'd have said yes. We'd have gone for dinner and drinks. I'd have kissed her.

It wasn't that long ago I actually had a life that would have rendered that a real possibility. And I will again, no matter what it takes.

Sofia's huge chocolate eyes flick open at the noisy commotion down the hall.

'Is Lula back yet?' Sofia's sister has a habit of going AWOL, determined to run in the wrong circles.

I shake my head, clicking my stiff neck. I didn't want to budge even a millimetre in case I disturbed what little rest she might get.

A deep wheeze rattles through Sofia's frail ribcage. The coughing starts again. She's always coughing.

She's sicker than she looks. Some sort of rare genetic condition. With no money and no medical aid, the odds of her making her twenty-fifth birthday are slim. It doesn't stop me praying for a miracle, spending every waking moment thinking of ways to save her.

I pass over the litre bottle of water I bought with the change Ryan came back with earlier.

When the coughing finally subsides, Sofia takes a sip and passes it back with a grateful smile. It doesn't reach her doe-like eyes. Taking my huge hand in her tiny one, she squeezes with an earnest expression.

Spending weeks on the streets has a way of making you feel invisible. Most people walk past, averting their eyes. They don't want to see the horrifying reality of it. So in contrast, the intensity of Sofia's stare makes my insides flip.

'Jayden, I need you to make a promise to me.' Cold fingers trace the back of my hand. 'If you ever escape this life, please drag my sister with you.' Instinctively, I pull her into my chest, wrapping my arms around her thin frame. 'Of course. And you'll come too...'

She swallows thickly.

We both know her poor health means that's unlikely.

'Take care of her, if I'm not around.' Her words are choked with sorrow. 'All I ever wanted was to get her out of there. To give her a chance in life.'

'I promise you, Sofia. No matter what happens, I will take care of your sister.'

Chapter One

CHLOE

Liberated is my middle name. Well, almost. Technically, it's Liberty, but you get the gist. My slightly bohemian, feminist mother picked it in the hope I'd courageously blaze a trail through the limited ideals imposed on women by society.

When it comes to business, I'm confident I've surpassed expectations. Hers, not mine. I'm just not sure she'd approve of the way I pursue my personal preferences.

I'm the queen of one-night stands, but believe me when I say the crown is heavy. Sex with strangers is rarely sublime. The satisfaction is minimal, but then again, so is the risk of getting hurt.

Is there something dead inside of me? It's almost as if, when my parents died, a piece of me died too. The piece that falls in love like normal people. I thought I was in love with Ethan, but when he left, my pride was more wounded than my heart.

Prising open my sleep-filled eyes, I'm met with two eager, espresso-coloured ones.

'Good morning, gorgeous.' Tanned, thick fingers sweep across the underside of my jaw. I've suffered through enough romcoms with my sisters to realise it's supposed to be sexy. To me, it's suffocating.

Mark is gorgeous and kind, the same as every other guy I've been with. I just don't feel anything for him past the physical.

'Morning.' Slipping from between the crisp cotton sheets, I stride naked and shameless towards my en-suite bathroom. With hazy flashbacks of last night's alcohol-fuelled activities replaying like a slideshow through my brain, there's zero point being shy now.

Mark's company is one of the primary sponsors for a Formula One event my company organised. I shouldn't have slept with him last night.

I blame the cocktails.

I need him to leave immediately so I can get back to my perfectly neat, regimented life.

I don't do repeats.

Dinner, drinks, parties, fun? Absolutely. Anything more than that is a resounding no.

'Chloe, what's the rush? I thought perhaps we could...'

The en-suite door clicks behind me and I breathe a sigh of relief. Sex is one thing, but sharing a bed with someone you barely know is a whole different level of intimacy. One I usually avoid.

I step beneath cool cascading water and lather coconut shampoo through my thick chestnut hair, mentally running through the day ahead.

Launching a startlingly successful business at such a young age might be immensely rewarding, but staying in Dubai for more than three years was never part of my plan.

I may have carved out a luxurious life for myself, but there's something missing, a hollowness in my chest that no amount of success has been able to plug.

Maybe I need to take Liberty Events Management to a

global level. A second branch in another country. Perhaps that will give me the internal validation I'm searching for, if that's what it even is. I try not to question it too much because even if I could somehow magic up the answer, I'm not sure I'm ready to hear it.

Fifteen glorious shower-soaked minutes later, I wedge a towel round my tanned torso and step back into the bedroom.

The bright morning sun blazes through the open balcony doors overlooking a glistening turquoise sea as it crashes against Jumeirah Beach, mere metres away.

October to May boast perfect balmy days in Dubai. After that, the humidity becomes insufferable. I'm Irish. I'm not designed for that level of heat.

Mark is thankfully dressed, wearing last night's suit, which is slightly crumpled from where it lay discarded on the floor. His eyes rake from my head to my toes as he exhales a long, low wolf whistle.

'Give over, will you.' I shake my head and jovially throw a pillow at him.

His eyes twinkle. 'Can't blame a man for trying.'

I fling open my walk-in wardrobe and grab the first outfit my fingers find, a high-necked yellow pencil dress with elbow-length sleeves. It's one thing to occasionally break Dubai's decency laws in the privacy of my own villa, but I'd be a fool not to respect them in public. I'm not going to risk a spell in a Middle Eastern jail, no matter how draconian their laws.

'Do you want me to call you a cab, Mark?'

His hand streaks across his chest as though he's been shot. 'Ouch. My heart bleeds.'

My eyes roll skywards. 'Come on, you knew what you were signing up for. Don't go all soft on me now.'

'I wouldn't say I'm soft exactly.' He crosses the room, his

hand brushing against my naked shoulder with a lascivious smile.

I gently brush him off and grab a pastel pink lace bra and matching thong from my top drawer. Everything has to coordinate. It's one of my many quirks. 'Mark! Seriously, we had fun. That's it. Now go, before you miss your flight.'

'Perhaps next time I'm in town we could...' Hope glints from beneath those huge puppy dog eyes.

'Mark.' An unmistakable warning piques my tone.

His hands fly up in reluctant acceptance. 'Ok, ok. You don't do repeats. I remember.'

With a palm lightly between his shoulder blades, I usher him out of my bedroom towards the stairs. 'I had a great night, Mark. Thank you.'

It's a kind, white lie.

I've yet to meet my sexual soulmate. Last night was as average as every other encounter I've had over the previous years. And I'm pretty sure that has nothing to do with Mark, and everything to do with me.

As he lingers by the heavy front door, he shoots me one last smile weighted with regret.

'Safe flying, Mark. Take care.'

It's barely nine o'clock and I'm emotionally drained. If a one-night stand can do this to me, how would I cope with an actual relationship?

I have no idea how my sister, Sasha, does it. I never imagined she'd be the type to settle down, but since she's been with Ryan, she's been positively glowing.

I take a croissant and a Nespresso onto the balcony to FaceTime her. I miss her so much my chest physically aches. There's less than a year between us and our bond is as strong as identical twins.

I hate being so far away from her, but it couldn't be

helped. I had to get away from Huxley Castle, our family's stately home, before the walls closed in on me permanently.

With the time difference, it's still ridiculously early in Dublin. Sasha hates my wake-up calls, but it's too tempting not to see her stunning, sunny face. Besides, someone has to rouse her, if her rock star fiancé hasn't beaten me to it.

Gross.

It's one thing knowing your sister's having mind-blowing sex with America's hottest rock star, and entirely another to get a first-hand glimpse of it, no matter how close we are.

With the warmth of the morning sun on my face, I sink into a cushioned chair and tap Sasha's name on my iPhone while soaking up the surrounding scenery. A foliage of greenery spans decoratively across my terracotta terrace, a poor replacement for the lush emerald rolling landscape of home.

Sasha answers on the first ring. Her grinning face fills my screen.

'You're up early this morning.' My eyebrows arch in an unspoken question.

'Not as early as my fiancé.' Her accompanying wink leaves nothing to the imagination. Behind her, the familiar living area comes into view. Majestic navy curtains are still drawn, blocking out the dark Dublin morning.

I might miss my sister, but I don't miss the weather.

'At least someone round here is satisfied.'

'The desert still running dry over there?' Sasha's cherry-coloured lips form into a sympathetic pout.

A sip of black coffee burns the back of my throat as I conjure up the appropriate words to describe my current sorry state of affairs. 'I wouldn't say dry exactly. It's just almost impossible to fully satiate a woman, if you know what I mean.'

'Say no more.' Sasha's splayed fingers make a poor attempt to cover her eyes. 'You know, sis, I worry about you.'

'Me? Why on earth would you be worried about me?'

Slim, dainty fingers slip from her eyes and her engagement ring glitters brightly enough to be spotted from space. 'Having a bit of fun when you're in your twenties is all well and good, but even though you're going through the motions, you don't seem to be having much actual fun.'

She's uncannily right. Sporadic nights with strangers are becoming less entertaining with each passing year, but how do I rectify that without lowering my carefully constructed guard?

'Don't worry about me, Sash. You have enough on your plate. I'm great, honestly. Everything is fine.'

She swallows hard. 'I love you, that's all. I'd like to see you happy.'

'I love you too, sis. But your idea of happy and mine just look a bit different, you know?'

Am I trying to convince her? Or myself?

My fingers automatically ping the ever-present elastic band on my wrist, a tip from a therapist after my parents died. I didn't finish my counselling sessions, but I never stopped using the technique. Anytime I feel stressed, I ping it against my flesh. Supposedly, it trains the brain to avoid stressful thoughts.

Manic days at work pass and I forget it's there, but the second a conversation becomes too personal, I start snapping like twigs under winter boots.

'So where is Ryan-Rockstar-Cooper this morning?' The quickest way to divert the subject away from me is to ask about my future brother-in-law. It sends my normally sensible sister gooey-eyed.

Their wedding's booked for the end of the year, and despite my own romantic reservations, I can't wait to watch my sister marry the only man she's ever loved. Her happiness ebbs through our freaky, sisterly bond, flooding me with joy.

'He's gone for a run to clear his head. We're in the final negotiations of his farewell tour with his record label, Diamond Records.'

'How's that going?' Ryan's plans to hang up his stage microphone to focus on writing and producing albums have sent half the world tizzy. Contractually, he's obliged to do at least one more tour, but since he's fallen head over heels in love with my sister, he's been doing his utmost to get out of it.

Madness, if you ask me. If I were Sasha, I wouldn't hesitate to go on tour with him. Huxley Castle's manager, Megan, is more than capable of running the place, and with our youngest sister, Victoria, heading off to college later this year, there's nothing holding her back.

Apart from the fact she's a massively unapologetic homebird, the polar opposite to me.

Sasha pulls her dressing gown tighter around her lithe frame, familiar bottle-green eyes glinting with a hint of devilment. 'Actually, I wanted to talk to you about that.'

'The tour? You want me to mind Victoria?' She's months away from turning eighteen, but with very different upbringings, she's lacking in the maturity we had at her age.

'Actually, I was wondering if Liberty Events would be interested in organising the tour?'

I almost choke on smooth, rich coffee as it splutters down my throat.

'Me? You want me to do it?'

Ryan's farewell tour is already set to be one of the most anticipated music events of all time. His departure from the industry, as a performer at least, will be devoured and dissected by the entire world.

Every woman in the world would likely sell their soul for a

ticket to one of these exclusive gigs. Money won't buy one. They'll be snapped up by celebrities and high-flying billionaires, desperate to say they were a part of musical history.

My company organises conferences, horse racing events, music festivals, charity galas, exclusive celebrity parties and once even a Lebanese royal wedding, plus facilitating regular Formula One after-parties. (Let's hope next season they have a different sponsor.)

I'm exceptionally good at what I do. The extensive array of business awards lining the walls of my open plan office overlooking the city's skyscrapers are testament to it.

But is it enough to qualify me to take on something of this size and magnitude?

'Yes, you. Who else would we trust with such a monumental task? If it's left to the record label, god only knows who they'd subcontract to. We'd both rather it was someone with a proven track record of class. Someone who's familiar with Ryan's style.' Sasha flicks her hair from her shoulder as she waits for my shock to subside. 'You mentioned at Christmas you were thinking of expanding out of the Middle East.'

'I did, didn't I?'

Managing an event, or a consecutive string of events like these, I should say, would undoubtably propel my company to the next level. A global level.

Everyone who's anyone will be watching. It's an opportunity to branch out from a country where my hands are bound by laws that no feminist could endure long term, no matter how much luxury she has access to.

I'll never get another chance like it.

I can't turn it down.

I don't want to turn it down, even if I'm nervous about what could potentially go wrong with half the world watching.

'I'll do it.' I send up a silent prayer I'm physically able. There's no doubt I'm going to need help, though. A lot of help. Events of this scale have a lot of potential to go wrong. And even though I'm a huge music fan, I don't have much experience of the industry.

Sasha claps her hands and squeals in delight. 'Fantastic. Thank you so much!'

'No, thank you.' We both know it'll be a game changer.

'Obviously you'll have to attend each concert, reap the rewards of your hard work, and oversee it personally. Which means you and I will get to spend more time together than we have in years.'

My heart soars. Time with my gorgeous, sweet, sunny sister that doesn't involve a heart-wrenching trip back to Ireland. Sign. Me. Up.

'There's just one tiny detail Ryan is insisting on.'

'What?' I knew it sounded too good to be true.

'You have to collaborate with Jayden. As Ryan's agent, he'll be equally involved in the organisation of the event. He has all the inside knowledge.'

'That smug-faced twat? You've got to be joking me.' Not only is he Ryan's agent, Jayden's also his older brother. And a top-notch dickhead. Conceited, arrogant and infuriatingly attractive, and my god does he know it.

If he were a bar of chocolate, he'd devour himself whole.

'I'm deadly serious. Play nicely now. When Ryan and I get married, you'll be related.'

'Ugh, don't remind me.'

'He might be a little arrogant...'

'A little? Who are you kidding?'

Sasha clears her throat with her big sisterly air of authority. 'He might be a little arrogant, but he's the best agent in Hollywood. He knows his stuff. The two of you combined are going to make a formidable team.'

I huff like a teenager. 'Fine.'

'Just don't fall into bed with him.' Sasha pokes her tongue out at me in jest. 'Turns out he's even more emotionally unavailable than you.'

She's certainly changed her tune. At Christmas she was all "Ryan's got a brother."

Finally, she must see him for the obnoxious, self-righteous prick that he is.

'Dubai will freeze over before that happens. Apart from the fact I can't stand the sight of the man, I'm a professional, I'll have you know.'

An image of Mark in my bed a mere twenty minutes earlier pops into my brain.

But that was different. Mark's a decent human being. Nice. Too nice for me.

Jayden Cooper is a different animal altogether.

Chapter Two

JAYDEN

'I can't work with her. The woman has a silver spoon stuck so far up her ass she'd need twelve hours of extensive surgery to have it removed.' The luxury of my own surroundings isn't lost on me. An enormous triple-height kitchen. Elaborate marble flooring. Enormous windows overlooking my own private pool, glistening under the moonlight.

The difference is, I wasn't born with a silver spoon up *my* ass. I worked damned hard to ram it there. And despite my opulent lifestyle, I like to think I'm still me. Still grounded.

I drive a Ferrari. I live in a mansion on Santa Monica Boulevard. I'm the highest paid agent for the most ruthless record label in LA, but I know where I came from. It's etched into every cell of my DNA. My father's rotting in an Irish prison cell, for fuck's sake.

Definitely no silver spoon here.

My brother's heavy sigh resounds through the receiver from across the miles. I balance my phone between my ear and shoulder, open the American-style fridge and help myself to an ice-cold Budweiser.

'She's about to become my sister-in-law,' Ryan reminds me.

As if I could forget.

Ryan's upcoming marriage will turn my jet black hair grey before my thirtieth birthday and it has nothing to do with the lavish nuptial exchange that half the world is desperate to witness and everything to do with the fact he's desperate to re-negotiate his contract with Diamond Records to spend every waking moment with Sasha Sexton.

She's hot. I get it. They're in love. Even I can see that. But is any relationship worth giving up everything you ever worked for? Not in my book. I've learnt the hard way that one way or another, they never last.

Still, I suppose if it doesn't work out, Ryan will be able to revive his career in a heartbeat. America has never seen a more successful rock star than my kid brother. The world is obsessed with him. And now they're obsessed with Sasha, too.

'Does Chloe even have any experience with this type of thing? This tour has to be mind-blowing. Mon-u-fucking-mental. You only have eight concerts. Eight cities. It has to blow everything that ever occurred before it out of the water and into oblivion, I tell my brother.

It took a huge effort to get the record label to release him from the previously agreed world tours. They only bent when Ryan offered to continue writing and recording for them exclusively, which he can do from anywhere in the world.

Why he'd want to return to our cold, dreary homeland permanently is beyond me. Trust my little brother to propose to the only woman in the world who won't drop everything to be with him here in Hollywood.

'Chloe is the CEO of her own events marketing company, Jay. She's really talented.'

'And what exactly does she do, by the way? Organise tea

parties for ladies who lunch while their ex-pat husbands strut around the golf course talking shit?' I pop the lid from the bottle and take a huge glug of beer, revelling in the way it fizzes down my throat.

'She has a contract with Formula One. She organised one of the Sheik's weddings, for crying out loud. She's twenty-seven years old and she's already created one of the most successful events management businesses in Dubai.'

Thankfully, this isn't a video call because my eyebrows shoot skywards. The Formula One gig is pretty impressive, to be fair.

'She has the experience,' Ryan continues. 'She just doesn't have much experience with the music industry.'

'Which is precisely my point.' The marble flooring's cool beneath my feet as I strut across the open plan area and crash on one of three grey suede couches in the spacious sunroom. A myriad of stars glint in the navy night sky through the slanted roof composed entirely of glass.

'Look, she's hoping to expand. To branch out of the Middle East. This will give her the foot up she needs.'

'It's more than a foot up, Ryan. You know it and I know it. Having her name associated with this tour will set her up for life.'

'Why are you resisting this so much?' Frustration tinges his every word. 'Is this because she knocked you back at Christmas?'

My scoff lodges in my throat. 'No one knocked me back at Christmas.'

'Oh, come on. I saw the way you were looking at her. Which isn't a good idea, by the way, given the circumstances.'

'I was just winding her up. She's so uptight. Watching her pretty little face get all riled was too entertaining ...'

Ryan tuts. The subject of his future sister-in-law organising arguably the biggest tour of his career is clearly not up for negotiation.

'Look, Chloe's family, ok?' A distinct firmness resides in his tone.

Family has always been important to me, blood relations or not, even if I couldn't always do the right thing by them.

'Jayden.' He says my name like it's a question, but he's not asking me. He's telling me. He's the rock star. I'm his agent. I might be the older brother, but I can't pull rank here.

'Fine. But I'm not holding her hand the whole fucking time. She'll have to work as hard as the rest of us.'

'If Christmas was anything to go by, I don't think you need to worry about holding her hand.'

'Hmm.' I have no choice but to accept my fate.

'You know you love a challenge, Jayden. Working with one of the few women on this planet who's immune to your charms is precisely that.'

'No one is immune to my charms, Ryan.'

'Prove it. Work with her. For Christ's sake, Dad's responsible for the death of her parents. If she can work around that, the two of you should be able to work around anything. I'm not asking you to bed the woman for god's sake, just cooperate with her. Try to support her.'

Ryan and I have a complicated interlinked history with the Sexton sisters. It's not for the faint-hearted. Courtesy of some super tight NDA's with everyone involved in Dad's case, the media haven't got wind that it was our father behind the wheel of the car which ran Mr and Mrs Sexton off the road all those years ago yet, but I don't doubt they will one day.

Bedding Chloe would be a challenge, no matter what I said to Ryan, because she genuinely seems immune to me. Or if she isn't, she does a damn good job of hiding it. Although they say there's a fine line between hate and love.

Admittedly, Chloe is stunning, but her edges are as sharp

as her tongue. Definitely not my type. I prefer less complicated women. Models or actresses. Even if they do bore me
after a few weeks.

'I'll set up a Zoom meeting for tomorrow and we can
throw some ideas around, but you should probably get
together in person for a few days to hash out the theme and
the logistics of everything. The first gig's only eight weeks
away. I want this tour over with.'

No fucking shit, Sherlock.

'Anyway, it'll be no harm to spend some time together.
After all, you guys are going to be family soon.'

Don't remind me.

The following afternoon I'm lazing on a poolside lounger
with my MacBook on my lap while Kim, my feisty no-
nonsense PA, works in my home office. Kim's been with me
for years. With a quick, dry wit and bigger balls than most
men, she's easy to be around.

Colton, my silent and brooding security detail, is the total
opposite. If he has a sense of humour, he's yet to find it
beneath his bleach blond shaggy locks.

Busying himself installing a new elaborate home security
system, he's barely said two words today. Thankfully, he's not
here for his personality. Like the twelve cameras surrounding
my property, he's a necessary evil when your brother's a rock
star.

Is it any wonder I prefer backstage to centre stage?
Where Ryan was created specifically to shine under the harsh
glare of the limelight, and to be devoted to one woman, I was
created for drinking whiskey in dark bars with scores of
women. Sadly, the media didn't get the memo and have plastered us both over every tabloid at any opportunity.

Kim stalks out of the house, hopping onto each decorative but impractical stepping stone that lines the pathway from the house to the pool.

'Declan's on his way over,' she says, biting her lower lip in an unusually serious fashion.

'What's up with him?'

Declan's one of the few childhood friends I kept in touch with. He moved to LA from Ireland five years ago, setting up a top secret, but highly lucrative business for celebrities and high-fliers, who pay him huge amounts of money to find something, and even more when they want something hidden. Declan's methods aren't always legitimate, but he always gets the job done.

Wisps of her blonde shoulder length hair catch in the light breeze, whipping across Kim's lips. 'He finally found her.'

She doesn't need to say who. The solemnity of her tone tells me everything I need to know. I've been searching for Lula Flores for almost nine years. For nine long years she's managed to stay out of every system Declan's capable of hacking.

My throat tightens. I lurch forward, placing my laptop down beside me. 'Is she alive?'

Kim nods curtly. 'She was working illegally in a Mexican restaurant when the place got raided. She needs a place to stay and a visa ASAP. She was close to being deported before Declan intervened.'

I swallow the lump in my throat.

'Is he bringing her here now?'

Kim nods again. 'They'll be here in just over an hour.'

'Will you ask Sara to make up the guest room?' Sara Garcia used to be Ryan's housekeeper. When he moved back to Huxley Castle, I snapped her up. Sara's loyal, discreet, and she makes the best steak sandwiches this side of the Atlantic.

'Sure.' Kim squints at her watch. 'Don't forget you've got

that Zoom meeting with Ryan and the Sexton sister in ten minutes.'

My eyes roll skywards. 'Don't remind me.'

Today is shaping up to be one hell of a day.

I text my best friend, Gareth, to cancel tonight's drinks. We meet most Thursdays to shoot the shit and, more often than not, pick up women. Tonight, though, I've got more important matters on my mind.

A million questions for Lula buzz through my brain. They'll have to wait.

I have a date with the ice queen and her silver spoon.

I log on and wait for my brother to let me in from the waiting room. When he does, an image of Chloe Sexton's glowing face appears on my screen. My chest involuntarily tightens.

Light freckles adorn classic high cheekbones, dazzling cyan eyes pop against her sun-kissed skin. Thick chestnut hair, which was so gorgeously free-falling at Christmas, is twisted into some sort of elaborate knot on top of her head, bar a few loose tendrils framing her heart-shaped face.

The top half of her dress visibly clings to her womanly frame without revealing a millimetre of skin. She's as stunning as ever. It's just a shame she's a complete and utter pain in my ass.

My brother's grinning face takes up the other side of the screen. 'Hi guys. How are you both?'

'Fine.' Chloe glares at me.

'Thank you for collaborating on this. You're the two best people for this job. As you know, this is my final farewell. I need it to be incredible. To give the fans something to remember forever.'

'I appreciate the magnitude of the situation. Some of us *do* have experience in the industry.' It's a dick move, pulling rank already, but it's out of my mouth before I can stop it.

Chloe's jaw ticks. Her disdain is palpable, even from another continent.

'Right, and Chloe has a huge amount of experience in large-scale event management and exclusivity, so you guys are going to be perfect together.'

Ha. Unlikely.

Ryan's mobile rings in the background. He glances down at the screen. 'Guys, sorry, I have to take this. Start brainstorming. I want this entire tour over and done with well before the wedding. The first concert is only eight weeks away. We don't have a lot of time to come up with something epic.'

His stream remains open but his voice disappears into the corridors of Huxley Castle, Sasha and Chloe's family home, the place we all grew up. Although Ryan and I were raised in an on-site cabin and not within the lavish castle walls.

'So...' Chloe attempts to take command of the situation.

I recline in my chair, grateful for the poolside firepit. March isn't nearly warm enough in California. The urge to feel some real heat is beginning to eat me.

'So...' I echo. If she wants to assume control, let's see her try.

She leans forward to squint at the screen 'Do you always conduct your meetings poolside or do you actually have an office? Scratch that. I don't care either way.' She shuffles some paperwork and continues, barely pausing for breath. 'As you know, there's probably nothing that truly hasn't been done in some capacity. I spent last night researching the most iconic concerts to date and I've come up with some innovative twists.'

I suck air into my cheeks before exhaling in a deliberately patronising manner. 'I doubt that, Princess.'

I can practically predict what she's going to say. Fireworks. Disco balls. Circus animals. Whatever. We need something that each city is going to remember. Something that speaks to them on a personal level.

Chloe adjusts her camera slightly and I snatch a brief glimpse of her office. It's huge, open plan, and she has at least thirteen people working alongside her in the background. Floor-to-ceiling windows showcase the manic Dubai skyline where skyscraper upon skyscraper punctuate the otherwise flawless azure horizon.

Once again, I'm reluctantly impressed. Even if she is a royal pain in the ass.

'Well, seeing as the tour's called *It's Always Been You,* I was thinking we could spin it to make each city feel like Ryan is singing specifically to them.'

Her idea's dangerously close to my own, but I can't help the low sigh that whistles from my lips. 'Princess, I'm not sure how many concerts you've been to, but spoiler-alert, the artist performing does generally sing specifically to the people of that city.'

The glare she shoots me could slit my MacBook in half. 'First, I'm not your princess. Second, you didn't even hear me out. I'm well aware of the concept of a concert. I attended nine last year alone. What I'm trying to get through your stupidly smug head is that we need to have a different theme for each city. One which specifically targets them.'

It's not actually a bad idea.

Most tours pick a theme and run the same tricks across every single venue. It would certainly spice things up a bit. Not that I'll admit that out loud, of course.

Thankfully, my sunglasses hide any flicker of interest sparking. Chloe and her silver spoon don't need any encouragement. 'Go on.'

Dusting an imaginary fleck of lint from her slim fitting dress, she pauses dramatically before elaborating. 'So, as I was saying, the theme would be tailored around celebrating each city's biggest achievements, to create the illusion that Ryan's referring to the residents of each city when he sings, *It's Always Been You.*

I hate to admit it, but the feelgood psychology of it is exceptional.

'It's a possibility, but something like that would require a phenomenal amount of work.'

She arches one perfect eyebrow in a challenge. 'Afraid of getting your hands dirty?'

'My hands are the epitome of dirty, but why get dirty unless it's necessary?'

Chloe shuffles in her seat, then takes a sip from a glass. Is she thinking about my hands? Or other parts of me?

For fuck's sake, Jayden, get a grip. She's not the first attractive woman you've ever met, although she might possibly be the most uptight. What she needs is a really good...

'Thankfully, I have more than just you and your dirty hands to rely on.' Her voice cuts off that train of thought before it can go completely to the gutter. A slim index finger rises on the screen, twisting in a slow circle, motioning to the staff surrounding her. 'Plenty of hands, actually.'

'Fine. Let's explore the idea further. When can you fly in?'

'I'm up to my eyeballs here with the Prince's twenty-first birthday party. Realistically, I can't fly anywhere until the end of the month.'

I said I wanted some sunshine, and Dubai is warmer than here, even if only just.

While I'm there, I could meet Aurelia Arlington, the only artist I manage in the Middle East. Her contract's up next month and I need to negotiate and renew on her behalf.

'I have a client from Abu Dhabi I need to meet. I could potentially fly there instead of bringing her here. We need to finalise the plan before the end of the month in order to source whatever we need, even if it's just for the first concert, which is in...' I open up the confirmation email from Diamond Records, but Chloe interjects before I locate it.

'Sydney.' Superiority taints her tone, like she can't believe I had to check.

It's okay for her, but I'm currently representing fourteen other artists, seven of whom are touring this year.

Using the biro she's clutching, she sweeps her hair behind her ear in a quick, feline gesture. 'Email me your schedule and my PA will make the arrangements.'

'It's a date.' I can't help poking the angry bear.

'It most certainly isn't,' she snaps and hangs up without so much as a goodbye. Whatever. I've got bigger fish to fry.

Chapter Three

CHLOE

With Friday being a holy day in Dubai, Sunday is technically Monday, and by Tuesday, I'm ready for a few sneaky midweek drinks. If I get through today, I don't doubt that feeling will only have intensified.

Jayden-smug-face-Cooper is due to arrive this afternoon.

It's been over a week since our initial Zoom call. In between organising the most lavish twenty-first birthday any billionaire prince could dream of, I've been sourcing a magnitude of information to present to Mr Dirty Hands himself.

Personalising each concert won't need half as much work as some of Ryan's previous tours if Jayden signs off on my idea, but knowing him, he'll block me every step of the way simply to goad me. He seems to get off on it.

'Chloe.' Ruby, my best friend-come-eccentric-office-manager, shouts across the room. London born and bred, she's been with me for five years, arriving in this humid state almost a year to the day after me. Together we've been through the good, the bad and the ugly, of which there have been plenty.

Ruby's the only one of my staff who would dare to shout

at me. The rest scuttle towards my desk with hushed tones and apologetic expressions. My resting bitch face is my armour and my shield. Despite the open plan office, I deliberately segregate myself socially.

Business is business. Lines in this office blurred before when I foolishly dated my first office manager, and it almost cost me everything I ever worked for. I can count my friends on one hand, and that's a statement I'm more than comfortable with.

Glancing up from my window-side desk, my eyes lock with Ruby's huge blue ones. 'It's time,' she mouths, scraping her trademark crimson talons through her sharply bobbed ebony hair. Everyone else keeps their eyes fixed forward, engrossed organising the six very different projects we simultaneously have on the go.

Ugh. Of the three million people who live in this crazy city, why do I have to be the one who has to drive to the airport to pick up my sister's future brother-in-law?

I never expect anyone to pick me up from the airport. In fact, I positively discourage it.

Sasha warned me to make him feel welcome. If I had a dirham for every time she's said that this week, I could retire. Although, I could probably retire anyway on the back of this twenty-first birthday. Party planning for the super-rich and royalty is a lucrative business. But then what would I do?

I live for the challenge. The next gig. The next event. Let's be honest, it's not as if I have much else going on in my life. My business *is* my life. My palms rub my sternum as if to plug the hole in my chest.

Ruby strides towards me, her crimson patent heels clicking on the floor as she approaches.

She's fully aware of my utter disdain for Jayden. 'You ready to make a deal with the devil?' Her voice drops low enough to be lost amongst the low office chatter.

My PA, Izzy, sits at the desk next to me, involved in a heated discussion with one of our regular suppliers. From what I can gather, the price per head has increased by twenty-five percent since the last time we used them.

I resist the urge to take the phone from her and give whoever's on the other end of the line hell. Not because Izzy isn't doing a stellar job, but because the satisfaction that follows when I resolve these types of issues gives me such a buzz.

Ruby shoots me a warning look to leave well alone.

Shoving my chair back with my backside, a sigh slips from my lips. 'As ready as I'll ever be.'

'You've got a great pitch there. Knock the bastard dead with it.' Ruby offers an encouraging wink.

She's right. I have a great pitch. Primarily because everyone in our office spent two days straight throwing ideas round the boardroom, leaving only to pee and eat, until we were all one hundred percent satisfied we'd nailed it.

But however ready I am for the pitch, nothing can prepare me for spending time with Jayden, and it has nothing to do with the fact his father is currently languishing in jail for killing my parents with his erratic driving and everything to do with the man himself.

His personality.

His arrogance.

His demeanour.

The way he lives to torment me with stupid one-liners.

The fact he breathes the same air I do.

My blood boils in his presence. I can't help it. He radiates this innate air of superciliousness, grating every nerve end inside of me, leaving me seething with irritation.

He's self-righteous, conceited and condescending, all rolled up in an infuriatingly self-appreciative parcel. And the fact he looks like a goddamn male model only serves to infuriate me further.

'See you tonight.' I wave to Ruby before grabbing my oversized handbag and riding the elevator thirty-six floors down to the underground car park to find my convertible BMW in the same space I always leave it. What can I say? I'm a stickler for routine.

With a warm gentle breeze blowing deliciously through my hair and the sun beating down on my face, I navigate my way through the early afternoon traffic to the airport.

I'll pick Jayden up, drop him off at whatever hotel he's staying at, and be on my merry way. Tonight, I have plans. Tomorrow, we'll talk shop.

In the arrivals lounge, I clear the twenty-two emails which have landed in my inbox in the forty-minute window since leaving the office. All around me, people hustle and bustle to greet loved ones. It's utterly alien to me. On the rare occasion I return home, I lie about my arrival time. My sisters think I hate the fuss, but actually I hate the idea of anyone I care about risking their life on the road because of me after what happened to my parents.

A problem Sasha and Jayden obviously don't have.

Each time the automatic doors open behind me, a fresh wave of heat bursts through from outside. So when every minute tiny hair stands to attention on my forearm and my heart lurches skywards in my chest, I know without a shadow of doubt it's not because I'm cold.

He's arrived. The fizzing, excruciating stirring in every vein and artery beneath my skin proves it.

I glance up and my breath catches in my chest as I spot Jayden's enormous frame. The man might be an exasperating alphahole, but he's one handsome bastard.

Women stare open-mouthed as he struts cockily towards

me, radiating a commanding presence, a condescending smirk curling his lip to one side.

Ink-coloured hair, cropped into a short snappy style, matches the dark stubble dotting his sharp jawline.

It's his eyes that get me though.

Every single fucking time.

Deep swirling silver pools blaze with a heat every bit as blistering as the Asian climate. The deliciously distinct after-shave he wears plumes the air around me, tinged with his own unique masculine scent. Intoxicating. I mean, infuriating.

'Sorry to keep you waiting, but as they say, good things *do* come to those who wait.' Hot lips linger against my cheek in a greeting that's too intimate to be polite.

Ugh. How can one sentence cause every hair on my neck to prick up?

Cocking my head to issue a sideways glare, I forget Jayden typically favours the French greeting. When his lips land on my face for the second time, instead of meeting my other cheek, they land squarely on my parted lips.

Jolting back like I've been electrocuted, blood flushes my face. Steely grey eyes glitter with unashamed delight at my social faux pas.

I stalk across the gleaming polished floor to put some space between us. He follows hot on my heels, dragging a charcoal-coloured Samsonite case behind him.

'I knew you didn't truly despise me, but you know, I thought kissing in public like that was illegal here.'

'Trust me, I do despise you. And if you recall correctly, it was your lips that landed on mine.'

'They did, didn't they?' His accompanying grin is enough to ramp up my fury to the next level.

One more wrong sentence from those ridiculously full lips and I might actually blow.

What is it about him that drives me to such an aggravated

state? I've encountered more than my fair share of over-confident men along the way. Men who were equally attractive.

Ok, that last part isn't strictly true. Jayden Cooper is other-worldly sexy, but he knows it. He's only been here approximately three seconds and it's apparent he's still a total asshole.

He lets out a low whistle as I unlock the convertible. 'Nice ride.'

Why does everything seem to be a double entendre with him? I swear the man delights in winding me up. I'm not a silly teenager anymore.

'Want me to drive?'

I count to ten before spitting, 'Why would I want *you* to drive *my* car? Because you're a man and I'm a woman? Could you be any more chauvinistic?'

'You seem a bit flustered. Is the heat getting to you? Or is it those unruly pheromones around me again?' He tucks his suitcase into the boot before hopping into the passenger seat.

His hand brushes mine over the gearbox. The contact lasts for less than two seconds, but it's like an electric shock.

'Oh, would you ever fuck off?' Slamming my foot on the accelerator, the car lurches forward, narrowly missing a flashy red Lambo.

Jayden sniggers, and even though he doesn't utter another word, his silence still screams, 'I told you so.'

When we're safely out on the highway, I allow my gaze to slant briefly in his direction.

'Which hotel are you staying at?'

His eyes widen mockingly, exuding a deliberately false show of innocence. 'What do you mean? I'm staying with you, aren't I?' Laughter lines crinkle the corner of his eyes.

The urge to scream is suffocating. 'You are joking, right?'

'I'm deadly serious. After all, we're practically family, right?'

Chapter Four

JAYDEN

Staying at Chloe's place was too tempting. Apart from knowing it would irritate the life out of her, and she's smoking hot when she's irate, we genuinely have a lot of work to do, and only four days to do it.

Plus, if I stayed in a hotel, Colton would insist on coming. A private residence is safer from the paps and other prying eyes.

I soak up the scenery, relieved to escape LA, my new house guest and the momentous commitment I've just signed up to.

Sasha thinks I'm mad. Ryan thinks I have a weird god complex.

If I were to overthink it, I'd never go through with it, but there was no way I could allow Lula to be deported. Apart from the fact she's spent the last eight years building a life here, I swore to Sofia I'd help her.

Pushing all thoughts of Lula out of my head, my gaze slants towards Chloe. White fingers clench the leather steering wheel.

Uptight doesn't even come close to describing her. I

shouldn't tease her, but it's too much fun. Making light of things is my favourite distraction from my own darkness.

The tyres of the BMW screech to a standstill on the driveway of a whitewashed, beachside villa. The sound of the sea soothingly slaps the sandy shore. Scents of seaweed and sun cream linger deliciously in the air.

I need to get the business part of this trip done because every bone in my body's craving pleasure in the form of sea swims, good food and serious soaking in the sun, somewhere where I'm anonymous.

The engine stills and Chloe hops out of the car, darting towards the modest entrance.

'I guess I'll carry my own case then.' My joke's answered with a scoff and Chloe's raised middle finger.

I follow her into a bright white hallway. The place is immaculate, taking the term minimalistic to the next level. A few nondescript canvases decorate the walls. There are no photos. No feminine touches.

Interesting.

Is Chloe as cold at home as she pretends to be outside of it? And why do I care either way?

'This is nice,' I say.

It's a fraction of the size of my pad.

Fuck, maybe I am an arrogant twat, like she broadcast three times on the way here? No, it's simply an observation, not a judgement.

The villa is gorgeously Mediterranean in style. I'm just used to everything being super-sized in the States. I've become used to my own particular style of silver spoon.

Chloe doesn't offer me a tour, but I follow her anyway, this time to the kitchen, which coincidently is also white with zero personal effects. I'm sensing a theme.

Chloe marches to the fridge, removes two bottles of water

and hands me one. I unscrew the lid and sniff it to make sure it's not poisoned.

'Believe me, if I thought I could get away with it.' Her jaw locks and I can only imagine the pressure her molars are under.

I spot double doors leading onto a spacious terrace, and pad across the room for a better look. Terracotta tiles adorn a high-walled outdoor area. A cosy looking L-shaped couch flanks a small rectangular coffee table, and two sun loungers perch hospitably next to a fifteen-metre pool where the water glitters tantalisingly below the balmy afternoon sun.

It might be smaller than my place, but it's so inviting. If only my host was a fraction as welcoming.

Brightly coloured plants and flowers line the perimeter, offering vivid pops of personality. The question is, whose personality? Is this Chloe's doing? Hard to imagine her tending to these daily.

As if reading my mind, she says, 'Naveesha, my house-keeper, is mad into gardening. She's Sri Lankan. She says the flowers remind her of home.' Chloe shrugs in a gesture of disdain.

A pang of pity startles me and the reality of her situation hits me square on the chin. From what Ryan told me, Chloe bolted from the place we all called home the day after she turned twenty-one. She couldn't get away quickly enough.

Was it any wonder?

I don't have to imagine what it was like losing both parents as a teenager. Even though the circumstances were wildly different, I can relate. Maybe she's not as cold as she seems. Maybe she just has to be more careful with her emotions.

'Don't look at me like that, Jayden.' The warning's clear in her tone.

'Like what?'

'Like you're about to bring up the past.' Man, she's astute.

I have to. It's the elephant in the room. Although I had no idea, I can't help but feel partly responsible. For all the codding and winding her up, family is something I'd never joke about.

'Let me say it once, then I promise to never bring it up again.'

She shakes her head resolutely. 'No need.'

Turning on her four-inch heels, she stalks back inside before calling, 'FYI, your father running my parents off the road has nothing to do with the fact I can't stand you, and everything to do with the fact you're an asshole.'

All my pity evaporates as an indignant snort spurts from my nose.

'You know, it's a fine line between love and hate.'

'Yeah. I love to hate you.'

So much for business before pleasure. Chloe feigns a headache and locks herself in her bedroom the second she shows me to mine. It leaves me with no other option but to dive into her pool and bask in the sunshine.

A couple of hours later, a clicking sound from above the pool area draws my attention to a second, smaller terrace. This one appears to extend from Chloe's bedroom. Apparently oblivious to the fact I'm sunbathing below, she shimmies out, wearing the most decadently indecent cerise underwear showcasing a body worthy of a professional lingerie model.

Holy fuck.

A flimsy layer of lace supports the most beautiful natural cleavage, tanned and ripe, just begging to be unwrapped. A flat, sun-kissed stomach paves the way to a flimsy, transparent hot pink thong.

She's even more stunning than I imagined. Not that I've spent much time imagining her in her underwear. Much. My dick twitches in my shorts.

At this rate, I'm going to have to get back in the water. But even the subtlest of movements risks drawing her attention. I want to sit here and relish this resplendent view for as long as possible.

It's been months since I've been intimate with a woman and the signs are on me.

Chloe has her mobile phone pressed to her ear, a rare smile flashing across her face. A flicker of envy rips through my chest. Who's inciting that reaction? The only emotion I get from her is hate.

'See you soon.' She disconnects the call before running a hand over her lace clad breast.

An appreciative sigh slips from my lips and her head whips downwards.

'Jayden, what the fuck? Are you spying on me?' She grabs a towel and wraps it round her body with a glare.

'Excuse me, Princess, but I was here minding my own business when you walked out into the broad sunlight like you were a Victoria Secrets model strutting the catwalk. What did you want me to do? I'm only fucking human.'

Even with the blush creeping into her cheeks again, she looks hot as fuck.

'Human? You're a goddamn animal. Your reputation precedes you.'

'Sweetheart, if the truth of my reputation really preceded me, you wouldn't hesitate to come down here right now and let me bury my tongue between those heavenly legs.'

Yet again, my mouth opens before I have time to question the consequences of such a galvanising statement. I can't help it. Chloe Sexton is hot as fuck and right this second, I'd give my right arm to taste her. To witness her controlled exterior crumble and come undone under my touch.

What goes on tour stays on tour, right?

I'm in no position to date her. But if her own reputation is correct, she doesn't do relationships, which suits me down to the ground.

A final fling.

Ryan's words echo through my head.

Don't fuck things up with Chloe.

Does fucking her count? Because right now that's exactly what I'm contemplating, regardless of my other commitments.

Those commitments are merely a business transaction, after all.

Winding her up gives me a bigger thrill than what's good for me, but truth be known, I've wanted her for years. And just like a fine wine, she's got more alluring with age.

Eyes, a sinful shade of blue, flick over my naked torso in a betraying display of interest. Her tongue darts over her lips and I glimpse a sliver of raw humanity that sends a jolt of electricity surging straight to my dick.

Alas, her mouth refuses to conform to her body's desires.

'In your wildest dreams, Jayden. Apart from the fact I can't stand you, and I wouldn't let your dirty hands or mouth anywhere near me, we're practically family, right?'

The echo of my earlier words is the last thing I hear before she slams her balcony door closed.

It may have been brief, but it was there.

I can sniff out bullshit from a mile away. And the only scent Chloe exudes is a raging musk of desire.

Given half the chance, I would actually put pleasure before business. Or at least blend the two for a few days. If only she'd give into me. I'd luxuriate in unwinding every uptight bone in that beautiful body and removing that silver spoon with my exceptionally talented tongue once and for all.

Here in Dubai, away from all my LA obligations, I can be myself again, even for a few short days.

I drag myself out of the pool and back into the villa in search of something to eat. I'm shamelessly raiding the fridge when Chloe finally emerges from her room. She's wearing a full face of make-up and a figure-hugging black satin dress.

'Princess, you look stunning, but you didn't need to go to any trouble for me.' Though winding her up is my current favourite hobby, there's an underlying truth to my teasing.

I shoot her a salacious wink. 'I actually preferred you without the dress.'

Her icy laughter slashes through the humid air like a freshly sharpened knife. I deliberately didn't put a t-shirt on, and her eyes are once again drawn to my body. A body that I work ridiculously hard for. Physical pain leaves less time for overthinking. It's why I spend a lot of time in my home gym.

It's also an effective way of avoiding my new house guest, Lula. I had no idea what I was signing up for. Still, I promised I'd help and that's exactly what I intend to do.

'It's not for your benefit.' Chloe's hands skim over her curves in a deliberate tease. Our eyes lock in an explosive, invisible short-circuit before she announces, 'I actually have a date.'

She stalks across the lounge and out to the pool. I follow her and dive back in, hoping the chlorine will wash away my irritation. When I emerge at her feet, I have a clear view of hot pink beneath the satin. The thought of another man getting to unwrap that perfect package blasts a hit of heat through my blood.

'A date, huh? And when were you planning on doing some work exactly? In case you've forgotten, you have the biggest gig of your life to organise.'

That at least incites a hard swallow alongside her oh-so-familiar glare.

'Tomorrow. You're in my diary for nine o'clock sharp. Stupidly, I thought you might be swanning round some fancy hotel, living it up. I didn't realise you intended on spending the entire four days of your trip with me swinging from your coattails.'

In one swift leap, I'm out of the pool and close enough to inhale her deliciously exotic perfume. 'Oh, Chloe, if I had my way, you'd be spending the entire four days of my trip swinging from the chandeliers. And you'd luxuriate in every single second of it.'

'Promises, promises...' She rolls her eyes dramatically skywards.

Before I can think of a suitable reply, the doorbell chimes. Chloe turns on her stilettos, waving her fingers in a patronising farewell. 'Naveesha left a lasagne in the fridge. Don't wait up.'

She loiters in the patio doorway long enough for me to wonder if she's changed her mind. 'Oh, and I hope you've got earplugs.' Her painted lips part into a wicked grin. 'I'm a screamer when I get going.' She winks and shakes her sensual hips.

Chapter Five

CHLOE

Tuesday is Ladies' Night in Dubai. It drives men out in force like a pack of starving animals hunting for prey.

Ruby and I dwell at one of our usual haunts, an exclusive bar called Tonic, near the Burj Khalifa. During the day, it offers breathtaking views of the city. At night, it offers a different perspective on the country entirely.

The opulent décor is otherworldly. Black granite lines the floors. Exquisite chandeliers shed soft light on the patrons enjoying themselves below, and an addictive bass sets my toe tapping in time to the rhythm. With two potent cocktails lining my otherwise empty stomach, a fuzzy buzz slowly diffuses the tension of the day.

Ruby perches across from me talking to Brad, her on/off American investment banker boyfriend of a year, while I'm surrounded by half the English soccer team. I don't follow the Premiership, but I gather I'm supposed to be impressed by their celebrity status.

Obviously I'm not, given my sister's engaged to one of the world's most famous stars.

To my left, the captain of the team flanks me. He's a tall,

broad-shouldered blond with bright piercing eyes. His cedar-wood aftershave envelops me. It's nice. Not knicker-drop-pingly nice like the intoxicating, masculine scent that's currently, and unwelcomingly, wafting through every room in my house right now.

To my right sits the team's tipsy, opportunistic striker.

Initially, their attention is flattering, but fumbling hands repeatedly wander further than I'm comfortable with. It's time I extract myself.

'I'm going to the bar.' I turn to the captain, Carl, I think he said his name was. His thick toned thigh is pressed closely against mine.

'Sit down. I'll ask one of the boys to get the drinks.' A firm hand presses on my thigh, preventing me from standing as his lips twist into a devilish smirk.

Quintessentially, he's my type. Good-looking and unavail-able for anything long-lasting, but I'm getting a weird vibe from him. From both of them, actually.

I try to catch Ruby's attention across the table, but she seems to be engaged in a heated discussion with her boyfriend, Brad.

'Order some shots, then we can take Clara for some real fun.' The striker leans across me, wedging me tighter between the two of them, as he grabs his crotch.

I bite back my snort. Neither of them are scoring here.

Infuriatingly, the only person I'm fantasising about tonight is my vexatious, but sexy, house guest, Jayden. Two cocktails in and I can't shake the image of his shirtless body. The perfectly sculpted planes of his ripped torso. The way they angled into a delicious V above the waistband of his swimming shorts.

Even with all his trashy one-liners, his stare provokes a heated promise within my core.

I don't doubt he'd deliver in the bedroom.

Or any room, for that matter.

Jayden is fiercely competitive. The best agent in Hollywood. The fastest on the ice rink at Christmas. The first to run into the sea for the Boxing Day dip. When he commits to something, he does it with a passion. It's like a weird personal mission.

I'm pretty sure he'd devote the same fervid passion to his lovers. Of which, by all accounts, there have been many. I'm ashamed to admit I know more about him than I should. I've scoured far too many news articles about him, googled his name more than is healthy, purely with a curious disgust, of course. Not that you can avoid it. Every few weeks, his picture is plastered across the media with a different conquest on his arm.

I'm no virgin myself. So why does the thought of him with anyone else send a fresh ripple of irritation coursing through me?

'Do you think you could handle two of us?' The striker's breath brushes my ear.

My head whips round to face Carl, certain he'll shoot his teammate down, but he shrugs and smirks. Looks like anything's on the table. Including me, apparently.

Liberated or not, I'm not interested in either of them, let alone both of them. Time to extract myself. Quickly.

There's zero chemistry.

Not like the toxic crackle I suffered when Jayden offered to bury his tongue between my legs, as he put it.

Speak of the devil. He appears like a vision before my eyes.

A crisp white shirt hugs his taut chest. His sleeves are rolled to the elbow, revealing tanned powerful forearms dusted with a smattering of dark hair. Navy jeans hang from his narrow hips like a goddamn work of art. His usual teasing expression's been replaced with an unnerving glower. Steely graphite eyes glint in a manner that has me half terrified and half intrigued.

As he stalks across the room, he oozes an aura of dominance, power and authority. Women, and men, gape open mouthed.

His narrowing gaze focuses intently on me. Specifically, my thigh, where the captain's hand is still lingering. A vein pulses furiously at his temple.

Carl leans into my ear, his hand tracing higher up my thigh, squeezing suggestively, inching beneath the hem of my dress. They're assuming I'm a forgone conclusion.

'What do you think?' Alcohol fumes sting my eyes.

What do I think?

I think you're way out of line and the only man my errant lady parts are screaming out for is marching across the room with the expression of a trained killer carved on his exquisite face.

Jayden grabs both my hands, jerking me up onto my feet. 'We're going.'

'Hey, she's with us,' Carl protests.

'Actually, she's with me. Get your fucking hands off her.'

Ruby's huge blue eyes widen from across the table. Jayden Cooper needs no introduction.

'O-M-Fucking-G.' She mouths through the noise and escalating tension. Crimson nails fly back and forth in front of her face as she dramatically fans herself at Jayden's blisteringly hot arrival.

Anger fumes from his broad frame in ferocious, palpable waves. Carl jumps to his feet, his hand catching me by the wrist. His features twist into a sneer.

Jayden's menacing hiss is weighted with a warning The Hulk himself would be foolish to ignore. 'Get your hands off my woman while they're still attached to your body. I won't say it again.'

The grip on my arm drops and I'm ushered away from the table by a hot palm nestling against the base of my spine.

I don't know whether to be relieved, flattered, or downright incensed. Okay, I was uncomfortable, but I had the situation under control. I don't need a hero. Especially not Jayden.

'Your woman?'

'Yes. My woman. And you're welcome, by the way.'

As much as I hate to admit it, possessive Jayden is even hotter than infuriating Jayden. I'll die before I admit that out loud. Resentment ripples through me even as his huge hand lingers on my spine, sending delicious hot tingles in every direction.

As we reach the door, I glance back to check on Ruby. She waves from across the room, motioning she's staying with Brad.

'You want me to thank you for barging in on my night?' I snarl as we reach the lift.

Why am I being such a bitch? He saved me from a couple of creeps. I should be grateful. Instead, I'm livid with him once again for charging in and taking over.

I'm even more livid with myself for the way my heart hammers in my chest in his presence.

'From where I was standing, it looked like you were about to be coerced into the front pages of tomorrow's tabloids. Do you know who those guys were?'

'Soccer players, apparently. I don't follow sport.'

'Do you follow the news by any chance? They were both arrested last year for sexually assaulting two eighteen-year-old girls,' he hisses. 'They got off with it. It's hard to prove assault when the girls willingly went home with them. God knows what they'd have done to a gorgeous piece of ass like you.'

'Oh, I'm a piece of ass, am I?'

'To them. Not to me.' He tuts, resting back against the

mirrored glass in the lift as we descend ninety floors. 'To me, you're the finest piece of ass I've ever seen. It's just a shame about the silver spoon that's rammed up it.'

My palm connects with his right bicep, shoving him indignantly before bouncing straight off it.

'Careful, Princess, you might break a nail,' he smirks.

'Just when I didn't think it was possible to despise you any more...' Heat blazes through every single cell of my body.

'Oh, you don't despise me. That's red-hot desire rolling from your every pore.' His confident tone's tinted with glee.

'It's red-hot hatred. You ruined my night. Who says I even want to go home?' I flick my hair from my shoulder.

Intense steely eyes bore into mine. 'Who said I was taking you home?'

'Funny, Jayden.' My hand lands on his chest. It's intended as another shove, but my fingers didn't get the memo. Instead, they linger over his shirt, revelling in the tautness beneath the brilliant cotton noticeably longer than necessary.

'Seriously though, are you ok?' All trace of his usual tormenting humour is replaced with solemn concern. 'They didn't... touch you?' His voice drops lethally low.

'I'm ok. I can handle myself.' Doubt creeps in as my fingers trace the wrist that was held so tightly.

'Princess, I don't doubt it, but while I'm here, you won't have to.'

Usually, when he calls me Princess, it triggers a fury in my stomach, but this time it ignites a spark between my legs. Nobody has ever protected me like that before. The feminist in me should be horrified, but she's been replaced by a sexually stimulated, pheromone-infused hot mess.

'So, this is your idea of a date, huh?' Thick, dark eyebrows arch.

'Technically, Ruby was my date until she ran into Brad

again. They've been off and on more times in the last year than my vibrator, Perky Pete.'

'Perky Pete, huh?' His smouldering black pupils dilate. 'That's something I'd like to see.'

'In your dreams.' Just because he pulled me out of a sticky situation, it doesn't mean I'm going to invite him into another, even if the chemistry is sparking like a badly wired plug.

'Admit it.' Hot eyes sear my soul. 'You like me.'

'I can't stand you.' I poke my tongue out like a child. 'How did you know where I was, anyway?'

'It's Tuesday night and according to our respective siblings, you're a stickler for routine.'

'So you came down here to what...?'

'To take you on a proper date...' His tongue darts out over his lower lip. 'Then, I'm going to find out first hand if you really are a screamer...'

The doors finally open as we reach the ground floor, but the heat outside has nothing on the temperature inside the lift. Or my underwear.

Chapter Six

JAYDEN

When Chloe strutted out of the door dressed to kill, there was no way I could sit in her empty villa and simply wait for her to come home. As fate would have it, Aurelia is performing in Dubai tonight.

'Where are we going?' Chloe asks as I hail a taxi.

'The Madinat.'

'What's at the Madinat?' she huffs.

'Dinner hopefully. I'm starving.'

For once, she doesn't argue.

When we arrive, the place is absolutely thronged. I've been here several times over the years, but its grandeur never ceases to take my breath away. As the largest resort in Dubai, it's like a mini city within the emirate, composed of lavish five-star hotels, ornate souks and tourist-infused beachfront hotspots.

'It's busy tonight,' Chloe muses, glancing out of the window as the taxi slows to a halt. 'There must be something going on.'

I slip the taxi driver a wad of notes and he attempts to hand them back. 'Too much, sir. You overpay.'

'It's fine. Thank you,' I insist. These guys work hard. They deserve it and so much more.

'Very generous, sir.' Turning to Chloe, the driver says, 'Aurelia Arlington is performing at a charity function.'

Chloe's eyes light up. 'I read about that. Aurelia Arlington is my absolute idol. I saw her twice in concert last year. She's such an inspiration, the way she came from nothing to become an ambassador for her country and for women in general.'

'If only we had tickets.' It's a battle to suppress my smile.

As I hop out of the cab, thanking the driver again, I offer Chloe my hand. She glares for a half a second before sighing and accepting it.

Her fingers slip into mine and three thousand volts of sexually charged energy surge up my forearm, raising every single nerve ending in my body. The need to act on it magnifies with every passing second.

Ryan was right about two things. First, she did knock me back at Christmas. Second, I live for a challenge.

Even as a teenager, she had an exquisite, alluring appeal. Her curvaceous figure was all woman, but she was unequivocally underage. I wanted her so badly my balls physically ached anytime she was near.

To obliterate thoughts of all the different ways I could take her virginity, I distracted myself fucking one of Huxley Castle's lacklustre but obliging chambermaids, Jacinta. Not my finest moment, admittedly. I only did it because I couldn't have what I really wanted. Chloe.

However stunning she was at seventeen, at twenty-seven, she's magnificent.

'Come on.' I link her arm through mine, leading her towards a starlit entrance. For once, she doesn't resist.

'What are you doing? There's no way we'll get in there.'

Her footsteps slow, imposter syndrome oozing from her usually confident core.

She might be used to organising events like these, but she's obviously not used to attending them. I make a mental note to check who Aurelia normally hires for events management and pass on Chloe's details.

I give my name to four burly bouncers and much to Chloe's obvious shock, we're welcomed like visiting royalty.

'Aurelia insisted you sit at the front. She signed the paperwork you couriered over. It's at the front desk,' a security guard says, leading us to a lavishly decorated round table a couple of metres from a huge gold emblazoned stage.

The bouncer pulls out Chloe's chair, and she sits wide-eyed, drinking in every single inch of the extravagant decor.

Sitting at the table beside us are four British royals, two world famous golfers, and an academy award-winning actress and her twenty-years junior husband.

Chloe turns her awe-inspired gaze to me. 'How?'

Aurelia emerges from behind the curtain, popping her head discreetly out. 'Jay, I heard you'd arrived!' She darts over and I rise to greet her, pressing a kiss on both her cheeks.

'It's so good to see you.' Dainty arms reach around my neck, yanking me into a warm, all-encompassing hug.

'And you, Aurelia. You look fantastic, as usual.' Her perfectly poised exterior is a far cry from the tattered looking teenager who mailed me a badly recorded demo tape, desperately seeking a way to escape her poverty-struck life in Brazil.

The quality of the recording might have been poor, but her star quality was unmistakable. I signed her in a heartbeat, changing both of our lives for the better. We've been firm friends ever since.

'Who's this lucky lady?' She turns her attention to Chloe, who's unusually quiet for once.

'I'm Chloe Sexton. It's an absolute pleasure. I'm a huge

fan.' Cyan eyes continue to dart inquisitively between Aurelia and me.

'She was at two of your concerts last year, apparently.' I chance draping an arm across Chloe's shoulder, drawing her closer into the conversation. Goosebumps chase across her bare skin beneath my hand. When my thumb strokes her soft flesh, she trembles.

Has she finally got the memo we should embark on the hottest fling of both our lives? I'm playing with fire. I know I am, but I can't stop myself. Away from Ireland and Huxley Castle, Chloe's silver spoon doesn't seem nearly so deeply inserted.

Even her sarcastic retorts are growing on me.

'Ahh, thank you so much. I'll send you tickets for next year, if you'd like? Or perhaps Jayden will bring you again?' She shoots me a conspicuous wink, knowing as well as I do the Pope will get married before that happens.

Current outstanding obligations aside, I don't do relationships.

Four weeks is my longest relationship to date, and I was out of the country for two of them. Flings, on the other hand, that's a different matter. I'm a pro. As long as everyone knows where they stand and nobody gets hurt, what's the harm?

This time around, discretion is essential, though. There are bigger things at stake, namely the promise I just made to Lula. Being photographed publicly with another woman would certainly jeopardise the fiancée visa she's applying for.

In the past, women have agreed to casual sex, convinced deep down they'll be the one to change me. To fix me. It's never going to happen. If I thought for a second I could maintain a loving and committed relationship, something that had potential to turn into the traditional love and marriage, I wouldn't have signed away my chances of finding it by offering to help Lula get her green card.

Chloe seems refreshingly like me, liberated and uncompli-cated. It doesn't take a genius to work out the hard exterior walls she's constructed are for her own protection, but even knowing that doesn't deter me from wanting to explore what's behind them, for a short time at least.

Aurelia's bodyguards approach and a six-foot five skinhead with an earpiece gently takes her elbow, informing her it's time to begin her show.

Blowing me a final kiss, she turns to Chloe. 'It was a plea-sure meeting you. Take care of this one.' She motions to me. 'Even the heroes need saving sometimes.'

I'm no hero. I couldn't save Sofia. That's why I have to save Lula.

Throughout Aurelia's performance, memories from almost a decade ago infiltrate my mind, piercing my heart. It's an effort to shake them off, though the ear-splitting pop and the proximity of the mysteriously deep woman next to me definitely help.

Throughout the show, we're treated to a sumptuous meal, course after course, following each other with little pause. So much food. Fresh lobster. Sorbet. Succulent steak. Truffles. Each mouthful increasingly more delectable than the one before.

Between gazing at her apparent idol and devouring each decorative plate set before her, Chloe's eyes intermittently slant towards me with a look of impressed bemusement.

At the halfway interval, she finally speaks. 'You and Aure-lia...? I mean, did you...?' She takes a huge mouthful from a crystal champagne flute.

I know exactly what she's referring to, but as ever, it's too tempting not to wind her up. 'Did we what?'

'Are you, I mean... is there something going on between you?' She takes another mouthful of bubbles.

'Would you be jealous if there was, Princess?' Leaning

closer, my hand cups her chin, tilting her gaze upwards so she can't look away.

I should tone it down. I'm in no position to be embarking on anything right now, but if the rumours are true about Chloe, then we could come to some sort of arrangement. The attraction between us is obviously mutual. It buzzes between us with a growing insistency. We could have some real fun on tour, if she'd only agree to it.

Chloe's huge cyan eyes gaze at me with a rare hint of vulnerability. It's my undoing. My lips seek hers, crashing against them with a hunger that could get me arrested in this country. Kissing her into oblivion. Doing what I wished I could have done years ago.

Hooded eyes flutter closed as her mouth fully submits to mine, parting just enough for my greedy tongue to slip in and devour her from the inside out. Our mouths fasten, slipping and sliding with a decadent hedonistic desire, igniting an inferno within. An urgent, feral need to claim her consumes me.

Calling her my woman was not for her benefit. It was for mine. I was marking my territory. Because she is mine, for the next few days anyway. The moment I hopped on that plane, deep down, I knew this was inevitable.

That energy between us was never hate. It was red hot vibrating molecules of lust.

A loud and deliberate cough next to us reminds me we're in a very public part of a Muslim country. Startled, Chloe jerks away, pressing her fingers to her lips like she's been burned. Shock, confusion and a sultry longing flashes in her dilated pupils.

'Now, this is what you call a date.' My mouth brushes the sensitive skin of her ear. 'Tell me again how much you despise me.'

Chapter Seven

CHLOE

When the show's finally over and Jayden collects the paperwork from the desk, we hop into a taxi, sitting decidedly closer to each other than in the last one we shared.

'Home?' I check, before directing the driver, trying not to dwell on how brazen that sounds and what might actually happen when we get there.

Jayden offers a swift nod, staring at me with unblinking intensity. His Adam's apple bobs through the half light of the moon.

The air crackles. He's a man on a mission and if that explosive panty-melting kiss was anything to go by, that mission is defiling me in what promises to be the most delicious fashion.

Heat suffuses from every inch of my skin as explicit images assault my brain of what the god-like creature sitting millimetres away from me might look like naked. If his top half was anything to go by at the pool earlier, I can't wait to see what other hard muscles he's packing lower down.

In a mad twist of a script I didn't write, the irritation I

usually feel for Jayden Cooper has ignited into an inferno of irrepressible carnal longing.

I've never denied he's devastatingly sexy. But to be so viscerally attracted to a man, that until an hour ago I could have cheerfully throttled, is a total mind-fuck for a self-professed control freak like me.

That kiss was out of this world. The kind of show-stopping cathartic moment you normally only ever see on the big screen. For that experience to stem from *him* has shaken the world as I know it.

From the day he and his rock star brother, Ryan, returned to our lives, he's tormented me. Flirted outrageously. Teased me for fun. Did he mean every word? Or is he as shocked as I am at the turn of events?

And who's to say he won't turn on me again? I've been burnt before.

Mind you, we're not kids anymore. Both consenting adults, apparently harbouring the same attraction to each other. Neither disillusioned with daft romantic ideals.

But despite the chemistry, I can't help the feeling I'm heading rapidly towards disaster. If I sleep with him and it gets out, the world will assume that's the only reason I was hired to help organise this tour. All my hard work building up my company will be forgotten. I'll be labelled another notch on the bed of one of LA's most notorious playboys.

Plus, there's the teeny tiny fact Sasha warned me off him. If my sweet, sassy sister thinks he's no good for me, then she's probably right.

While I've been preoccupied over-analysing every single thought that pops through my head, we've reached my front door and I'm nowhere near ready for what might occur behind it.

Jayden pays the taxi driver while I'm mentally willing my ass to move from the spot where I'm rooted.

I want him more than I've ever wanted anyone. The intensity of it terrifies me. It's not as if I can wave him off the next day and never see him again, like my previous conquests. Ryan asked us to organise this tour together. I'm going to have to face him not only at work, but at every major family occasion afterwards, too.

If we cross the line, how do we move past something like this?

And if we don't cross it, how will we ever get over it? Because I've never felt attraction like it, and if I don't get the chance to explore it, I'll wonder about it for the rest of my life.

Why, oh, why does it have to be him?

Jayden's firm fingers interlace with mine, tugging my hand, coaxing me out of the car. His grinning lips brush my ear. 'Come on, Princess, I want to hear you scream.'

I was only joking about that. No one ever made me scream before, except in frustration, of course.

My stomach flips and I can't work out if it's terror or lust. Probably both. Until this moment, I never realised they could exist in parallel.

On the doorstep, he surveys me. Anxiety must be rolling off me in waves. Or perhaps it's my trembling hands giving me away because the predatory look he's been sporting for the previous hour has suddenly evaporated.

Taking the keys, he unlocks the door, ushering me into my home like he's been there forever, not just a day.

It closes behind us. We stand chest to chest under the harsh light of the hallway, my ragged breath penetrating the air between us.

'You ok, Princess?' His velvety voice rumbles like a purr as he pins me in a pensive stare. My heartbeat goes haywire.

'Who even are you?' The question's out of my mouth before I can overthink it.

'I'm the idiot who should have kissed you ten years ago and I'm going to spend the next four days making up for that fact.' His full lips inch towards mine, a blistering masculinity emanating from every inch of him.

His intoxicating heady scent envelops me. I can't think straight. When his breath brushes my mouth, I stop trying, allowing our kiss to do all the talking.

Tongues dance and swirl exploratively. His fingers trace my collarbone, and then drift lower to cup the underside of my breast as he lets out a possessive growl.

There's no choice but to submit to the sensation. With lust gushing through every inch of me, I have no alternative.

'I've been thinking about your beautiful tits since I saw that indecent scrap of lace covering them earlier.' His words sink straight into my mouth as he palms both breasts appreciatively. 'Actually, that's a lie. I've been thinking about them since you were seventeen years old. I'm the type of man your mother probably warned you about.' Pinning me against the wall, he locks me into position with his hips, and there is no mistaking his desire. It's at least eight inches and deliciously wedged against me. 'You've met your match then.' My words fall in ragged breaths. 'I'm the kind of girl you'd never take home to your mother. I'm more interested in what you've got in your trousers than in your bank account.'

A playful grin rips across his face and his eyes dance with delight.

'Is that so? Well, it's great to see we can *finally* agree on *something...*'

He hitches my dress up around my waist, displaying the hot pink lace. A wetness pools at my centre. 'Do you have any idea what you're doing to me?' It almost kills me to say it.

He's barely touched me, and he's already blown every other sexual encounter I've had out of the water.

'Princess, I'm only getting started.' He palms my thighs

apart, nimble fingers darting beneath the lace, sweeping the length of me before darting out again. I've barely gasped before he has the same finger in his mouth, his dilating pupils penetrating mine.

He sucks without breaking eye contact. 'Mmm. For the next four days, you're mine.' It's not a request.

It looks like we're not entirely in agreement after all.

'No. Tonight, and tonight only.' My thighs press tightly together again as I pray he accepts the deal. 'I don't do repeats. Take it or leave it.' The nonchalant tone requires every bit of acting skill I can muster because if he doesn't take it, there's a good chance, given the way my body is alight with a fire only he can extinguish, I might actually beg.

'Never?' A thick, dark eyebrow arches and his fingers slip inside the lace again.

My head shakes, along with every other atom I'm composed of.

Darkening eyes bore into mine, alight with curiosity and unmissable desire. 'One night isn't enough to explore your fantasies, or to satisfy my own.'

'Fantasies?' I'm so close to blowing it's embarrassing. I let out a gasp as his finger continues to sensuously caress me.

'Yes, fantasies. The scenarios we each conjure up when we're touching ourselves, Chloe.' Hot ragged breath grazes my ear. 'I want to hear every single one of yours and bring them to life. For that, I'm going to need more than one night.'

'I can't...' Those magic fingers continue their delicious assault, lighting every single nerve end in my body. 'I did once. It didn't end well.'

'You'd give up four days of pleasure because of some idiot?' he murmurs, hot lips cruising over the sensitive skin of my neck and he slips another finger inside of me.

'I made a rule after him.'

'Rules are made to be broken. Believe me, I'm breaking them all right now.' His thumb circles my sweet spot.

'Not this one.' I swallow thickly, praying he'll go for it. 'Tonight. Now. Let's do it and get this out of our systems once and for all.'

'Didn't you hear? I'm ruthless when it comes to negotiating?' he whispers, as his hand slows to a stop, leaving me teetering dangerously close to the edge. 'Take the deal, Chloe.'

In a frenzied state of horny desperation, I do something I never do. I lay my cards on the table. 'Next morning's freak me out. Men always say they won't get attached, and then the next thing they're asking if they can see me again.'

His lips curl into a slow smile as his fingers resume the same transcendent motion. 'I promise you, I'm more unavailable than you could ever comprehend. You're worried I'll fall in love with you? I don't think I know the meaning of the word. When I get on the plane, that will be it.'

My release is building inside as he works my walls with expert precision. 'What about the concerts?'

'What about them? Princess, we'll be up to our eyeballs. There won't be time to piss. Plus, we'll be surrounded by my brother and your sister, and I'm pretty sure we should keep this between us. Because as they so often remind us, we're practically family.'

That single line rips through me and I still his hand, the one that feels so fucking good. 'Stop. We can't. Imagine the wedding. It'll be so awkward if we've hooked up. Everyone will know.'

'If we don't hook up, it'll be worse. The tension will be explosive. Did you ever wonder why there's so much friction between us? It's called chemistry. We need to blaze our way through it until we're both fully satiated and then lock it in the compartment called "good times."' He slides two fingers back inside me, my own fingers pathetically gripping his wrist in a feeble attempt to stop him.

'Stop, Jayden, please. You're killing me. I can't think straight when you're touching me like that.'

His hand slips out of the lace. He shrugs as my body shrivels in objection.

'When you *can* think straight, you know where to find me.' He nods towards his bedroom door, directly across the hall from mine, running his tongue seductively over his fingers before sauntering down the hall.

I might still despise him, after all.

No, what I despise is how much I want him.

And his ability to make me lose all control.

The distant wail of the morning call to prayer wakes me after a fitful night's sleep. I wish someone would say a prayer for me. For the life choices I'm making, for my dick and maybe my right hand, because if I can't get Chloe into bed with me, neither will be right ever again.

I almost had her. Her body trembled so responsively beneath my fingers. I can only imagine how satisfying that trembling would feel around my cock.

A weaker woman would have crumbled. The fact she didn't only drives me on in my quest. Chloe Sexton's just handed me the biggest challenge of my life.

For a million reasons, it's the one line I shouldn't cross. Apart from my promise to help Lula, we're virtually family. Not to mention we're stuck working together for the duration of this tour. But there's something about her that creeps beneath my skin, setting my insides on fire. She's so different from any other woman I've dated before.

Sharp.

Smart-mouthed.

Independent.

Sexy as hell and worryingly, she's everything I never knew I wanted in a woman.

I'm determined to be the man she breaks her rules for.

Slipping out of bed, I grab a pair of black boxers from my open suitcase. It's too hot to consider putting on a suit until I've eaten. Plus, Chloe seemed to like what she glimpsed yesterday. After her abrupt departure last night, I'm determined to remind her of that.

I brush my teeth in the terracotta tiled en-suite and stroll downstairs in search of coffee.

In the kitchen, Chloe stands in front of the machine with her back to me. Her hair's swept up in that elaborate twist again, exposing a long slender neck that begs to be kissed. A grey suit dress clings indecently to the swell of her hips, showcasing everything but revealing nothing. She oozes the type of class money can't buy.

'Morning, Princess.' I deliberately graze my bare chest against her back as I reach over her head to grab a coffee cup from a glass-fronted cupboard.

She leaps a foot into the air before spinning round with a palm pressed against her naked skin.

'Holy fuck, Jayden, you scared the shit out of me.' Her perfectly shaped eyebrows knit together in a frown.

'Did someone get out of bed on the wrong side this morning?' My lips smirk upwards in the precise way that seems to antagonise her. 'Or maybe you just woke up in the wrong bed...'

'Will you give it a rest? You're like the boy in the playground who pulls pigtails to express his interest. Last night was a mistake.' Her mouth says one thing, but amorous eyes blaze over my bare chest. That raspberry-like tongue darts hungrily over her lower lip.

I can't help myself. In one swift motion, I pin her against the kitchen worktop with my hips. She swallows thickly but doesn't protest. Her gaze angles upwards. Bright eyes burn with desire.

'The only mistake you made last night was not letting me make you come.' I shoot her a salacious wink before turning my attention to the coffee machine. 'It's going to be a long day at the office.' For me, more than her. At least she seems to have some level of self-control.

She scowls at me, red-faced.

'How do you like it in the morning?' I continue to poke the angry bear. 'Your coffee, I mean...'

'You are so irritating, it's not even funny.' She storms towards the kitchen door, pausing long enough to say, 'and put some fucking clothes on, will you?'

Why exactly is the thrill of the chase so, well, thrilling?

She'll cave. I'd put money on it.

And even if I regret it later, I'm going to make sure *she* doesn't.

Half an hour later, we're in her office, which is even more impressive than the brief glance of it I caught on Zoom. Open plan in its design, Liberty Events Management & Marketing occupies the entire thirty-sixth floor of a sleek modern skyscraper overlooking Dubai Creek below. Skyscrapers crest the horizon. It makes my office look like a dump.

'This is Izzy, my PA.' Chloe introduces some of her employees, drawing my attention away from row upon row of awards lining the white (surprise surprise) walls. 'Jack, Sarah, Mohammed, Jordan, Michelle, Paul, Sebastian and you sort of met Ruby last night.'

Ruby, a mass of dark hair and red nails, shoots me a knowing wink and a wave. The others barely lift their gaze.

My reputation must be worse than I thought. It's almost as if they're intimidated.

'The others are out pitching various projects. You'll meet them later.' Chloe's tone is curt, cold and commanding.

Shit, it's *her* they're intimidated of, not me. Holy fuck. CEO Chloe is seriously fucking hot.

'Grab your iPads and we'll convene in the boardroom,' she barks and the staff scurry to their respective desks to gather their things.

While she collects her own personal effects, I rest my backside on the edge of her desk, deliberately invading her personal space.

'Boundaries? Much?' She shoves past me, and I follow closely on her tail, admiring the swaying of her backside as she struts in four-inch heels.

The smile stretching my lips isn't just to annoy her. It seems to be a natural fixture in her presence. 'Princess, you're sexually frustrated. Don't take it out on me.'

She whirls round, colliding full frontally with my chest, a tremulous finger pressing firmly against my sternum. 'Don't you dare undermine me by calling me "Princess" within these four walls. Do you hear me?'

'So it's okay outside of these four walls?' Oh, it's too much fun. How will I ever bring myself to leave in three days when I could happily spend a lifetime winding up my super sexy, almost sister-in-law? 'What's it worth, Princess?'

'It's worth me not ramming my stiletto so far down your throat, you'll never be able to utter that word again, to me or anyone else.'

'Tut tut. Is that any way to speak to your brother-in-law's brother? I've got a better idea. One that's much more appealing.' We continue through to a large boardroom housing an ornate oval oakwood table, flanked by high-backed chairs.

'I doubt that. Unless it involves you signing off on all my

ideas for the tour and hopping on the first flight back to the States.'

'It involves swimming in your pool this evening.'

Bright eyes glare at me, silently searching for the catch. I don't leave her wondering too long.

'Naked.'

She scoffs, hand on hip. 'In your dreams.'

'What's the matter? Can't trust yourself, Prin...' The rapid rise of her right hand signals me to stop before I finish my sentence.

'Either I can give you free rein on this project or I can fight you every step of the way. Which is it going to be?' she says.

'You wouldn't dare.'

Her hands rest on her hips in a silent challenge. 'Try me.' She takes the chair at the head of the table. 'Sign off my suggestions for the tour and don't call me that name for the duration of the day and I'll think about it.'

'Don't make me bend you over the desk. I don't care if it's open plan and the whole damn world is watching. Yes or no, Pri-'

A flush inches up her delectable neck as her staff flock around the table, closing in on us. Inquisitive eyes dart between their boss and me. Flustered is clearly a new look for her.

She bites her lower lip and shakes her head. 'Fine. I'll swim with you. You win.'

'I think you'll find we'll both finish on top.'

The others silently assume their seats. Chloe shoots me a warning look as I take the seat to her left.

'What was that about the desk?' Ruby takes the seat to the right of Chloe. She's not just a friend. She's clearly Chloe's right-hand woman.

'Shh! Nothing.' Chloe glares a warning at both of us. Ruby smiles knowingly.

Settling back into my seat, my mind reluctantly returns to business. After all, it's the sole reason I'm here. Well, almost. I can only hope to god Chloe's ideas aren't egregious. I'd hate to have to shoot her down and forfeit my end of the bargain.

Her team launches into a strategic proposal with 3D images of potential themes and stage props sourced and priced in each city. I have to admire the thoroughness of their research and uniquely thought-out suggestions.

'That's not the best part.' Chloe nods to a red-headed guy. I think she introduced him as Jack.

'We were thinking of taking some pressure off Ryan by using a local legendary support act for each concert. Let him duet with someone they already love as much as him. One of their own local treasures.'

A list of suggestions for each city floods the projector to the left of the table.

I have to admit they're onto something. Using a local support act would allow Ryan to perform for a shorter time and uniting him with a hero of their own is solid gold entertainment butter. It's actually fucking genius. Especially if we could keep each duet a secret, ramping up speculation.

'What do you think?' Chloe demands, rhythmically tapping her pen against the desk.

I think I'd love to rhythmically tap your ass off that desk.

'I'm impressed, honestly.' The staff glance round each other, relief rolling between them like cresting waves.

'There's just one tiny thing. That's an impressive list of potential artists to collaborate with there, but has anyone reached out to any of them to discuss the opportunity?'

'You're the agent. The ruthless negotiator, by all accounts.' Chloe scowls at my hand. The same one that graced her underwear last night. 'I thought you were happy to get your hands dirty.'

'Oh, I am, Prin–' I catch myself. 'Email that list and I'll run through it with Ryan. Great work everyone. This is shaping up to be epic.'

Though not nearly as epic as my evening's shaping up to be now Chloe and her team have done most of the legwork. Ryan was right, again. She really is talented.

Beneath this very conservative dress, a painfully blistering fire blazes through every fibre of me. Jayden was right. I should have let him make me come last night because I can't think about anything else. I gave him a desk farthest from mine so he can scan our earlier proposals for himself, but the distance doesn't offer even a modicum of relief.

He's the one itch I know I shouldn't scratch, but doing something I shouldn't, only enhances the appeal.

The day's dragging. Probably something to do with the deal we made.

In theory, it's an horrific proposal, but after last night, the thought of being naked with him sends a jolt of arousal pulsing between my legs.

The fact he's left me with pretty much no choice if I want this tour to go my way should make me angry. But oddly, there's something disturbingly hot about the power he wields over me to get what he wants. About him wanting me so desperately that he's happy to relinquish his say in organising this tour.

Clearly, I have bigger issues than I realised.

In the past, some men have been intimidated by my success. Others have tried to take it from me. I don't think I'm going to have either problem with Jayden.

No, I think I'm going to have a bigger one.

He might just be the best I ever have, which would prove to be a monumental problem. Because even if I was brave enough to embark on an actual relationship again, clearly LA's biggest player is the most unsuitable candidate.

His head jolts up from across the room. I look away, feigning interest in a spreadsheet on my computer, but there's no denying the spark fusing across my spine.

How can a person flip from being so infuriating to so alluring in a single day?

Oh, Chloe, his allure was never in question.

Maybe it's not him who's the cause of my infuriation. Maybe I'm annoyed with myself that I'm attracted to him in the first place. He'll use and discard me like he does with everyone else.

But am I really any better? I'm probably slightly more discreet about my, well, indiscretions, that's all.

He was my first crush.

Back then, before the harsh reality of real life took hold of me, I hoped he'd be more.

I scrutinised every picture ever printed of him. At the time, I thought it was out of disgust. What if it was because I secretly wanted him?

I don't want a relationship with him, but I'll take his body in mine.

Is it possible that all the things I don't like in Jayden are a mirror image of the things I don't like in myself? I snap the elastic band on my wrist and ping away that thought before it consumes me.

I don't need to glance up to know his eyes are firmly fixed

on me. The heat of them sears my soul from across the room. I'm practically ready to blow.

No matter how spacious the office is, it's nowhere near big enough to hold the magnitude of sexual tension radiating between us. 'Hungry?' I mouth, looking for any excuse to get out of here for an hour.

Cool grey eyes drop deliberately to my breasts.

I roll my eyes even as my thighs press together. Turning to Ruby, who's on the phone to a supplier, I whisper, 'I'm bringing our guest to lunch. Can you man the fort?'

She presses her hand over the receiver. 'Not fair.'

I shrug, my nonchalance fooling nobody, and grab my clutch from my drawer. 'Got to keep him sweet, I suppose.'

'I'm sure you can think of better ways... if you haven't already?' She wiggles expectant eyebrows, but I shake my head. She leans across her desk and whisper-shouts, 'Did you add him to the list of your breakfast dates yet?'

What is it with Ruby and Sasha and this obsession with my breakfast dates? If only they knew the truth, that I kick them out before breakfast. Eating breakfast together is every bit as awkward as waking up with them.

'No, I did not.' My lips twitch at the prospect of what might happen later. 'But ask me again tomorrow.'

'Oh, you bad girl.' Ruby raises her hand and gives me a high five. 'I need details.'

Jayden joins us from across the room. 'Listen hard from wherever you are in this city, and you'll get your "details."'

Ruby picks up a stack of papers from her desk and theatrically fans herself.

'Don't mind him.' I shoot her a wink. 'He's from Holly-wood. He has a flair for the dramatics.'

'We'll see about that, Princ- Chloe.'

I stalk towards the elevator to hide my grin, with Jayden following closely on my heels.

'Where are we going?' he asks as the chrome doors slide shut.

Resting my bum against the metal handrail, I reapply a touch of lip gloss. 'For lunch, I told you. Mexican, Italian or seafood?'

A frown flickers across his face. 'Not Mexican.' Snatching the tube from my fingers, he says, 'And you won't be needing that.'

His hot breath brushes my lips as he lowers his face to mine, licking the gloss with torturous strokes of his talented tongue.

'Strawberry. Not bad.'

'Boundaries? Much?' Apparently, he's as ruthless in his pursuit of his conquests as he is in business. I'm torn between outrage at his audacity and a blinding lust.

It's just a crying shame the source is the man I'm supposed to hate.

The lift pings a split second before the doors slide open. Thirty-six floors suddenly seem like an inadequate journey. After sharing Jayden with my entire office all morning, I'm enjoying this brief stolen time together.

Strolling side-by-side down the busy sidewalk, the scorching sun feels weak compared to the heat flooding through me.

'We're not seriously going back in there after lunch, are we?' His eyes home in on mine.

'I agreed to swim with you tonight, not skive off for the afternoon. What kind of example would that set for my staff? We have a lot of work to get through. Business before plea-sure, always.' It's one of the few mottos I live by.

'Huh. Normally, I'd feel exactly the same, but the way I see it, you've got this entire tour completely under control.'

'That's exactly the way I like it.'

'Seems like we have more in common than we originally thought.'

I look at him to see if he's winding me up again, but for once his features fan into a serious expression. A troubled flicker creases his brow before he catches himself.

I steer him into The Marriot. Gi Gi's, one of three restaurants in the hotel, boasts the best seafood on the marina.

In the doorway, his mouth drops to my ear. 'I'm taking control tonight though, and if you run away from me again, rest assured, this time, I *will* run after you.'

The air-con is useless. His eyes hold mine as they set me on fire.

'A table for two?' A South African waitress greets us.

She's stunning. Blonde, tall and a few years younger than me. Ethan, my ex, would have been all over her like prickly heat. Unbelievably, Jayden doesn't seem to notice. His palm settles on the base of my spine as we follow her across the room to a window seat with panoramic views of the marina. Bright blue skies loom overhead while the still navy water mirrors the adjacent granite-coloured skyscrapers.

I slip my heels off beneath the table and order a bottle of chilled house white. 'What did you think of the proposal?'

'I think it's going to be mutually exhilarating.' The smirk is back.

'I meant the tour.'

His expression narrows thoughtfully. 'I think you've nailed it. There's only one suggestion I'd make. I notice you have Ahlam Alshamsi down for the Dubai date. Would you consider switching for Aurelia? I know she's not technically native, but she's been in the Middle East so long they've claimed her as their own. She's a better match.'

My heart skips in my chest at the mention of my idol. Hard to believe anything could trump meeting her last night, but somehow Jayden's touch obliterated everything else. 'Do you think she'd do it?'

'I know she would. I'm her agent, remember?' He flashes his Hollywood smile.

'That would be unbelievable.'

'Also, I'm loving the Arabian Nights theme, but I think the genie might be a step too far. Tacky rather than trendy.'

'Yeah, that was Ruby's idea. She's a six-year-old Disney fanatic trapped in the body of a twenty-six-year-old. I'll make sure it's cut.' The waitress returns with two wine glasses. She uncorks the bottle and pours an inch into my glass to taste, but I wave her on.

If Jayden's pissed neither of us thought to invite him to taste it, he doesn't mention it. Maybe he's not the alphahole I assumed. The jury's still out.

'The thousand diamonds representing glittering stars can stay, though. This country loves to promote its wealth.' Jayden gestures round at the grandeur of the restaurant. Gi Gi's might be my favourite, but the country's full of amazing places to eat.

'And the camels?' I'm dubious about them.

'Two, in a corner somewhere. They're great for people flying in specifically for the tour. Not so interesting to the locals, I'm sure.' He presses his wine glass against his lips and I squirm with envy.

'Yes, sir.' I offer him a military salute.

His irises darken two shades. 'Finally, you've stopped questioning who's in charge.'

'Know that it physically pains me to admit this out loud, but it's actually a relief to have someone with your experience to check in with. This tour is a big deal for all of us.'

He sets his glass down and knits his fingers together. 'It will separate Liberty Events Management from its competitors. It's an opportunity like no other.'

I take a sip of wine and my mind strays to my main competition in the Middle East.

Ethan Harte used to be my office manager. And my boyfriend. Ruby calls him Ethan-Has-No-Heart. He screwed me, literally and figuratively. Robbed me of the ability to trust anyone when I was already raw and stole my clients at the same time.

Eventually I clawed them back, and so much more. But the snake's still out there, slithering round the desert.

I figure the best way to get my own back is to become the most successful events management company the world has ever seen. Bring in new clients. Get more exposure. And put some distance between us and give myself a clean slate in the process.

Ruby is more than capable of overseeing the Dubai branch of Liberty Events Management. One day, I'd like a branch in every city in every country in every continent in the world. Ambitious perhaps, but I didn't climb this high to develop a fear of heights halfway.

'I'm ready to get out of here.' My hand sweeps the air around me.

Devilish pupils gleam. 'Why didn't you say so?'

'I meant the Middle East. I need more. There's something missing. I feel like I've got more to give. So much more. And I know I can do it. I've already proved I've got what it takes, but if I'm going to make the company a truly global brand, I need to make a success of Ryan's tour. And as much as I hate to admit it, I need your help to do it.'

Jayden's features rearrange into genuine resoluteness. 'I promise I'll do everything to help make it happen. Even if you wear your disdain for me like a mask.'

Does he mean it? Or is it because he just wants to get into my knickers? I don't know. He's so hard to read. Hell, for all I know, it's because he feels guilty about my parents' death, blaming himself for his father's recklessness, even though Jayden had nothing to do with it.

Aurelia made some passing comment about him saving everyone. Does he have some sort of god complex? Or does he genuinely care?

Either way, the wine's loosening my tongue.

'That's what it is, a mask.' Suddenly I'm confessing secrets I only admitted to myself this morning.

Fuck it, he'll be gone in a couple of days, anyway. 'Of all the things I know about you, you're one man who's unquestionably capable.'

He runs a finger over the back of my hand. 'Was that actually a compliment, Princess?'

'Careful. It'd be a shame to get arrested when we're supposed to be going swimming later.' When it comes to my body, I'm far from shy. It's just a body. We all have one. It's what lurks beneath my skin that I worry about revealing.

Yanking my hand away, I ask him the one question that's been bugging me for months.

'Why do you insist on calling me Princess?' I can't work out if I'm supposed to be insulted when he says it with borderline affection.

'Because you *are* a princess. You were born in a castle, for Christ's sake.'

'Far from royal, as you know...'

'You're pretty fucking majestic from where I'm sitting. It's taken me ten years to get my hand in your royal underwear, although it wasn't there nearly long enough.'

'Huh. That was because you were busy with your hand in a certain chambermaid's underwear, if I remember correctly.'

My remark is blasé but the memories of that day are all too vivid. I hadn't realised how much it's been pissing me off all these years. I thought he liked me.

That day sparked a jealousy inside me which I channelled

into hatred towards him. A hatred which finally dissipated last night.

'You have no idea, do you?' The intensity of his stare trebles. 'I used her. Because she was there, willing and easy, and my balls were about to explode with carnal thoughts of my landlord's daughter. You were only just legal. I was two years older than you. Those two years make a big difference at such a formative age. It would have been so wrong.'

I swallow hard as his words sink in, softly soothing the insecure seventeen-year-old lurking inside. I wanted him so badly back then. The same way I do now.

For the first time in my life, I might not be entirely averse to a breakfast date.

Chapter Ten

JAYDEN

The evening sun lowers over the terrace. Pink and orange streaks illuminate the sky, casting an alluring reflection on the pool, and that's even before Chloe gets anywhere near it. The need to make good on our deal consumes me. There's only one problem - a five-foot Sri Lankan woman by the name of Naveesha.

She shuffles around Chloe's kitchen with a bright smile and kind eyes. If I could have chosen a mother for myself, it would have been someone like her. Warm and approachable. Though any mother would have been a novelty. My own walked out when Ryan and I were toddlers. If she hadn't fallen pregnant, I'm pretty sure she'd have left dad long before then. Perhaps that's one of the reasons I can't sustain a relationship long term? If my own mother didn't love me enough to stick around, why would I expect any other woman to? Maybe, deep down that's why I don't ever keep the same woman around to give her the chance.

'Miss Chloe,' she calls up the stairs. 'I do your ironing tonight, no?'

No is the only word for it.

Chloe went upstairs five minutes ago with the excuse of putting on a swimsuit, leaving me to work on getting rid of the only person she'd need to wear one around. I take five hundred dollars from my wallet and hand it to Naveesha.

'We have some very important business to do here for the next couple of days. We need a little privacy.'

She pushes the money back towards me even as her eyes widen at the sight of the crisp notes. 'Sir, I cannot take this.'

'Naveesha, please, take the money.' I'll do Chloe's damn ironing myself, if necessary. There's no way I'm having a chaperone here tonight, or tomorrow, for that matter. Not when I'm so close to nailing the most elusive conquest of my life. My dick's been pulsing at the prospect all day.

'Miss Chloe wants you to take a few days off. Three, actually.'

Naveesha's earnest expression searches mine. She points to the terrace. 'What about the flowers? Miss Chloe always forget to water the flowers.'

Ushering her towards the front door, I add another hundred-dollar bill to the wad of cash. 'I'll water the flowers. You have my word.'

'What about dinner?' Naveesha's gaze returns to the kitchen doorway and her voice drops to a whisper. 'Miss Chloe burns everything.'

I suppress my snort. 'I'll take her for dinner. Trust me, she won't go hungry.'

Naveesha pats her black, thinning hair as her head bobs from side to side in contemplation. Before she can decide, Chloe emerges from her bedroom, gracefully sauntering down the stairs wearing nothing but a tiny black bikini.

I nearly trip over my dick, ushering Naveesha to the front door.

'Miss Chloe, you want me to come back tomorrow?'

'The day after will be fine, thank you. I'll pay you for both, of course.'

'No need.' Naveesha's trembling hands hold up the bundle of cash in wonder.

'That's a tip. Wages as usual.'

No one's more surprised than me when Naveesha throws her tiny frame at me, wrapping her arms around my body in what I can only assume is gratitude. I sidestep so she awkwardly cradles my ribs. The poor woman would be traumatised if she accidentally brushed me full frontal at this precise second.

'You are very generous, sir.'

Hardly. Impatient is more like it. Though I can't deny the warmth that surges through my bones from making Naveesha's day. If only all the problems of the world could be solved as easily. I pat her arm in a weird side-hug.

Chloe rubs Naveesha's back as they walk to the door, giggling and whispering in hushed voices. I get the impression I'm not the only one to have maternal thoughts about the housekeeper.

The door closes and finally we're alone.

'You're overdressed.' I focus in on the dark triangles of Chloe's itsy-bitsy bikini, which do little to hide the beauty beneath.

Arousal thrums between us, growing with every passing second.

'I agreed to swim naked, not permanently walk around starkers for your entertainment.' Her lips roll in an amused smile and my chest swells almost as rapidly as my pants. It's the first genuine smile she's ever given me, and it possesses an unnerving ability to bring me to my knees.

That doesn't mean I'm not going to enjoy rearranging those lips into a parted O of pleasure.

Chloe grabs a bottle of champagne from the fridge and

two flutes from a cupboard before strutting confidently to the terrace, her peachy ass cheeks ripe for grabbing. 'Are you coming, or what? Let's get this over with.'

She's fooling no one. Desire smoulders in the air between us. The question is, tonight, will she give into it?

I follow her onto the terrace, unbuttoning my shirt as I walk, discarding it on the couch as I pass. By the time I'm outside, I'm down to my boxers.

Chloe puts the champagne and glasses on a tiny table between two sun loungers and strolls to the deeper end of the pool. With the sun setting rapidly behind her, her curvaceous silhouette is bathed in a majestic golden sheen.

It might be a nickname, but the truth of it isn't lost on me. The woman is a goddamn princess. Given half the chance, I will serve her body like a loyal subject.

She stands poolside, ready to jump. Oceanic eyes glitter brighter than the water as they skim across my torso and lower. I haven't had this much fun in forever. Who'd have thought Miss-Silver-Spoon-Sexton would be so easily corruptible?

'That bikini looks unbelievable on you, but it wasn't part of our deal.'

Fiery eyes hold mine defiantly as she slowly unties the lycra, discarding it with a brief flick of her wrists. Her confidence is as sexy as her full, round breasts.

My eyes drop, noting the absence of tan lines. Topless in her garden is clearly not a new look for her. Perfect nipples point directly at me, silently screaming to be sucked.

This deal might have been my idea, but there's no mistaking who's in control, for now at least. I can't tear my eyes from this semi-naked goddess.

Why on earth did I think she'd be shy? Sasha told me she's no wilting virgin. Her experience is obvious. She's empowered by it and it's sexy as fuck.

Dare I believe I've finally met my match?

The timing couldn't be any worse.

'Pop the bottle, will you? Anyone would think you've never seen a topless woman before.'

Head in the game. I can berate myself later. It's something I've gotten good at over the years.

'Princess, the deal was naked.' My tongue darts over my lips as I drop to a lounger, relishing the show.

'Good things come to those who wait, isn't that what you told me yesterday?' Her fingers skim across her smooth flat stomach, skimming the waist band of the remaining lycra. My dick stiffens noticeably in my boxers.

I didn't realise it was possible to get any harder.

She's good.

Really good.

To hell with the consequences. I can't wait to make her come undone.

As I pop the cork, she dives into the pool, surging through the water to materialise at my feet. An outstretched hand silently demands her drink.

Holding a glass of fizzing bubbles deliberately out of her reach, I nod towards the water that envelopes her lower half. 'Loose them.'

She shrugs, slips out of the bikini bottoms, a hand emerging a few seconds later and slapping them straight into my palm. Oh, I am definitely keeping these as a souvenir.

I hand her the glass and clink my own against it in a toast. 'Cheers to our deal. A pleasure doing business with you.'

Evocative eyes dart towards my boxers. 'I'm still waiting for you to hold up your end, though.' She sniggers at her own joke.

I'm pretty sure they can see my end holding up in Timbuktu right now. And I thought I was the funny one.

'Good things come to those who wait, remember?' Placing

my glass and the rest of the bottle next to the glittering water, I drop my underwear, revelling in the way she swallows hard at the sight of my erection. In one swift jump, I'm in next to her.

'Now we're even.' I bob in the water, mere inches from her.

It occurs to me that even though I have every intention of lavishing her with a never-ending stream of multiple orgasms, she mustered enough control to stop me last night. Who's to say she's going to let me take her now? She could be the biggest prick-tease ever.

She wants it, whatever this thing between us is, but she's got more self-discipline than most. So, before she has time to back out, I reach for her bare shoulder, using my index finger to trace lower over her collar bone.

She doesn't flinch.

My fingers skirt lower, dropping to worship those glorious tits. 'You are fucking magnificent, Chloe.'

'You're not so bad yourself, considering I hate you and all that.' Her hand extends to palm my pecs as lusty eyes comb every inch of my bare skin.

My mouth dips, capturing her breast while my fingers dart beneath the water. When her legs part willingly, a primal urge to satisfy her takes over.

This needs to be the best she's ever had. It'll only ever be a fling, but I want this moment to mark her forever. To be her comparison point for all eternity.

Slipping between her folds, my fingers glide over her slickness. A whimper slips from her lips as my mouth captures her nipple.

'You hate that too, Princess?'

'It's ok, I guess.' She might joke, but there's nothing funny about her breathy tone.

The carefully built wall of control's lowering, but nowhere

near low enough for my liking. I won't be satisfied until she's begging for it, screaming my name and utterly at my mercy. I've had too much time to imagine this moment. Over ten years, to be precise.

Upping the pace, my fingers work her over, again and again. 'What about that? How are my dirty hands working out for you now?'

Gone are her tongue-in-cheek remarks, the promise of impending release too deliciously close for her to risk it.

She grips my shoulders, kneading and squeezing the tautness of my skin. When she parts her legs further, I slip two fingers inside, using my thumb to massage her clit.

'Jayden, it's been too long... I'm so fucking close.' Her heated whisper brushes over my chest, scalding me inside and out.

It has nothing to do with how long it's been and everything to do with what I'm doing to her, but she'll learn that first hand in a minute.

I'm going to make her come. Again. And again. And again. As much for me as for her. Being able to touch her there, to get her off and watch her sharp edges soften is the biggest turn on of my life. I'm going to remove that silver spoon once and for all.

Trailing tiny kisses up and down her neck and back across her breasts, I whisper, 'Come on my hands, Princess.'

Hooded eyes flutter up and her mouth parts as she arches her pelvis against my fingers, crying out my name.

A shiver rips down my spine. That's what I wanted. What I needed. As much as I hate to admit it, Chloe Sexton affects me like no other woman I've ever known.

Chapter Eleven

CHLOE

My whole body shakes, bathed in the aftermath of shockwaves from the explosive orgasm delivered at the hand of the one man I'm supposed to hate.

Why couldn't Mark, the Formula One sponsor, have that effect on me? Or anyone else? Things were good with Ethan before he fucked me over, but were they ever *that* good?

Honestly?

Nowhere near.

However smug Jayden was beforehand, he'll be a million times worse after this. For a woman who was oozing confidence not ten minutes ago, I can barely raise my face to meet his dark penetrating pupils.

When I do, he's staring, transfixed. That smug smirk is definitely pinned back in position, but it's accompanied by a look of what could definitely be mistaken for awe.

Beneath his sculpted body, I'd almost swear his heart's hammering as fast as mine. 'You're so fucking beautiful when you come.'

'Sorry, I didn't mean to lose control like that.' My teeth

nip my lower lip. His hand sweeps under my chin, angling my face towards his.

'You're apologising? For orgasming? Princess, you just made my year.' Full hot lips capture mine, his excitement pressing against my stomach, and I'm shocked to find the satisfying ripples being rapidly replaced by greedy new ones.

The prospect of feeling those eight inches inside of me is enough to get me off again.

My hand drops, fingers gripping his excitement. His head rolls back, an animalistic sound groans from his throat.

I can deny it until I'm blue in the face, but the truth is, I've wanted him for years.

Thick fingers find mine, unwinding them from his throbbing shaft, placing my hands firmly on either side of my body.

'Not yet.' Sculpted arms lift me effortlessly from the water and onto the side of the pool. Broad muscular shoulders part my thighs, as Jayden inches his perfect pecs between my legs.

I need to feel him. To have him fill me up. The way he's drawing this out only makes me want it more. And he knows it.

Greedy hands grip my backside, inching me towards the slippery ledge of the pool until I'm hanging on the edge.

'I want to taste you.' His lips brush my inner thigh and my sex throbs in response. *Traitor.*

How can I be ready again so quickly?

Because Jayden Cooper is the hottest man you've ever laid eyes on, and right now he's naked between your legs.

Add in the alfresco part and I'm pure putty.

His hot tongue dips over my sex. I cry out in sheer uninhibited pleasure. 'Are you trying to kill me or what?'

I feel his grin, but he doesn't stop those slow, maddening strokes. The man is insanely gifted. He knows exactly what to do with a woman's body.

Because he's had hundreds. A ripple of irritation spreads across my spine.

As if sensing it, his thick fingers grip my thighs, securing my legs in position as he ups the pace with that talented tongue. Every delicious stroke reassures me it's me he wants.

Dizzying hot waves of bliss pulse repeatedly through me. I'm so close it's blinding. Just as my orgasm's building at the back of my eyelids, he stops, pulls back and gazes up at me with a cruel, gorgeous smirk. 'Tell me again how much you hate me.'

He's ruthless in bed as well as business.

My white knuckles grip the side of the pool as I shimmy further forward, closer to that clever mouth. 'At this precise second, I really fucking hate you.'

'You want more?' Dark pupils glint mischievously. 'Is that what you're telling me?'

He has me exactly where he wants. And he knows it. But I'm too lust-riddled in this moment to care. A hot quivering mess. In all my one-night stands, I've never known desire like it. I need him.

His fingers continue to pin my thighs apart as his eyes drink me in. 'Say it, Princess, and it's yours. Tell me what you need.'

'Jayden, I need you to make me come.'

'How?'

'With your tongue.'

'Say it. Say "Jayden, I need your tongue on my clit."'

Nobody has ever had this effect on me. I'm far from shy, but fucking hell, he's pushing my limits in the most deliciously decadent way.

Careful what you wish for, right?

I groan as his tongue flicks over me persuasively before darting away again. It's unbearable in the most hedonistic way.

I submit. 'Jayden, I need your tongue on my clit.' I'm too turned on to be embarrassed.

'Good girl. Now, eyes open. I want you to watch.'

Oh my god.

When I thought this couldn't get any hotter, he cranks it up another hundred degrees.

Our heated eyes lock as his mouth captures me and I groan in sheer undulated pleasure. He lets out a moan of approval as I tilt my pelvis up for him.

What he's doing to me is sexy as hell, but what's really getting me off is the way he's watching. Like he's enjoying this as much as I am. He has an innate way of making me feel like I'm the only woman in the world.

My climax pushes tantalisingly close to the surface again. When my thighs begin to tremble, he slips two fingers inside me, his tongue continuing to swirl in maddening circles.

My fingers claw his shoulders as my orgasm rips through me with a paralysing intensity that's so transcendent it's life changing.

It's carnal.

He's ruined me.

As I slowly come back down to earth, he plants a final kiss down there before hoisting me into the water. Strong arms envelop me. My hands palm the back of his neck, legs wrapping around his waist. When the tip of his erection grazes my entrance, it's too tempting not to slide straight onto it. I'm not sure which one of us is more shocked.

Hot lust dances in his widening eyes. Firm hands grip my backside, both supporting me and stilling me. I'm playing with fire, riding him bareback, but the man stirs something feral in me that no one has ever done before. In this moment I need to feel him.

'Do you want to come inside me?'

'Chloe.' It's a warning, but his voice is pained, torn between knowing what's right and wanting what's wrong. 'Are you on the pill?'

My lips press tiny teasing kisses across his neck, feeling the throb of his racing pulse beneath his skin. Why is the prospect of doing something so bad, so damn good?

'I get birth control shots and I've always been careful. Have you?'

'Of course. The last thing this world needs is a mini-me.' He stands rigid, caught between risk and reward. 'I always use protection.' He bites his lower lip.

'Not so smart now, are you?' I tease. 'Cat got your tongue?'

'No, it's got my cock.'

Even though it was sexy as hell, he's going to pay for making me beg for it. I clench around him, revelling in the way he fills me. It's my turn to watch him unravel. 'Say it and it's yours.'

He hesitates for half a second until his hips decide for him, bucking back before slamming into me. 'I want to come inside you. I want to mark you from within.'

I was supposed to be unravelling him, but his dirty mouth has me in a frenzy again. Grinding myself against him, he levers my back to the pool wall, driving himself inside me, matching fire with fire.

His mouth dips to my breasts but his eyes remain locked with mine as ever, both of us luxuriating in each other's lust. It's primal. I'm unrecognisable, even to myself.

A million stars gather before my eyes as my legs tremble again. As my world explodes for the third time, he pumps harder, fingers digging into my backside as he spills himself into me.

Our groans of satisfaction mingle in each other's mouths as our hearts hammer together, synced, chest to chest.

'Don't even think of telling me that's a one-time thing, Chloe Sexton. I'm going to spend the next few days joined to you with my mouth or dick. Preferably both.'

I can't even argue with him. For the first time in a long time, one night isn't going to be enough.

Chapter Twelve

JAYDEN

The wailing call to prayer wakes me for the second morning in a row. Thankfully, last night my own prayers were answered.

Multiple times.

Although that doesn't stop the blood rushing rapidly to my dick again where it's pressed up against Chloe's smooth naked backside as she sleeps peacefully beside me.

Who knew she'd be fucking dynamite in bed?

She always gave off that elusive posh girl vibe, and the prospect of corrupting her was half the appeal, but never in my wildest dreams did I imagine she'd be so responsive.

It was explosive.

Worryingly, I think there's a real chance I've finally found my sexual soulmate. My exes have been pretty predictable in and out of the bedroom. Within a matter of weeks I'm bored, ready to move onto the next conquest. The way I feel right now, I could fuck Chloe all year and never tire of it. Sadly, that's not an option. She made that abundantly clear.

I was so determined to be the best she'd ever had, it didn't occur to me for a single second she might be the best *I've* ever had.

Thick chestnut hair spills across the pillow and I sniff it, memorising its exotic fruity scent.

Get a grip, for fuck's sake.

'Did you just sniff my hair?' Amusement rings through Chloe's sleepy tone.

Busted.

'Good morning, Princess.' I nudge my throbbing dick against her.

'It's looking that way alright.' She wriggles her ass backwards, inching herself onto me, slick and ready.

After her hallway confession two nights ago that she doesn't do repeats, I had to wonder if she was going to weird out on me this morning. No fear of that, apparently. Hard to feel awkward around someone when you shared what we did last night.

My hands reach round for her nipples, rolling them between my fingers as I slide in and out of her at a deliciously languorous pace.

If I could pause this moment forever, I swear I would. I've found my own personal heaven. Sex with Chloe Sexton is practically a religious experience.

I nudge her onto her stomach and onto her knees, inching myself into her as deep as physically possible. Reaching round her waist, my fingers find her sweet spot, slowly circling as my lips press against the back of her neck and my tongue rolls down her spine.

When her legs begin to tremble, I use my free hand to part them wider, slamming myself into her until her back arches in pleasure and she cries out my name like a plea and a prayer rolled into one.

I'm right behind her. My orgasm rips powerfully through

me, wave after wave of heady pleasure floods through every inch of me.

With my heart hammering in my ribcage, I can't even articulate what just happened between us. Again.

'Can we agree to do that solidly for the next...' I glance at the Swiss watch on my wrist, the only item I'm wearing, unless you count Chloe who's still clenched around my cock, '... forty-two hours?'

Chloe slides off, flopping onto her back. My eyes dart between her magnificent tits and huge turquoise eyes. 'Now, Jayden, you know I don't do repeats. I warned you.' She pokes her tongue out. From the way her eyes glint, I can only assume she's joking.

Elevating her arms above her head, I tower over her, pressing tiny kisses along the sensitive skin of her neck as she squirms deliciously beneath me. 'Princess, do I have to pin you down here and tie you up for the day? If that's the case, then so be it because I am nowhere near done with you.'

Before she can answer, the shrill ringing of my mobile phone pierces the air. I glance at the screen out of habit, annoyed at the intrusion.

It's Kim, my PA.

I hover over Chloe, torn between burying myself inside her for the day and facing the responsibilities of the real world.

Burying myself wins. I cancel the call. So much for business before pleasure. One night with Chloe and I'm unrecognisable. My lips resume their position, skirting lower over Chloe's collarbone. Who knew collarbones could be so sexy?

'We should get up,' she whispers.

'I am up.' I nudge against her entrance.

'Again? You are insatiable.'

'It's a talent and a curse.'

When the phone rings again, I know there's a problem.

With an indignant growl, I snatch my mobile. 'Yes?'

'Jayden, it's Mia.' Kim's panicked tone makes me sit up and take notice.

Mia Sweet is an up-and-coming female artist I signed last year. I only sign the cream of the crop. If they look bad, they make me look bad.

'What's up with her?' I'm not negotiating her contract again. She already earns more than most of my female artists.

'She was photographed off her face in a nightclub last night. The media's having a field day with it.'

What? Sweet isn't just her name, it's her nature. She came straight out of the Disney Junior Club, for Christ's sake. Agents were tripping over themselves to sign her.

'She's adamant someone slipped something into her drink. I'm inclined to believe her.'

'Is she ok?'

'Not great, to be honest. She's in hospital undergoing blood tests.' Kim's tone cracks across the phone. She's fond of Mia. We both are. 'She's had some sort of allergic reaction to whatever substance she ingested.'

'Fuck.' I sit bolt upright, raking a hand through my hair.

I might have a reputation for being one of the most ruthless agents in Hollywood, but the one thing I can't stand is a woman crying.

You can't save them all.

A niggle in my subconscious attempts to rise to the surface. I squeeze my eyelids shut, forcing it out.

I might not have been able to save Sofia, but I'll be damned if I don't see Lula right. Even if it's costing me more than I ever thought I'd give.

'There's more as well. The cops found drugs in her apartment. Enough to send her down.'

'What? That's ridiculous. The girl is as innocent as a newborn baby. That can't be right.'

It can't be. Because if it is, it means I was wrong. My bull-shit radar was off. And that's simply not possible.

'Can you come home? The media are all over it. Things are spiralling out of control. The paps are crawling around the hospital and her apartment and even her family home in Orlando. Disney is threatening a lawsuit on top of everything too. It's a fucking mess.'

It *is* a fucking mess. For all of us. If Mia is as innocent as I think she is, someone's framed her as well as drugged her. And if she's not as innocent as I think, I've fucked up and risked my reputation along with her own.

As much as I hate the thought of leaving Chloe, I have no choice but to deal with it.

'Ok. Book me on the next flight.'

'I'll email you the details.' Kim exhales a long, deep breath.

'Send them on to Colton, too. Have him collect me from the airport.'

'No problem.'

I hang up and kiss the back of Chloe's hand as I commit the image before me to memory. The woman is a fucking work of art. Every inch of her silky skin begs to be worshipped. I might have to go now, but I'm nowhere near done with her yet.

I know she has this one-night rule, but where's the harm in extending it a little longer when she's safe in the knowledge it will end naturally after the tour?

I wasn't joking when I told her I'm utterly unavailable.

Other than our respective siblings' wedding, we're never going to cross paths again. But until then, I need more of her. The sex is other-worldly. I don't care how busy the tour dates are. I've nowhere near had my fill.

'I'm needed in LA.'

'Well, it's a good job you gave me the green light to bull ahead with my extraordinary ideas.'

'There's nothing good about it.' My eyes roam over her nakedness. 'I need more of you. Of this.'

Chloe gazes at me with an enigmatic expression. 'Let's not pretend this is something it isn't.'

'We agreed four days,' I growl.

'No, you demanded four days. What we actually agreed is that you'd let me take charge of the tour and I'd swim naked with you. Everything else was a bonus. I gave you one night, Jayden, to get it out of our systems. I think it's safe to say we milked every minute.'

Slinging my clothes into my suitcase, I tell her, 'I'm nowhere near done.'

'You are.' There's no malice in her words. No regret. She's simply stating a fact. But her facts are wrong. Because when this tour kicks off, I'm going to take her in each of those eight cities. I don't care how busy it is. I'll make time. And she might fight me on it, but just like last night, she's going to love every second.

'The beauty of having sex repeatedly with the same partner is the uniquely gratifying intimacy that comes with familiarity of another person's body. Knowing what they need. Knowing it'll be delivered in the most delicious manner,' I tell her.

Hooded eyes stare back at me and I'm ninety percent convinced she's on board.

'Start compiling that list of fantasies, Princess, because I'm going to tick off every single one of them.'

At some point, this thing will wear itself out. It has to.

The alternative is too terrifying to think about.

Chapter Thirteen

CHLOE

It's been eight manic weeks sourcing a magnitude of weird and wonderful props for Ryan's farewell tour. Busy isn't the word for it. It's the biggest opportunity of my career and I've invested every ounce of energy into ensuring it will be as epic as I've promised.

Sadly, even that isn't enough to prevent vivid, multi-coloured mental images of Jayden and his exceptionally capable body from assaulting my mind multiple times daily. And don't get me started on the nights.

Fantasies?

I have them in spades. Nothing too wild or kinky, but they're enough to set my pulse racing and my panties wet.

There's been no one since him.

Even if I wasn't up to my eyeballs with work, how could anyone else compare?

No wonder he's been walking around this earth with that smug expression on his face his entire life. He knew what he was carrying around in his pants. Hell, I'd be smug too.

'You all set, Chloe?' Ruby calls across the office.

Izzy flew out to Sydney four days earlier to get everything

organised and Ruby's staying here, much to her disdain, to manage the office and oversee our other events. Everyone's gone home for the day, leaving us to lock up. Not that it'd matter if we didn't. Dubai has a practically non-existent crime rate.

'I'm all set for the tour.' Nervous energy thrums through me as I rummage in my handbag, triple-checking I have my passport, purse, and phone. 'What I'm not set for is Jayden Cooper.'

Obviously, I told Ruby everything. I couldn't keep it from her if I wanted to. If my grinning face and sunken eyes didn't give it away, the John Wayne walk definitely would have.

'You are *so* going to have sex with him again.' A scarlet talon pokes my arm as she passes by on her way to the watercooler.

'I *so* am not. Been there, done that.' As the words fall from my lips, even I have to question the sincerity of them.

'Aside from the fact I'm going to be busy working, my sister will be with me twenty-four seven. We're rarely in the same country. We've got to make the most of it.'

'Huh. You're rarely in the same country as Jayden Cooper's magnificent dick. If I were you, I'd be making the most of that instead. Priorities, my friend, priorities.' Her tongue pops out theatrically as she makes what I think is supposed to be a cross-eyed "come face."

'Ruby, please, that face is seriously disturbing.' I find a packet of mints in my bag, unwrap one, and pop it into my mouth.

'There's nothing disturbing about it. You should see the expression Brad pulls when he's seconds from blowing his load. Seriously, they don't call it "the vinegar stroke" for nothing.' Her face rearranges into an expression even more disturbing than the first.

'It wouldn't be nearly as bad if I'd got there first,' she snorts.

My hand flies to my eyes. 'For fuck's sake, Ruby! You know I'm normally all about the details, but there is such a thing as too much information.'

'Trust me, there isn't. It's the most natural thing in the world. You know, I think Jayden was onto something,' she muses.

My hand lowers as my head whips up. 'Like what?'

'Maybe there is a silver spoon stuck up your ass?' She screeches with laughter and ducks as I hurl a mint at her.

I shake my head, regretting ever opening my mouth.

'I'm just saying you can FaceTime your sister anytime. You can't FaceTime Jayden's dick.'

Believe me, on the nights I'm hot and restless, I've seriously thought about trying.

We've spoken almost daily. I was worried he'd drop his signature innuendos after he got what he wanted, worried about giving the game away to his brother and my sister, but he's remained every bit as suggestive.

Outwardly, I shrug off his remarks with as much disinterest as I can muster. Inwardly, my stomach never fails to flip.

It was probably a blessing in disguise he got called away because I wouldn't have had the willpower to kick him out of bed, which would have only made things harder in the end.

He took me like no one has ever done before. Or probably will again. He destroyed me in the most delicious way. His hands. His mouth. His body. But the biggest turn on was the way he owned me. As if he was the only one with the power to push me to my limits and blast me into sexual ecstasy.

Deep down, I've been obsessed with him for a long time. It's going to take a frickin' superhero to beat that.

Aurelia Arlington's words resurface out of nowhere for the hundredth time. *Even hero's need saving sometimes too.*

I've over-analysed them more than is healthy. I don't even know him that well. Is it possible there's more depth to Jayden than I've ever given him credit for? That perhaps underneath all that teasing and tormenting is a decent guy who's secretly as fucked up as the rest of us?

It doesn't take a shrink to work out my trust issues arose after the Ethan debacle, but what happened to Jayden to make him the way he is? Or was he simply born that way?

I'm pretty sure it'll remain as one of the wonders of the universe, because outside of the boardroom I've never heard a serious word fall from his notoriously filthy mouth.

Although I keep my own cards close to my chest. It's not just the Ethan scenario that scarred me.

The night I lost my parents flashes to the forefront of my mind and I force it away again, pinging the elastic band on my wrist to snap me back into the present.

Ruby perches on the desk opposite mine. 'I know you have this one-date rule thing going on, but rules are made to be broken.'

'Funny, that's what Jayden said.' I fluff my hair, which I had professionally blow-dried at lunchtime, just in case.

'If some gorgeous Hollywood playboy offered to tick off every one of my sexual fantasies, I wouldn't say no. What I wouldn't give to meet somebody decent. You know I've always had this feeling that when I meet the right person, I'll know right away.'

'Too many Disney movies, Rubes.' If only it were that simple. 'Besides, if that's the case, why are you wasting time with Brad?'

'That's a good question, and one I've been asking myself a lot lately.' Ruby drains the water from her paper cup before slam dunking it into a recycling bin. 'Come on, or you'll miss your flight. Hope you've packed condoms. Lots of them.'

A blush inches up my neck. That was one reckless detail I deliberately omitted.

First class is busier than usual. Like everything in Dubai, it's extravagant. The Middle Eastern airlines are no different. Ruby privately insists someone somewhere in this country is compensating for something. Personally, I just think most of the investors have more money than sense.

'A penny for your thoughts,' a man sitting in an adjacent seat says. He's wearing a well-fitting suit. Light brown hair falls in floppy waves framing bright green eyes that dance with devilment. With a roman nose and bone structure that most women would kill for, he's attractive, but not in a predatory way like those soccer clowns all those weeks ago.

'I was thinking I was enjoying the peace after yet another busy day.' My eyebrow arches instinctively and even I have to wonder about this silver spoon everyone keeps talking about.

It's not that I think I'm above anyone. I'm just really careful about who I allow access to my energy. It's not being cold, it's being cautious.

Besides, I'm not in the mood for small talk. Not when all I can think about is the next three days ahead of me, the concert, my sister and, of course, her new brother-in-law-to-be.

'That's me put back in my box.' His head cocks to the side as a chuckle gurgles in his throat.

'Sorry. I didn't mean to be rude. I'm just preoccupied.' I sip my drink.

I have at least another thirteen hours on this flight. I suppose I might as well relax a little.

'So, I take it this trip,' his strong smooth-looking hand gestures around us, 'is business and not pleasure.'

'Strictly business.' Am I telling him or reminding myself?

'Surely you could make it both...' He sips honey-coloured alcohol from a shot glass. 'I'm Levi, by the way.'

'Chloe.' Reluctantly, I tip my glass, and its rapidly depleting contents against his.

A smile lifts his lips. 'That's the spirit. Business and pleasure always mix well for me.'

'Oh, there are so many reasons that won't work for me. Don't even get me started.' Levi's not the only one on his second drink.

'Like what?' He sits up straighter, like he's genuinely interested. He'll be kicking himself in under thirty seconds, but now I've started, it's a relief to talk about it. Especially since we'll never see each other again.

'Like he's my colleague on this project, at least. Not to mention my sister's about to marry his brother.' I knock back the remnants of my gin and tonic and ask a passing cabin crew member for a refill.

When she hands over my third drink and disappears, I add, 'And sleeping with him was the best and worst decision of my entire life. The best because it was the best sex of my life, and the worst because it can never happen again.'

'Ah.' Levi's bright eyes dance with mischief again. 'You mean it was the best sex of your life *so far?*'

'I'm pretty sure it'll never be beaten.' I take another huge glug from my glass, grateful for the paracetamol in my handbag which I'm undoubtably going to need before this flight lands.

'In that case, hunt him down. Do it again. You only live once! Do you want another drink?'

My shoulders shrug in a why not gesture.

Levi is easy company. Something about his casual forwardness reminds me of Ruby.

BJ, as I refer to it in my mind, Before Jayden, Levi might even have been my kind of companion. AJ, I can't so much as summon a single butterfly.

It's true, I've been ruined.

Possibly forever.

Chapter Fourteen

JAYDEN

Sydney

Sydney might be cooler than LA at this time of year, but my body temperature's running hotter than ever. Between the singer I'd secured to duet with Ryan backing out and the prospect of mind-blowing sex with Ryan's sister-in-law again, I'm more than a little hot under the collar.

Thankfully, the air-con is on full pelt in the arrivals lounge. It's my turn to wait for Chloe. She just doesn't know it yet.

Hiding behind a pair of aviator sunglasses, I can actually breathe without Colton or one of Ryan's security breathing over my shoulders. I know they mean well, but it's so suffocating in LA, where someone constantly demands to know my whereabouts.

Through a fresh influx of tired looking travellers, Chloe Sexton stands out like a diamond. Is it any wonder I call her princess when she radiates a sublimely sexy regal aura? The second she emerges with her luggage, my eyes are drawn to her, the same as every other male in the room.

In a cream silk sleeveless blouse and fitted navy jeans, she is the epitome of every fantasy I've ever had. Glossy chestnut locks bounce over her shoulders as her long, shapely legs stride across the room.

A guy in a suit jacket and jeans falls into stride with her. She laughs at something he says before shaking her head. When he reaches into his pocket and hands her a card, a fire ignites in my chest.

My forehead creases into a frown. It takes me a minute to figure out the red-hot emotion racing through my blood is jealousy. It's not an emotion I'm used to.

Chloe runs her slim fingers over the card and flips it over in her hands twice before stuffing it into the pocket of her navy ass-sculpted jeans. The second I wiggle them off, I'll be sure to throw it in the trash. She's mine for the next few weeks. She just doesn't know it yet.

When he kisses her cheek, it's a battle not to run over and rip him off her.

For the past eight weeks, I've battled wicked thoughts of all the things I'll do to her given half the chance, even though it's wrong on a million levels.

Hell, who am I kidding? I've had these thoughts for ten years. But since our time together, I haven't so much as looked at another woman, because apart from the fact I'm supposed to be keeping a low profile, no one else can soothe the itch I have to scratch.

For me, it's unheard of.

Which is precisely why there's no way I'm going to let some jumped up travelling companion move in on her now.

Hypocrite.

This is supposed to be a quick fling.

You should let her find someone who has a chance of offering more than you can.

I swat my conscience away, not wanting to hear it.

It took a bit of digging, but I found the company she booked a private collection with and cancelled it. As if I'd miss her arrival. The concert's in two days' time. I plan on utilising every free second, starting right now, in the back of the limo Diamond Records hired to transport their biggest rock star.

We're booked into the same stunning five-star hotel on Sydney Harbour. With a little persuasion in the form of a ticket to my brother's concert, I convinced the manager to relocate me into the suite next to Chloe's.

Chloe's bright eyes dart in every direction, scanning the crowd for her driver. Eventually, they land on me. Time freezes as the air sparks and crackles between us.

I stalk across the room. 'Welcome to Sydney, Princess.' As I press a kiss to each of her cheeks, I inhale her familiar scent.

For a woman who's spent fourteen hours on a plane, she's as fresh as a daisy.

'What are you doing here?' Her forehead furrows in a frown, but her dilating pupils don't lie.

'Overseeing my brother's final farewell concert, the same as you.' I take her luggage and drop a hand to the base of her spine, attempting to usher her towards the exit.

She resists, her cream, open toe stilettos glued to the spot. 'Smart ass. I have a car coming to collect me.'

'Actually, you don't. I cancelled it.' I bite back the smirk as her eyes widen in genuine indignation. She might be secretly happy to see me, but she's still under the illusion she's in control, something that will rapidly change when I get her into bed later.

'You're kidding, right?' Tanned arms fold across her curvaceous chest and her mouth curls into a grim line, a poor attempt at disdain. I've come to recognise that expression well.

'So, we're back to this again? You pretending to hate me, right up until the second you slide onto my dick. Because we both know it's going to happen. Again.' My breath brushes her ear and goosebumps ripple across her bare skin.

'Jayden.' Her pejorative tone does nothing to mask the way her eyes flicker with arousal.

Hundreds of people mill around us, but all I see is her. Everything else fades in her presence. I wrap an arm around her shoulders and draw her in for an innocent-looking hug, pressing my hips against hers, intentionally demonstrating the effect she's creating in my pants already.

'Chloe.' An excited shriek echoes across the room and we dart apart like two wayward teenagers.

Sasha Sexton, Chloe's sister, and my future sister-in-law, has the worst fucking timing in the world. I subtly attempt to readjust my junk in my pants as they embrace like it's been years rather than months.

'Sasha, what are you doing here? You know I prefer to make my own way from the airport.' Something in her delivery makes me think she genuinely means it.

'As if I was going to let you land here to nobody.'

When they finally break apart, Sasha's gaze rakes curiously over me. 'Jayden. What are *you* doing here?'

'There were a couple of last-minute technicalities that needed Chloe's expertise, but I'll grab her for a few minutes later on. Where's Ryan?'

'Back at the hotel. The limo's missing and Pierce forbade him from going anywhere without tinted windows. The groupies are on high alert with the concert this weekend.' Her eyes dramatically roll to the ceiling.

'*I* took the limo. I thought you two would never drag yourselves out of the bedroom.' I shoot her a wink. Ryan says she's insatiable. I'm hoping it runs in the family. 'Come on ladies, let's get back to the hotel. I'm starving.'

I usher the two of them towards the exit.

This time, Chloe doesn't object, not that I believed her earlier protests for a second.

Sexual tension thrums between us like a live wire. Miraculously, Sasha doesn't seem to notice.

The hotel is absolutely stunning. I'm used to luxury, but this is next level. One side, overlooking the harbour and the bright lights of Sydney, is composed entirely of glass. Inside it's spacious, modern and almost offensively bright to my tired eyes.

My top floor suite is bigger than my entire office in Dubai, the bath big enough for four.

As I hang my dresses in the walk-in wardrobe, my mind inevitably wanders to Jayden. He's as infuriatingly sexy as ever. The only difference is now I'm painfully aware the fire burning through my blood every time I see him isn't rage, it's pure lust.

Ignorance really was bliss.

A gentle knock sounds at my door. It's him. I know before I even open it. As Shakira said, the hips don't lie and mine, along with every other inch of me, hums to life. Blood crusades through my chest, pounding in my ears.

It's tempting to let him in, now I know what he's capable of, but I can't. No matter how badly I crave his touch, no matter how alive he makes me feel, there's a reason I don't do repeats.

Letting people in results in heartbreak. If I'm this obsessed after one night, what would a second do to me?

I can't afford to find out.

Warily, I crack the door open to peek out.

Jayden's huge, bulky frame rests casually against the wall. That brutally attractive face stares knowingly at me, like he can read my mind, sensing my wavering sense of self-control.

With billboard worthy bone-structure and lips that part to reveal the perfect all-American smile, his allure is inescapable. And don't get me started on the sculpted planes of his body, barely concealed by a fitted white shirt, sleeves rolled up to the elbow, as if he's oh-so-willing to get those hands dirty again.

He wears his sexuality like a weapon.

Grey eyes roam lasciviously over me, silver flames of desire dancing in his irises. He shoves the door open and lunges at me like a lion pouncing on its prey. That expert tongue dips deliciously inside my mouth as the heavenly scent of his aftershave intoxicates me.

This wasn't the plan.

This isn't the plan.

This is the biggest opportunity of my life. I can't fuck it up by fucking my almost brother-in-law. Again. I just can't.

He growls as I dart back, running my fingers over my bruised lower lip. Hot, barely controllable desire flames through me, scorching me from the inside out. 'We can't, Jayden, okay? This thing between us is over.'

He takes a step back, resting his shoulder on the door-frame like he owns the place. 'I'm going to let you in on a little secret, Princess.' Leaning forwards, his lips brush the sensitive skin of my earlobe. 'This thing between us is only just beginning. It's only over when I say it's over.' He winks before disappearing down the corridor, and I don't know whether to be relieved or terrified.

Thankfully, I don't have too much time to dwell on it before Izzy arrives with a checklist for the concert, reminding me of the reason I'm here.

Sasha, being Sasha, has organised for the four of us to have dinner together in the hotel's Michelin star panoramic restaurant. She knocks on my door as Izzy is about to leave.

'Sasha, this is Izzy, my PA. I don't know if you've been formally introduced?'

Izzy looks a little star struck, gazing over Sasha's shoulder, probably hoping to catch a glimpse of Ryan, the main man himself. 'I saw you in passing, but it's lovely to meet you.' Izzy extends a trembling hand, reminding me of the time Jayden introduced me to Aurelia Arlington. I'm as bad as Sasha now. Every little thing seems to lead me back to Jayden.

'Ditto. I know Chloe only hires the best, so you must be very talented.'

'I try.' Izzy stares at Sasha's outfit, a black silk dress with a cowlneck. No doubt it's an Evangeline Araceli number, a super famous fashion designer from the States who took a shine to my sister. Thank god we're the same size because Sasha doesn't go anywhere near enough places to wear all the dresses she gets sent.

She prefers the comfort of the castle where we grew up. The castle I abandoned the day after I was old enough to leave.

Even thinking about it now widens that hole in my chest. So many memories. So much guilt. So much heartache.

I was seventeen when my parents died. It was the worst

time of my life. And when Sasha lost the baby she was carrying, I had to wonder if the damned place was cursed.

Almost seven years later, it's clear it isn't.

Sasha's about to marry the man of her dreams. They've built a huge extension at the castle and are making millions catering for Ireland's biggest celebrities. Hopefully they'll fill the place with babies one day too. Sasha will make a fabulous mother. She's had plenty of practice raising our kid sister, Victoria, who turns eighteen in a matter of weeks.

'Are you planning on changing?' Sasha gestures to my jeans.

'Give me five minutes.' I nod towards the enormous bathroom. 'Is your suite the same as this?'

'Embarrassingly, it's even bigger.' She struts towards the minibar and retrieves two miniature bottles of Moet and a couple of glasses. 'We may as well have a little apéritif while you get ready.' She shrugs with a lopsided smile.

Grateful I don't need to wash my hair after yesterday's blow dry, I take the quickest shower of my life before joining Sasha on the queen-sized bed for a sisterly catch up.

'So, are things still running dry in the desert?' She smirks, nodding at the towel wrapped around my nether regions, which I've waxed to within an inch of their life at Ruby's insistence, just in case.

'Huh! I've been too busy working on your fiancé's tour for anything else.'

I normally share everything with my big sister, but I feel weird admitting to shagging her brother-in-law. Apart from the fact she warned me off him, it feels borderline incestuous. The last thing I need is a lecture on how we're about to be family. I'm all too aware.

'You know Ryan has about fifteen burly, hot security guards here, plenty of choice for some Aussie action over the next few days.'

From the way Jayden looked at me earlier, it'll be a miracle if I escape without any Aussie action. It just won't be from one of the bodyguards.

When we arrive at the restaurant, Jayden and Ryan are deep in conversation. They're tucked away from the main restaurant in a private booth in a cosy corner overlooking the twinkling harbour lights below. Through the twilight, it's breathtaking.

My stomach flips. The glass of champagne earlier has done nothing to ease the nervous energy thrumming through my core.

What if Sasha and Ryan guess that there's something going on between me and Jayden?

What if he touches me inappropriately?

What if he *doesn't* touch me inappropriately?

Shit, this is exactly what I was worried about. I ping the elastic band on my wrist, trying to snap some sense into myself.

Jayden's head whips round as I approach. He pats the seat, encouraging me to sit next to him. As if I have any other choice.

Hungry eyes rake over the white chiffon dress that clings to every curve of my body. I bought it weeks ago, specifically with Jayden in mind. Is it so wrong that I want him to find me attractive?

Sasha orders a magnum of champagne the second the waitress approaches us.

'Chloe, you look positively delectable.' A wicked grin rips across Jayden's face. Is the same scene flashing through his mind, when he went down on me alfresco by my pool?

Of course it is. Energy pulses between us. An explosive energy like a grenade ready to blow.

'In your dreams, Cooper.'

'No, in yours, Sexton.' His tongue darts over his lip and I force myself to look away.

He's not wrong.

My sister fawns all over Ryan in an embarrassing over the top public display of affection. Yuck. Jayden could probably eat me out on the table right now and they wouldn't even notice. They're so completely into each other, it's sickening.

But underneath my crisp tailored dress suits, isn't that exactly what I've always secretly longed for? A man who's so smitten with me that the rest of the world could spontaneously combust and he wouldn't even notice. That's not something I could ever even admit to wanting until now.

One day, I want to meet someone who will love me so hard that maybe, eventually, that hole pressing against my chest will close for good.

One day. I might not be ready for it right now, but maybe it's not as far away as I'd assumed.

Jayden's expression transforms from sexy to serious in a millisecond. 'You okay?' he whispers, concern etching into those huge, astute eyes. He's uncannily in tune with my moods.

I nod and shrug, unable to trust myself to speak.

I must be hormonal.

What is it about him that makes me lose all sense of control? Bad enough my body buckled beneath him, but now my emotions seem to be going haywire too.

Throughout the evening we're served seven courses of the chef's signature tasting menu, each one more mouth-wateringly sumptuous than the one before, yet I'm still hungry. And no amount of oysters, caviar, or crème brûlée is going to satisfy that.

Of all the people in the world, why do I have to be so attracted to Jayden-Smug-Cooper? Soul-piercing eyes stare at me like they can read my mind, and a trace of amusement crosses his lips. When Sasha orders another bottle of champagne, I figure it's late enough to excuse myself. I barely slept on the flight thanks to Levi's jovial banter and not only am I wrecked, my willpower is fading with every drop of alcohol.

'Want me to send one of Ryan's men to take care of you?' Sasha winks across the table, giggling.

Jayden's head jerks up. 'Did something happen?'

'Nothing happened.' Sasha laughs. 'That's the problem.'

'Is that right?' His husky tone sets my insides soaring. 'You know I could help with that too.'

'Colton?' Sasha scoffs. 'Please, he's way too conservative to be Chloe's type.'

'I didn't mean Colton.'

Oh god, is my sister really discussing who I should bed with the only person I want? Fuck my life. No amount of alcohol could prepare me for that.

'Just going to get some air. Back in five. Don't go yet, Chloe.' Sasha pulls Ryan to a nearby balcony with outdoor sofas and a futuristic-looking telescope.

The last thing I need is to be left alone with Jayden. I motion for him to go after them. 'Don't you want to see the view?'

'I already am.'

His soft hand slips across my thigh, inching under my dress as the waitress arrives with the champagne.

She takes forever to uncork it, and when she eventually pours me another glass, I can't speak to decline because Jayden chooses that precise second to slip his finger inside my underwear, which was ruined the second I sat next to him. The victorious curl of his lips proves he knows it.

His mouth grazes my ear. 'We are so not over.'

I cross my legs and press them together tightly in a vain attempt to halt his hand. 'So, we're back to this again?' I quote his own words at him.

'Yeah, and look how it ended the last time.' A goading arrogance dares me to contradict him.

'Lightning doesn't strike twice.' I remove his hand and smooth down my dress. 'Goodnight Jayden.'

'Oh, it will be.' He shrugs, delivers a sultry wink and picks up his glass.

What does that mean?

If I won't sleep with him, he'll find someone who will?

You're not supposed to care.

That familiar hot flush of irritation swells in my chest again. I stalk out of the restaurant without saying goodbye to Sasha and let myself into my lonely suite.

Despite the long flight and the jetlag, the second my head hits the pillow, my brain recalls every image of Jayden unwillingly planted in it. I should have just succumbed.

No, I did the right thing.

Right for whom?

The room's in semi-darkness. Partially open curtains allow the bright city lights to penetrate the glass. I flip the crisp white covers down to my waist and spread myself across the middle of the bed, my hands automatically skimming my skin as I recall the poster-perfect physique of Jayden Cooper.

There's something so inexplicably appealing about him. And it's not just the pretty parcel he's wrapped in. He's so much more than that. That ruthless confidence. His unashamed pursuit of what he wants. Intelligent eyes that notice absolutely everything, including the faintest chink in my armour.

My hair fans across the pillow, untamed, like the thoughts that run through my delinquent head. My fingers brush mindlessly over my chest before grazing lower across my stomach. Goosebumps ripple across my skin. Not for the first time, I'm filled with a longing so acute it's practically painful.

Where's Perky Pete when I need him? Though lately, even my trusty toy fails to fully scratch the itch Jayden incites.

How can I be so obsessed? I don't even like him. Well, he's grown on me, a little. Certain parts of him, at least.

'Fuck's sake, Jayden.' His name rolls from my tongue in a dreamy, exasperated sigh. Thank god he's not here to hear it.

Movement from the corner of the room catches my eye. My heart leaps into my throat as a strangled squeal bursts out. I grab the sheets, bunching them up over my chest as it heaves with erratic breaths.

'You called?' An amused, gravelly tone cuts through the air.

Liquid metal eyes glint across the moonlit room as Jayden's low, slow exhale plumes before him.

Speak of the devil and he arrives again. I'm going to have to call him Lucifer.

I jolt upright, yanking the duvet even higher, my heart pummelling my ribcage. 'What the hell, Jayden? How did you even get in here? You can't waltz in and stare at me. I'm pretty sure there's a law against that.'

'What can I say? Housekeeping are rather obliging.' He shrugs in a casual gesture, but there's nothing casual about the hungry glint he harbours.

'Huh, you always did have a way with the chambermaids.' I flop back onto the bed as my breathing finally slows to a near normal pace.

'I have a way with more than just the chambermaids, Princess. Judging by the way you pant my name, like seeing me is your dying request, you know it.'

He saunters closer, undoing his tie, discarding it at the foot of the bed. Nimble fingers roll up the sleeves of his shirt. Even through the dimness, the strength of those forearms is apparent. A heady glimmer of determination emanates from his eyes. He's looking at me like I'm his next course. I don't know whether I'm afraid or elated.

'I'll happily stand here and watch where that hand goes next, but if you want it done right, Princess, all you have to do is say it. Either way, I'm not going anywhere.'

My stomach flips. 'Did I mention I fucking hate you?'

Husky laughter echoes between us. In one swift motion, he drops to his knees and grabs my ankles, yanking me to the edge of the bed.

'Jayden.' The warning in my voice is clear.

'I know, Princess, you don't do repeats. But this isn't a repeat because it's going to be exponentially more mind-blowing than the first time.'

His tongue starts at my ankle before rolling up over my calf to the sensitive spot behind my knee. My pelvis arches off the bed and he's nowhere near it yet. His chuckle vibrates against the inside of my thigh.

That arrogant tongue is good for something, at least.

Who am I kidding? It's good at everything, just like every other part of him. The man is a fucking god in the bedroom. And if his reputation is anything to go by, he's pretty powerful out of it too.

'Say it, Princess, and it's yours. Tell me what you need.' His fingers pin my thighs apart as his eyes drink me in.

So, we really are back to this again.

I've always hated that word, the one he made me say last time. I'm too close to the edge to care about my dignity. 'I need your tongue on my...'

Before I can finish the sentence, it's there, right where I need it. My eyes roll back as my fingers shamelessly rake through his close-cropped hair.

With deft, expert strokes, he brings me to the brink in seconds before abruptly stopping.

I might actually die of lust.

'Look at me while I make you come.' It's a command, but there's an underlying tenderness there too.

Dark, compelling eyes hold mine as his tongue resumes its rhythm. The earth shatters around me, chasing the breath from my lungs as I ride wave after wave of ecstasy.

He drops his trousers before nudging me back up the bed. Why did I ever fight him in the first place?

Chapter Sixteen

JAYDEN

I'm giving away more tickets to Ryan's farewell tour than I've sold but needs must. Getting the night manager to give me a key card to Chloe's room was a definite need.

The chemistry between us is thick enough to warrant a weather warning. I can't see past it. I have no idea how to navigate my way through it.

I shouldn't be here. Shouldn't chase her. But I can't help myself. Everything about her completely undoes me.

Any time she's close, every inch of me burns to touch her. Drinking her in through the moonlight, I could watch her all night. I want to know more about her than I have any right to ask.

The Chloe I met at Christmas was so cold, so formal and so goddamned self-righteous. Breaking her walls down and watching her writhe at my touch is addictive. Intoxicating. Getting her off gets me off. She's so responsive. Three rounds later, we're both finally satiated, for a while at least. I've never known pleasure like it.

I'm no stranger to lust but my hedonistic lifestyle isn't a choice, it's a necessity. I fill my life with carefree blondes and fast cars to block out the demons of the past, of which there are plenty.

Flashbacks of the roughest days of my life assault my brain. The dark thoughts are never far away, but in the middle of the night, they're always that bit closer to the surface.

Sleeping under the starry sky with literally nothing to my name.

Bonding with complete strangers in the same situation.

Sharing what little food we'd acquired that day, praying we'd survive the night in order to see the day.

A shudder rips across my spine. Huge brown eyes haunt my subconscious and plague my dreams.

Ryan and I clawed our way up from the streets of LA to where we are now. Not everyone was as fortunate.

Chloe sighs in her sleep. I curl my body around hers, taking comfort I'm not sure I deserve.

Sunlight streams through the window and I wake more rested than I've been since my trip to Dubai. Getting out of LA suits me. Or maybe it's sleeping with Chloe Sexton. I'm not sure which is more damning, as neither is a permanent option.

Chloe rolls towards the edge of the bed, but I catch her wrist before she can make a run for it. I know she said mornings can be awkward, but I'm going to remind her we're well beyond that. My fingers roam curiously over the elastic band she never seems to take off. What's it even for? To tie her hair up?

She pulls away, flashing that rare glimpse of vulnerability again.

'Where do you think you're going?' I purr.

Bright blue eyes look anywhere but at me, but she doesn't move. 'To shower. I have so much to do for tonight.'

'I haven't finished with you yet.' I tug her back into bed, pulling her into my arms. Her lithe frame is stiff initially, but when I pull her on top of me, she doesn't resist.

I guide her head to rest on my chest. A mad urge to kiss her forehead takes over and when I do, instead of bolting for the bathroom, her body slumps further against me, shoulders sinking as the tension she's holding eases.

Her gaze finally tilts upwards to meet mine. 'What are we doing, Jayden?'

'We're embarking on the most fabulous fling of our lives.'

She drags herself onto her elbows, cupping her chin in her palm. 'Is that right?'

'Are you telling me you've had better?' I nudge my hips against her, the blood pumping low again.

'You are so annoying.' She closes her eyes for a long beat and exhales heavily.

'Just admit it, I'm the best you've ever had, and that's why you broke your own rule for me.' It's easier to tease her than allow the swelling surge of emotions to reveal themselves.

She sighs and shakes her head. 'Of all the men in the world, why did I have to give *you* that satisfaction?'

'Oh, Princess, please. The satisfaction was mutual, and you know it.' I nudge her thighs open with my knee. 'There's no point stopping now. The damage is done. You know what they say, right? Hung for a sheep as a lamb...'

'Jayden, I...' She bites her lip, and it's obvious she's torn.

'Look, Princess, whatever you're worried about, you don't have to be. We're not that different, you and me. I'm utterly unavailable for anything other than casual sex. So are you. Let's enjoy it for what it is. Eight cities. Eight weekends of sheer carnal pleasure.'

'What about Sasha? And Ryan? And the tour?'

'Sasha and Ryan are too wrapped up in each other to notice a damn thing and thanks to your hard work, the tour is better organised than a military operation. Relax. Now is the time to sit back and enjoy.'

Again, a hint of vulnerability flashes through her normally guarded eyes. 'Do you think it'll go ok? Is everything under control? I've never dealt with anything as big before.'

'Everything is under control. As much as it kills me to admit this, you've done a stellar job. Now, there are bigger things to deal with.' I nudge my cock against her and she lets out a groan.

'Are we really doing this?'

'We're doing this. I'll make it worth your while. Did you compile the bucket list?'

'Bucket list?'

'The fantasies.'

I want to know every dirty little perversion that goes on inside her pretty head, although if I were to shag her vanilla for the rest of my life, the way I feel right now, it would be more than enough.

She swallows thickly, as if she's contemplating.

I need this thing to burn itself out properly, because if last night was anything to go by, we're nowhere near done yet.

Her eyes bore into mine with an intensity that sends shivers rippling across my spine. When her legs part a fraction, I get the answer I'm looking for.

'This stays between you and me. The last thing I want is for the world to think I only got this job because I'm shagging Ryan's agent.'

'Yes, ma'am.' I salute her, grateful she's finally stopped fighting this thing between us.

'This ends when the tour ends. And don't even think about falling in love with me. Do we have a deal?'

'We most certainly do. I always find our deals to be so rewarding. I can't wait to hear what's on your list.'

She taps her temple. 'It's all up here. Nothing too wild or

kinky, but there are some things I've wanted to try that you can't just blurt out to a stranger on the first night...'

I dig my fingers into her hips, gripping her in case she tries to wriggle out of this intriguing conversation. 'Tell me more...'

'Well, you can already tick off dirty talk. Your filthy mouth is one of your most redeeming qualities.' She shifts against me, her silky skin sliding against mine.

'Is that right?' I love how she's so sexually forward. 'In that case, ride my cock like a good girl until you come all over it.'

I press my hardness against her like bait and she slides on, assuming control this time, although, when we're together like this, I don't think either of us is in control.

————

The Sydney Opera House is wedged with women shrieking my brother's name at an octave that's beyond uncomfortable. The atmosphere's electric as he belts out a new song from his latest multi-platinum selling album. The song's entirely inspired by his relationship with Sasha. Nothing new there, though. The man has been in love with her since he was eighteen years old.

The production is out of this world. Chloe and her team came up with the idea of recreating the Sydney landmarks on stage, constructing them with layer upon layer of shiny silver records. Light reflects in every direction, bright silver beams projecting over Ryan and the crowd. It emits total class while incorporating the personalised themes we discussed.

And when the original artist I'd lined up got laryngitis at the last minute, Chloe somehow persuaded one of Australia's biggest rock stars to come out of retirement for one night only for the duet we'd planned.

All in all, Ryan appointing her was a good call.

A very good call.

Thanks to social media, the entire world will have seen this set by tomorrow morning. Chloe's name will be associated with it. And a very select percentage will experience the epic wrap party she's planning, scheduled for after the last concert in London.

That will undoubtably give her what she truly wants, access to the world's hottest stars and the opportunity to show them what she's capable of organising, given the chance.

When the woman actually manages to take her company global, we could end up on the same continent.

Given my current situation, I should probably be worried.

Chapter Seventeen

CHLOE

In the ten days that have passed since Ryan's first concert, Liberty Events Management has acquired more work off the back of it than we can cope with, and that's before my epic end of tour extravaganza.

I wanted global. Boy, am I getting it.

To the point I'm wondering if I've bitten off more than I can chew. Instead of plugging the hole in my chest, it seems to stretch it wider.

I've coerced Ruby's sister to view several commercial properties in London for me on the promise I'll hire her if, and when, the time comes. London's a huge market to crack and doing so will rely heavily on the exclusive wrap afterparty.

I've had to recruit another fifteen employees for the Dubai office. Ruby's making enquiries into offices in LA.

If I had an office in every city in the world, I'd probably still base myself in Hollywood, but it has nothing to do with Jayden Cooper. Well, it didn't before we started having regular, mind-blowing sex. After all, it is the epicentre of the rich and famous.

At least in Hollywood, everyone's acting. It's not just me pretending to be something I'm not. Namely, ok.

'Are you telling me you'd seriously leave all of this?' Ruby's red talons sweep across the impressive hazy Dubai skyline.

We're at the Aura Skypool, a three-hundred-and-sixty-degree infinity pool, the highest in the world. Ruby might be right about this country having a small man complex. It's one of our favourite spots to hang out at weekends. The sushi is world class, and the cocktails are to die for.

I take a sip of my margarita. Salt frosts the rim decoratively and water beads the glass. It looks like it jumped straight from the page of a trendy food magazine.

I soak up my surroundings. The magnificent backdrop to the cool azure pool. The iconic Burj Al Arab glinting in the distance and The Palm. Of course, I'll miss it. I'll miss days like these. I'll miss my best friend.

'You know better than anyone, Rubes, I never intended on staying this long. This is what the business needs.'

Ruby sweeps her dark hair from her face before motioning to the crystal-clear glittering pool, the opulence and luxury at our fingertips. 'Let's not kid ourselves about the business. It's already more successful than you ever dreamed. Moving on is what *you* need. I just don't get why.'

I don't get it either. Just that I'm looking for something. There's an internal force driving me somewhere, anywhere, to try to find it. I've been here too long already. Any longer and I risk laying down permanent roots. And that terrifies me. The last time I had roots, they were ripped from right underneath me.

That night flashes through my brain.

The manager of my parents' hotel summoning me, stricken faced, to the grand hall to tell me about the accident. Having to tell my sister how our parents had been forced off the road on an icy December night.

There were so many tears. It was bad enough dealing with my own grief but I felt like I was suffocating in my sisters' too. The day after I turned twenty-one, I left.

My phone rings from my oversized handbag.

Ruby huffs. 'It's the weekend. Turn the damn thing off.' She signals to a passing waiter and orders two more drinks.

I grab the phone, cup it in my hands, and squint at the screen. It's blown up since the concert. I couldn't turn it off if I wanted to. Every time it rings, it seems to be with the offer of a brand new opportunity. And I don't just mean a lewd conversation with my lover.

Ugh. That word. Lover. I hate it, but what other word can I use to describe Jayden? He's certainly not my boyfriend.

Jayden's name flashes before my eyes and I bite back the grin before accepting.

'How's my Princess?'

'Technically, I'm not yours. I'm just on loan.' I stick my tongue out at him, even though he can't see me.

A low growl sets fireworks popping beneath my skin. 'You *are* mine until I say otherwise. I forgot to mention in Sydney that I don't share.'

His possessiveness stirs a longing in my loins. Nobody has ever dared to try to possess me before and surprisingly, I love it. 'Oh shit, I'd better tell the pool boy to put his clothes back on this second.'

I'm joking, of course. I can't tolerate cheating. Ethan taught me what it feels like to be cheated on and I'd never do that to anyone.

'Don't make me get on the next plane out there.'

I down the rest of the margarita before hopping into the water with a splash. 'Is there a reason you're interrupting my Friday afternoon? You know I'm absolutely submerged here.'

A groan sounds across the miles. 'Tell me you're not topless by your pool.'

'I'm actually at the Aura Skypool.'

'Topless?'

'No!' I shake my head at Ruby, who's straining so hard to eavesdrop that a vein is bulging in her neck. If she leans any closer, she'll fall off her sunlounger, face first into the water.

Jayden sighs, seemingly placated that I'm covered up.

'But my bikini is really tiny.' It's too tempting to wind him up.

'Chloe, that's really not helping my raging hard on right now.'

'So it's probably not a good time to run through that list you had me compile? I made a few new additions since the last time we discussed it.' I sing-song sweetly, examining my freshly polished nails.

'Seriously, Chloe, you're killing me.'

'You should be in bed. What time is it there?' I squint at my silver wristwatch, but between the blinding sun and the cocktails I can't make out the time.

'It's late. Or early.' Traffic rushes in the background. 'I'm just heading home now.'

'Alone? Careful you don't get papped. That *would* make front page news. I can just see the tabloids now. *Jayden Cooper, no longer super.*'

'Don't believe everything you read in those trashy things.'

'Oh, I don't, but they are kind of addictive. Reading trash about you has been one of my guilty pleasures.' Oops, the cocktails have loosened my tongue again. Though the papers have been oddly quiet about Jayden since Christmas. Has he been behaving? Or just gotten better at being discreet about his endeavours?

'Chloe Sexton, have you been stalking me all these years?' His voice is low, seductive, as if he kind of likes the idea.

Ruby's practically hanging off her lounger, trying to listen.

I shoo her away and scoot across the pool, out of earshot. 'I've thought of you more than I'd care to admit.'

A hiss slips over the phone line. 'And now you're finally admitting it, what did these thoughts entail exactly?'

'Honestly? Mostly carving you up into tiny pieces and feeding you to piranhas.' Old habits die hard.

'Huh. We'll see how funny you are when I'm fucking you with my tongue next week...' Even from halfway across the world, he turns my legs to jelly. Excited butterflies soar and swirl in my stomach. And lower.

'See you in Singapore.' My lips smack into a kissing sound before hanging up.

'Oh. My. Fucking. God.' Ruby stares accusatorially at me. A red talon reaches out to poke my shoulder. 'You've got it bad!'

'Me?' I shriek. 'Didn't you witness me hang up on him?'

'You might have *hung up* on him, but you're also *hung up* on his every word. Look at your face! You're literally beaming.'

'That's because the man's *hung* like a goddamn fucking donkey.'

Ruby's answering snort is distinctly donkey-like, too.

The waiter chooses this second to arrive with our cocktails. 'You're infatuated with your brother-in-law.'

'Technically, he's Sasha's brother-in-law, but I am not!' Hauling myself out the pool, face down onto my sunlounger, I bury my grin in my towel. 'It's just a bit of fun.'

'Yeah, yeah. That's what they all say.'

I can't deny how good it feels to have a man who calls daily to check on me. Someone to ask how my day has been. My hand instinctively goes to my chest. The hole feels smaller knowing he cares.

Jayden doesn't care about you. Not like that.

But if he doesn't, then why does he call me every day?

. . .

A text message wakes me at two in the morning.

It's a photo from Jayden. Despite being woken, I'm grinning.

I assume it's his private pool. He's drawn an X on mosaic tiles around the edge of it and inserted an emoji tongue that makes me laugh out loud.

I fire off a quick reply.

> It's the middle of the night.

Three dots on my screen inform me he's typing.

> I know. If I were there, I'd be waking you too. What's first on the list? I want to be prepared.

I throw the phone on the bedside locker and huff. The last thing I need is thoughts of Jayden Cooper and all the things I want to do with him infiltrating my mind when he's half a world away.

Thirty seconds later, the phone vibrates with an incoming call. I groan.

'Jayden, it's two in the morning.' I squint at the digital clock by my huge empty bed.

'Not here it isn't, Princess.'

'Tell me, do you ring all the girls you sleep with at ungodly hours?'

'Only the ones I want to have phone sex with,' he sniggers. 'Is it on your list?'

Blood pumps furiously below at the prospect. 'It's something I've never done before, so I suppose technically it *should* be on the list.'

'Me neither, but I'm rock hard and I can't get you out of my head.' His voice drops and he whispers, 'Touch yourself, Chloe. Tell me how it feels.'

My face burns at his request, but my hand wanders beneath the covers, regardless.

'Chloe, I said, how does it feel?'

'It feels...nice.' How can I be so forward with him, yet so awkward on my own?

'Nice isn't good enough, Chloe. I need it to feel explosive. Get your head in the game. I want to know every single thing about your body. Tell me what turns you on,' he growls.

'You turn me on.' I quicken my pace and a gasp slips out of my lips. His smile is audible across the miles.

'Good girl,' he murmurs encouragingly.

The idea of him touching himself while thinking about me sends a jolt of electricity surging through my trembling limbs.

'What parts of me turn you on, Chloe? Tell me.'

I sigh, picturing him in the darkness, wishing he was in bed with me instead of on the phone. 'Your tongue. Your dirty mouth. Those exceptionally capable hands and how you fuck me into oblivion.'

A low hiss of approval rings in my ear. 'And you say *I* have a dirty mouth? Tell me what's on the list, Chloe.'

'Public places. Toys. Being tied up and teased until I explode.'

'Oh my god, please tell me you're close.' His breath quickens.

My release builds with a shocking assault. I moan his name with a voice I don't recognise. 'Jayden, I'm close.'

His satisfied groans resound through my ear, tipping me over the edge. My body thrums to life, sparking and spasming as exhilarating electric pleasure pulses through me.

The rise and fall of our breath unites in the same pattern. Minutes pass. We don't talk. We don't need to.

Eventually he says, 'Imagine, I thought you were a good

girl, Chloe. I should have corrupted you all those years ago, after all.'

'Better late than never.' Sleep feels a lot closer now, more because of the comfort of his voice than the release.

'Sweet dreams, Princess.'

Sometimes sexy, sometimes smart-mouthed, Jayden's phone calls are rapidly becoming the most exciting part of my day and night.

The second he hangs up, I miss him. Whose idea was it though to space the concerts weeks apart?

I guess it's because there's an end date on our 'situation-ship' that I feel safe enough to allow myself to be drawn into this bucket list game.

Although somehow, this thing between us feels way more intimate than what either of us signed up for.

Chapter Eighteen

JAYDEN

Singapore

Trust Ryan to bring us to Singapore in the monsoon season. Angela, his PA, and her girlfriend, Jasmine, run through the doors of the lavish five-star hotel overlooking the bay at Merlion Park we're all booked into. They're dripping wet from head to toe from the rain burst they've been caught in, but the laughter between them is infectious, even to me.

Angela shakes her hair out like a dog, sending huge droplets cascading over Jasmine and the hysterics start again.

They're so in love, and for a split second a pang of envy shoots through my chest before I remember myself.

Love doesn't last. Well, except in the movies. Lust makes the real world go round. At least it's what I tell my reckless brain every time it bombards me with thoughts of Chloe.

She warned me in no uncertain terms not to turn up anywhere near the airport this time. Either she's got an airport complex or she's hellbent on preventing Ryan and Sasha from finding out about us. Given the current situation in LA, if Ryan had any idea how much time I waste obsessing about his fiancée's sister, he'd probably have more to say about it than 'it's not a good idea.'

So, instead, I wait in the plush hotel lobby with a fifteen-year-old bourbon, the next best option.

With my laptop perched on a mahogany table, I pass the time catching up on a few emails. My head's not in the game.

A low buzzing from my phone comes from my pocket. It has to be Chloe. Her plane landed forty minutes ago. I've been tracking it on my computer.

And I had the cheek to call *her* a stalker.

But it isn't Chloe. It's my PA. 'Kim?'

'Jayden? We have a problem.'

I groan. Just what I don't need right now.

'A video of Naomi Carden just broke the internet. It's not good,' she says.

Naomi is another of my recent signings, a sweet country singer from Texas. Talk about shitty timing. Bad enough all the drama surrounding Mia Sweet and the alleged substance abuse, which still hasn't been resolved. Thankfully, she's almost fully recovered, and her home security system captured two hooded men entering her home with the drugs, but still, it's far from ideal.

'What is it now?' I snap.

'A sex tape's been leaked.'

'Fuck. You are joking?' We've built Naomi's entire career on her innocent girl-next-door image and her church-choir lungs. 'This will ruin her.'

It could also ruin me, as her agent, if I don't do something to limit the damage. And fast. 'Set up a Zoom call. I need to speak to her PA, PR team, and her lawyer in the next ten minutes. This is a fucking shitshow and I want to know what we can do to kill it. Got that?'

'Consider it done.' Kim ends the call.

Twice in a matter of weeks.

I don't believe in coincidence.

A hot ball of rage blazes in my stomach.

Who would do that to these girls?

Who would do that to *me*?

How am I meant to present new artists to the biggest labels if I can't control the scandals surrounding the ones I already manage?

This looks really bad.

Unprofessional.

Sloppy.

Amateurish.

I have a reputation for signing only the best. I'll do whatever it takes to uphold that.

I dial Gareth, my Hollywood movie producer best friend and wing man. He answers on the second ring.

'So you *are* still alive?' he says mockingly. Born and raised in the wealthiest suburbs of Santa Monica, he's the epitome of everything I normally hate about Hollywood, but with a sense of humour that can cut you in two, he's impossible not to like.

'Yeah, sorry, buddy. It's been crazy busy with the tour and everything.' More like I've been driving myself crazy, busy imagining fucking Chloe Sexton on every leg of it, but he doesn't need to know that.

We've shared girls before, but the thought of sharing Chloe is an abomination.

I cup my hand over my mouth, glancing round to check no one is eavesdropping. 'I need a favour.'

'Anything.' Gareth's voice is suddenly serious.

I tell him about the Naomi Carden scandal.

A low sigh whistles from his throat.

'Tell me about it.'

'What can I do?'

'Help me spin this. I'm going to ask her team to put out a statement that she's involved in a campaign promoting awareness to young women about the risks of unauthorised filming and consent and that she's working with you on a campaign film. Can you say we've leaked the sex tape deliberately, as a PR stunt? I'll fund the campaign myself. Whatever it takes to preserve her reputation. Please, just help me make this thing legit.'

He blows out a low, slow breath. 'Fuck, you're good.'

'That's why they pay me the big bucks.' My thumb roams the stubble dotting my jawline. 'Let's just hope it works. I haven't seen the footage, but we can always say the original's been tampered with.'

'Have your people send it to my people and I'll make a statement from this side. Let's shut this thing down.'

'Thanks, man. I owe you.'

'You owe me nothing except a decent night out. It's been way too long.'

'As soon as I get back, I promise. Though you could always ask Kim for that drink...'

'Ha, maybe I will.' Gareth clears his throat. 'Do you think this is a coincidence? I mean, after what happened with Mia?'

I pause for a heartbeat. 'I don't believe in coincidences.'

'No, I thought not,' he says.

One Zoom meeting and two bourbons later, the crisis is certainly not averted, but we've twisted the story into something more manageable. Unfortunately, it's meant I've missed Chloe's arrival, but this is important. This is my reputation on the line.

We've agreed Naomi's PR team will announce her engagement to her childhood sweetheart in the next few days which should further divert attention. But nothing about this whole sorry saga sits comfortably with me.

You don't just find a sex tape. It takes knowledge, skill, or money. Or all of them. And if Mia's drink was spiked, like she says, then whoever is behind this is dangerous.

I slam my laptop shut and check the security cameras at home through an app on my phone. Everything's in order. Colton's Mustang is in the driveway next to Lula's Prius. He lives in the summerhouse for most of the week. If there was a problem, he'd have called, but it's reassuring to have extra eyes around the place at times like this.

It's not the first time I've been threatened, but it's the first time my artists have been targeted this way and I'm taking it personally.

It's no secret in LA that I give priority to artists who come from nothing over those acts born and raised in the wealthy Hollywood suburbs. They need the break so much more than some mediocre rich kid.

Plus, the demos they send are always more passionate. They always have more fire and raw talent than the ones handed everything on a plate by their Porsche-driving, hummus eating, pseudo vegan parents.

Aurelia Arlington was right when she said I'm no hero, but I try to offer the underdog first chance. After all, I was one myself not that long ago.

It hasn't made me popular amongst Hollywood's elite, but I pick my own acts, and I refuse to be swayed by politics. Or bribes. I hate this 'you scratch my ass, I'll scratch yours,' crap. I'll scratch my own, thank you very much. The thought of being beholden to someone churns my stomach.

God, I wish Chloe was here right now, but of course, there's no shagging sign of her.

I flip my phone back and forth in my hand, and eventually cave in and text her. I assumed she'd come to me. I should have known better. Even with the silver spoon removed from her peach-perfect backside, she's still as stubborn as a mule.

> Playing hard to get? Or are we checking off
> sex in a public place from your list?

I send the message, then discard the phone on the bed.

It vibrates with a response before it touches the duvet.

A picture of Chloe and Sasha in the hotel bar, pink cocktails in hand, fills my screen. Her grin could light up the city. Fire spreads through my core.

Desire or irritation?

Both, if I'm honest. Tomorrow night will be manic with the concert, so why is she wasting what little time we could have together? No, that's unfair. She needs time with her sister, but a ripple of something flickers through me. This time, I recognise it for what it is. Jealousy.

The royal blue dress she's wearing dips ridiculously low over her pert, tanned cleavage. Loose curls bounce over her shoulders, framing her striking face. And her eyes glint, bright and daring. I've never seen a come-to-bed-call like it.

Three tiny dots appear on the screen as she types.

> Will find you later. Don't worry, Ryan's
> security is keeping an eye on us.

I bet they are.

> Don't make me come and get you.

Three dots appear again.

> Don't you dare.

Oh, I dare alright, Princess. After talking the talk on the phone all week, what is she playing at?

The need to see her consumes me. I've missed her, and not just her body.

She does something to me, and not just in my pants.

Chapter Nineteen

CHLOE

I'm on my second Singapore sling. The alcohol crusades deliciously through my blood, heating my skin while the easy company of my sister warms my soul. Perched at the long mahogany bar, two of Ryan's security, Frankie and Archie, flank us. They're close enough to smirk at our stories, but far enough not to crowd us.

Sasha fills me in on the latest from the castle. Our youngest sister, Victoria, still lives at home, for another couple of months at least.

'So then, Vic pulls out Ryan's underwear from beneath the cushion of the couch, pinching it between her index finger and her thumb, her face screwed into a look of pure disgust. I wanted the ground to swallow me whole, I swear!' Sasha's fingers rub her temples at the memory.

'And you know what Ryan said? "Thanks Vic, I was looking for those." Like it was totally normal she'd found the boxers I'd ripped off in a passionate rush the night before.' Colour floods her cheeks as she sniggers.

'Young love!' I tease, unable to hide the envy in my voice. Sasha's eyebrows arch in what I assume is surprise. I take another sip from my drink before anything else stupid slips out.

'Anyway, you won't have to worry about it soon enough. She'll be gone to college before we know it.' I shake my head in wonder. The time's flown. Hard to believe our parents have been gone for so long.

Does it ever come between Sasha and Ryan? Does she blame his father's reckless driving for the untimely death of our parents?

I don't. Not entirely, anyway. Probably because I'm so consumed with blaming myself.

'I know, don't remind me. I don't know what I'll do with myself,' Sasha says. 'It'll be so odd. First Mam and Dad are taken. Then you move country. Now Victoria's going to Scotland.' She sips her drink, gazing into the distance.

The atmosphere's turned sombre in seconds.

To lighten the mood, I say, 'Imagine, Ryan will be able to bend you over the breakfast bar anytime you feel like it. Evangeline Araceli can send her dresses directly to me. You'll have no need for clothes at all!'

Sasha's lips twitch and the emotional crisis is averted. Thank god. I'm no good when it comes to discussing deep and meaningful. My reticence might appear cold or reserved, but it's just easier to pretend my parents' death didn't happen than to face up to the truth and process it all. If I did, I'm sure I'd crumble. I wouldn't be able to cope, so it's better if I bury my head in the sand and keep a stiff exterior.

'Who's bending who over the bar?' Jayden appears, a vision in a white ab-hugging shirt and navy jeans. Amusement hums from the same mouth that's oh-so-capable of committing unspeakable sins.

His familiar, enticing aftershave wafts between us and it's a battle not to throw myself into his arms.

The man is a fucking ride. Silver eyes gleam with lust-fuelled promise. Is it any wonder I've spent every waking second of the last couple of weeks composing my list of fantasies I want to live out with him? To the point it's beginning to terrify me.

It took everything I had not to run to his room the moment I landed, which is precisely why I hit the bar with my sister instead.

If I ran straight into his bed, he'd never respect me.

Although, why do I even care? It's not as if this is going anywhere. We're not in a relationship. It shouldn't matter, but it does, and the urge to separate myself from the millions of other women he's slept with gnaws at me.

'Chloe.' He drops a kiss on both my cheeks in his usual French greeting, deliberately lingering longer than necessary, although I don't miss the way he inhales the scent of my hair.

'Sasha.' He greets her the same way, but without the lingering or sniffing, before turning his attention to Archie and Frankie. If looks could kill…. I eye him with trepidation, silently willing him to be discreet.

They're only doing their job. It's not as though they're hanging out in the bar with us for fun.

Although Sasha promised to send someone up to me, so maybe that's why he's got the whole alpha thing going on.

Jayden signals to the barman for more drinks. 'I asked who's bending who over the bar?'

'Your brother is bending my sister over the breakfast bar, if you must know,' I say.

His steely eyes blaze into mine with a molten flame.

'What about you Chloe? Would that be a secret fantasy of yours?' Jayden hands over a wad of cash to the barman, winks at me, and deliberately presses his muscular chest against my back as he murmurs into my ear.

He balances an elbow on the mahogany behind mine, his

hip 'accidentally' bumping against my bum, leaving me in no doubt exactly how pleased he is to see me.

Why am I trying to play it cool? If I had any sense, I'd be tied to his bedposts right now, ticking off my BDSM fantasy.

Who am I kidding? I wouldn't need to be tied. I'd willingly lie there all night.

I press my thighs together to stop myself from squirming or combusting at the mental image.

From the periphery of my vision, I glimpse my sister's eyes widen and dart between us.

Fuck.

Jayden's less than discreet, and with Ryan in the gym with Pierce, Sasha's beady eyes are all too perceptive.

Jayden hands Sasha a cocktail. As she takes a large sip, she rocks back on her heels.

'So, Jayden. How long have you been fantasising about sleeping with my sister?'

'W-what?' The fruity alcohol splutters in my throat.

Jayden smirks and two firm hands slide around my waist. 'Since she was sweet sixteen.'

'Quit it, Jayden. Now, if you'll excuse me, I have some phone calls to make before dinner.' I down my drink and strut from the bar as fast as my peep toe Louboutin's will carry me.

I bang the bedroom door closed behind me and slide to the floor onto the thick swirling carpet.

Panic fills my chest, crushing my windpipe and stealing the breath from my lungs. My fingers instinctively seek the elastic band around my wrist. I snap it against my skin as I battle to process my thoughts.

What's wrong with me?

Why am I so worried about Sasha finding out the truth about me and Jayden when I usually tell her everything, anyway?

Because not only did she tell you not to, this thing with Jayden is different, and you know it.

It's not different. It's just sex.

It's sex on repeat, over and over. And that's something I haven't done since Ethan.

Urgh. It was only supposed to be sex. Simple and straightforward. But there's nothing simple or straightforward about any of it.

A gentle tap on my door sets my heart racing.

'Chloe, it's me.' Jayden's gravelly voice drifts through the thick solid wood door.

'Go away.'

'Don't make me break the door down.'

I stand with a huff.

As I open the door, Jayden barges in, towering over me. 'What's wrong with you?'

'I asked for your discretion. What was that in front of my sister?' I run my fingers through my hair, barely able to meet his gaze.

'Jesus, Chloe, I'm fucked if I do and fucked if I don't. In case you haven't noticed, I've been flirting with you since the day I met you.' He pinches the bridge of his nose. 'You sent me that picture and what was I meant to do?' He exhales and a hot puff of air brushes my lips.

That alluring aftershave assaults my senses again. It should come with a health warning. 'I've been counting down the seconds until I could finally get my hands on you again and you're playing some stupid game with me. It's not what we signed up for.'

He takes my hand and says, 'I was only teasing at the bar. Believe me, I understand why we can't let Sasha and Ryan find out. Ryan would fucking kill me if he knew.'

I used to be worried about what my sister and her boyfriend would think, but we're both consenting adults.

What's the problem? Maybe it would be awkward for a while, but it wouldn't last forever. No, the truth is I'm more worried about being labelled as nothing more than Jayden's latest squeeze by the tabloids..... and for the world to think that's the only reason I've been contracted to organise this tour.

It would obliterate my reputation professionally. And personally. How can I expect people to take me seriously when they find out I'm sleeping with one of LA's most notorious players? What kind of message does that send to the world? It hardly screams professional businesswoman, does it?

He's the only man since Ethan who has ever convinced me to break my own rules, but I can't explain why, even to myself. So how could I possibly explain to Sasha or anyone else?

Blood roars in my ears. Tension, desire, and fury rise like bubbling lava, ready to explode from the peak of a volcano.

'Are we having our first fight?' My lower lip catches between my teeth and tears unexpectedly well in my eyes.

I must be hormonal again.

'I didn't come here to fight. I came here to fuck. But I'll give it to you hard if it means you can tick "angry sex" off your list.'

'Keep your "angry sex." And everything else on the list. I don't want any of it.' I lie.

'Don't make me put you over my knee, Princess.' He pounces on me, that hot, full mouth capturing mine.

A feral need for him rips through my core. My lips can deny it all I like, but as ever, the need pulsating through every fibre of my body gives me away. I'm fooling no one. Not even myself. Still, I attempt to push him away, tearing myself away from his kiss, but he's relentless. Strong fingers grip my wrists, pinning them above my head and against the wall. Even his firmest touch is filled with a tenderness.

I need him to fill me up, but there's still a part of me that hates giving him the satisfaction.

I attempt to wriggle my wrists free from his grip, but he's too strong.

Fuck it. I can't fight him any longer. My body slumps in submission.

'Finally,' he murmurs into my mouth. 'Let me fulfil every fantasy you ever had.'

The old Chloe, the one who had full control of her senses, would have rather died. But this version nods in agreement, relieved to surrender to the flames of whatever this thing is burning up between us.

To something more powerful than my need for control.

Because I haven't been in control around Jayden in a long time.

Probably in forever.

Jayden makes me feel safe. I don't have to pretend to be something I'm not. He sees me. He gets me. On some level, he *is* me.

He releases my hands, tugging me towards the bathroom, heading, I think, for the jacuzzi bath tub, but instead he pushes me towards a sunken porcelain sink set into a lavish granite counter. Behind the sink is a mirror that runs the height and length of the entire wall.

'Bend over,' he commands.

I do as he instructs with my heart hammering in my chest.

I grab the granite as our gaze locks in the mirror.

My knuckles whiten as I cling on and a hot hand skirts under my dress, between my thighs, to locate a tiny scrap of lace. Magic fingers slip inside me. His name slurs from my lips, drunk on his every touch as we watch the sensual show together.

With his free hand, he lifts my dress around my waist before undoing his trousers, nowhere near quick enough for my liking. He shoves the lace to the side, and inches himself inside me, filling me up, captivating me with those arresting eyes.

'It's not exactly a bar, but I had to bend you over something,' he moans in my ear, as swift fingers work my sweet spot. He slams into me, over and over again. My eyelids flutter closed, my release boiling inside, ready to burst.

'Open them, Princess. I want to see you.'

We're locked once again in our own crackling current. Grey eyes pierce my soul as I shatter around him, exploding with ecstasy. He's seconds behind me, his firm fingers digging into my ass as he empties himself inside me.

The man who stares back at me in the mirror is so much more than the devil I thought I was making a deal with.

He's a fucking god.

Chapter Twenty

JAYDEN

New York

I persuaded Chloe to fly in three days early to spend a few nights in the Hamptons so we can work on the bucket list without being bothered by the paparazzi, our siblings, or any of my other impending commitments.

Truthfully, though, it's not about the bucket list.

I enjoy being with her. Not ideal, given the circumstances.

Using the security app on my phone, I check the cameras at my Santa Monica residence for any unusual activity. Something's still not sitting right with me about the Mia and Naomi incidents, but the only thing I see is Colton's Mustang and Lula's Prius in my driveway.

Lula's heading to Mexico tomorrow for two weeks to sort out some paperwork. She's probably stocking up my fridge with another endless supply of tacos, quesadillas, tamales and pambazos from the restaurant where she's back working. Even though I never eat any of it.

She's travelling with one of her colleagues, Diego. If the way she blushes when his name comes up in conversation is anything to go on, I assume there's something romantic going on between them. If only Diego would step up and make an official commitment, then I'd be off the hook and free to pursue a real relationship.

How times have changed. I gaze out across the Atlantic, wishing not for the first time this week that things were different.

'How long have you had this place?' Chloe's question drags me away from my mental "if onlys."

With a smile wide enough to light up the room, she takes in my beachside villa in all its pristine glory. Backing onto the high, white sand dunes and rolling waves of Cooper's beach, it is pretty spectacular. When I found this place, I knew I had to have it, especially as we share the same name. It felt like fate.

Trendy artwork lines the walls. The interior is entirely teal and white with the odd splash of bottle green, as if the designer simply replicated the colour scheme from outside. And with its huge soft furnishings and sandalwood floors, luxury really does blend with comfort here. 'About four years. I bought it to escape the rat race of LA.' I shove my phone into my pocket and settle my hands on Chloe's waist as she gazes out across the crashing ocean waves.

'Do you get out here much?' she asks.

I shake my head, unable to voice a reply.

I've never had anyone I wanted to bring before and coming here alone leaves too much time to think.

'Can we go to Kobe Beach Club?' Chloe asks excitedly.

'Only if you don't mind your face and ass being plastered all over tomorrow's papers.'

'Ah, right.'

She'll happily discuss her wildest fantasies with no shame, but she has a distinct aversion to being photographed with me. Given the fact I'm technically engaged to be married, even if it is one loveless transaction for the sake of Lula's green card, this should be a positive. Discretion is essential. So why does it grate on me?

I nuzzle Chloe's neck over her shoulder, taking in the view with her. 'Are you embarrassed of me?' My tone's jovial, despite the hint of doubt eating me. Even if I wanted to, I can't be seen with her because I don't want to jeopardise Lula's citizenship, but it still rankles my pride that she's so averse to it.

She always was a class above me, even when we were kids.

Chloe spins round, her lips inches from mine. 'No, I'm embarrassed of me.'

Her confession takes me by surprise. 'I don't get it.' My hands dig deeper into her waist. It feels so good to hold her without worrying someone might see.

'I'm ashamed I'm not strong enough to fight this thing between us.'

'And what is this thing exactly?' My hips press deliciously against hers.

'It's an infatuation.' There's no shame in the way she grinds back.

'Is the cold, sharp, ambitious ice queen, Chloe Sexton, actually admitting she's infatuated with me?

'Certain parts of you, at least.' She winks and grinds again.

'Just wait until we've worked through your list. If you're infatuated now, you'll be madly in love by the time I'm finished with you.' The words slip out before I can stop them.

Chloe stiffens.

I've gone too far. 'Let's start on that list right now,' I say, unbuttoning my trousers.

Chloe's gaze drifts to my hand as I free my hardening cock.

Relief reflects in her eyes.

We're back in more comfortable territory, happier, it

seems, discussing our sexual fantasies than talking about genuine emotions.

'Sex slave for the afternoon? Or sex in a public place? You decide.'

'Why choose?' She guides me out to the varnished decking where anyone could walk by, and drops to her knees, taking me with her mouth.

Fuck it, I could get used to this. With intelligence and sex appeal by the bucket load, Chloe Sexton is my ultimate fantasy. I'm going to tick her boxes so thoroughly, when she eventually settles down with someone she's not embarrassed to be seen with, she'll be forever tarred with memories of our time together.

'When you're finished, I'm going to carry you into the sea where you're going to wrap your legs around my waist and ride me, while everyone's oblivious on the beach. How's that for not choosing?'

Her low moan vibrates around my cock, tipping me closer to orgasm-induced oblivion.

It's been weeks since we started sleeping together and I'm nowhere near tiring of her. This isn't like me at all. Not one bit.

And it's becoming increasingly disconcerting.

After an afternoon of sun, sea and sublime sex, I order takeout from Serenity, a local restaurant specialising in fresh lobster.

Chloe carries plates from the kitchen and lays the table on the deck, like this is totally normal for us. As if we're a regular couple. And I like it. Lula is the only other person I've shared meals with lately, and even that's been a rarity forced on us by guilt.

'It's not exactly the Kobe Beach Club, but it's pretty damn

close.' She throws her head back in a laugh, exposing her long slender neck.

She's exquisite. The more time we spend together, the more I glimpse beneath the mask she wears for the rest of the world. She's amazing. If I had to write a list of desired qualities in a woman, she'd tick every single one of them.

Independent.

Driven.

Ambitious.

Beautiful, inside and out.

Her unwavering determination reminds me of Sofia.

I've had more than my fair share of physical encounters over the years, but I've never met anyone like Chloe Sexton. We connect on a much deeper level than simply the physical. Being with her makes me question what I truly want from this life. Worryingly, right now, the only thing I'm certain I want is her. It scares the fucking shit out of me, yet instead of shying away from it, I'm helplessly attracted to her like a starving bear to a sticky honeypot.

We're incredibly similar. We both have the same emotional scars and drive to succeed. We both need to take control even though life has taught us the hard way that we never truly are.

Is it any wonder we click?

But we're playing with fire because our lives are woven so intrinsically. My brother is marrying her sister, for fuck's sake. My father is in jail charged with the manslaughter of her parents.

We're supposed to hate each other.

I should be utterly unavailable.

It's so messed up, it's not even funny.

'After the Vegas leg of the tour, I want you to come stay at my house for a few days.' The words are out of my mouth before I can stop them.

Her head whips around, apparently as surprised as I am. I never invite women to my house. Apart from Lula, but that's wildly different.

Her mouth opens but she hesitates before answering, leaving me an opportunity for further persuasion.

'Imagine, we could have three more days of this.' My hand flicks between us.

Watching her taste the seafood, observing how her head tilts back before her low throaty laugh exits her chest, and just getting to know her better, has been the highlight of my day.

She stares at me for a beat, her head cocked to one side as if she's analysing me. Analysing the meaning of this growing intimacy between us.

I hold my breath as she contemplates my offer, my heart hammering in my chest. She has no idea how big a deal this is for me.

'Sure,' she says with a casual shrug.

There's nothing casual about any of it. I'm falling head-first into the deepest darkest manhole I've ever known, yet instead of fighting it, I'm free falling, cruising on the short-term rush, ignoring the inevitable looming crash to rock bottom, with consequences so devastating I might not survive.

We eat together on the veranda as the sun sets, the sky glowing pink and orange. There's no fucking denying it. I'm developing feelings for Chloe, even though I can't afford to for a million reasons, none of which are because I'm ashamed or embarrassed.

But I don't want to hurt her. Or let her down. Because that's what I do, isn't it? It's what I've always done, and a leopard doesn't change his spots just because he's falling in love.

Given my rapidly flourishing feelings for Chloe, it's probably a saving grace we've set an end date on this fling, because I've got a horrible feeling she might be the only woman I could truly fall in love with. And after losing my mother and Sofia, then watching Ryan's years of heartbreak, that's something I vowed I'd never do.

Chapter Twenty-One

CHLOE

Santa Monica

I glance around Jayden's swanky bachelor pad. I've imagined so many times what it might look like, his own private lair, while we talk on the phone for hours into the night.

Seeing the inside of someone's house is so personal, especially when you're staying in their bed. So why am I not utterly freaked out?

Because you're utterly obsessed with all the naughty things he might do to you here.

The house is everything I expected and more. It's miles bigger than my villa in Dubai and screams wealth and power. The back wall is triple glazed glass and overlooks stunning manicured gardens and an Olympic-size pool.

The kitchen is Nigella's dream, with marble counters big enough to carve a roast fit for forty. Naveesha would have a field day here.

I hate to admit I'm impressed, and not just with Jayden's house, but with the man himself. To think he and Ryan built themselves an empire from nothing.

Sasha mentioned they'd had some rough times. Sleeping on the streets of LA, for one thing, but in all the hours we've spent curled in our post coital, bliss-filled bubble, Jayden's never once mentioned it.

Not that I ever expected him to. I'm not his girlfriend. We're just sleeping together.

'I can't wait to get you into my bed tonight.'

I can't wait to get you into my bed tonight. It's so caveman. I love it.

Energy swirls between us, hot like a wildfire. Butterflies swell and dip in my stomach.

This thing between us is feeling dangerously close to something more than it's supposed to be. These past few weeks he's ignited something in me I didn't think was possible. It's probably for the best there's an end date in sight because I'd never forgive myself if I did something stupid like fall in love with Jayden-Super-Smug-Cooper.

'What are you thinking?' He closes the distance between us.

I almost blurt out, 'Reminding myself not to fall in love with you.' But I catch myself. 'The bucket list.'

'What's next?' he asks with a potent stare.

Carnal thoughts rip through me as he pins me against the countertop. 'Toys?' Who am I kidding? Perky Pete's been permanently relegated. My new favourite toy is in Jayden's pants, hard and ready.

Hot, full lips pave a trail along my neck, skirting across my collar bone. I yank off the top I'm wearing to showcase the lingerie I spent way too long selecting to impress a man I'm simply having a fling with.

Dark eyes rake appreciatively over the black transparent lace. 'You know, you're nothing like I imagined.'

'Is that right?' I reach for his belt buckle as he tugs my bra down, spilling my breasts over the top of it. His mouth captures my nipple, and I let out a gasp. 'How did you imagine me exactly?

'Cold. Unresponsive. In need of corrupting.' His teeth nip at my sensitive flesh, sending shivers rocketing through my entire body.

'And now?'

'Now I think you're the hottest woman I've ever met. If anything, you and your list are corrupting *me*.'

'Oh, I doubt that somehow. I saw the tabloids. A different woman every few weeks. How many have stood in this very spot, listening to the same words?' My head rolls back blissfully as his tongue travels lower towards my belly button.

'None. I never bring women home. I promise, that's the truth.'

'Never?'

He shakes his head as a tingling sensation courses from my head to my toes and everywhere in between. I'm flattered. And seriously struggling to discern what this even means for us.

I don't get a moment longer to contemplate it.

Raw possessiveness blazes in his eyes as he drops to his knees before me. 'But was that jealousy I detected in your tone?' he asks.

Lie. Lie. Lie. Jealousy equals caring past the immediate physical gratification. Caring equals vulnerability. I swore I would never leave myself vulnerable again after Ethan.

But my body doesn't know how to lie to him. My pelvis arches longingly and he grins.

'Say it, Princess, and I'll make you come so hard they'll hear you back in Sydney.' He unzips my skirt, and it falls to the floor, leaving me in just the lace and high strappy stilettos.

I don't know why I fight it. I might be assertive in the bedroom, the kitchen, or wherever else he takes me, but he's always in control. And he has an uncanny knack of extracting the truth from me, even if his methods aren't entirely fair.

'I'm jealous of every woman who came before me.'

His mouth presses against my inner thigh. It travels upwards until his tongue darts expertly around the scrap of material. Every single cell in my body jolts to life. I'm hopelessly addicted to his touch. 'Just as I'll be jealous of every man who comes after me,' he mumbles

After?

I've deliberately pushed the thought of life after Jayden from my brain because it doesn't bear thinking about.

I don't want to give him up. Not now. Probably never. I don't want to give up the phone calls and the stolen dinners. But most of all, I don't want to give up being truly seen. Understood. Appreciated. Cherished. Because even though this was supposed to only be sex, that's exactly how Jayden makes me feel.

My hands rake through his inky hair as he glides his tongue through my centre, up and down, relentlessly bringing me to the brink of an explosive release. 'You're unbelievably talented with that tongue.'

I feel his smug grin against my sex, but I don't care. My lust is primal. Blinding. As my orgasm crests, washing over me, I'm already thinking how I can get my next fix.

It's official. I'm ruined.

In one swift motion, he's up from his knees and hoisting me onto the marble counter.

'I know you said toys, Princess, but will this one do until I get you upstairs?' He pushes his length at my entrance, and I yank the lace to one side in response.

The man's a mind reader on top of everything else.

'I'm beginning to realise toys are overrated. Give me the real deal.'

He slides in, gently easing himself into my space, and something unspoken passes between us. An intimacy that goes way beyond anything we agreed. It's etched into every line of his face, a tenderness I never believed he was capable of.

'This is the real deal, Princess.'

He's right. It *is* the real deal. The world around me falls away into nothingness. And there's no denying I have feelings for him.

My insides ignite with a stupid but incessant spark of hope when there really is none. Even if I wasn't such a staunch commitment-phobe, Jayden most certainly is.

I wake from a deep jet lag slumber, snuggled under the comfort of Jayden's silk sheets. There's nothing awkward about waking up with him, apart from the sheer size of him pressing against me. The heat pulsing between us is hotter than the desert, though not as dry. Prising myself from his solid arms, I slip out of bed and creep down the corridor in search of a glass of water.

The house is gigantic. Three doors line the long corridor, all slightly ajar. My curiosity piques, I can't resist taking a peek while Jayden's still sleeping.

The first door leads into a bathroom bigger than my bedroom. A whirlpool bath sits beneath a huge circular window overlooking lush gardens and greenery while deep green walls contrast the brilliant white bathroom suite. I'm drawn in and stand before a mirrored cabinet where I glimpse my matted hair. An unmistakable luminous glow replaces my usual dull skin.

Instinctively, my fingers reach for the cabinet. Row upon row of neatly stacked toiletries stare back at me. Cleansers, moisturisers, day creams, night creams. Who would have thought the most masculine man I've ever met has a skin care regime? I silently close the cabinet and creep back into the hall.

The second door off the corridor opens up into what is obviously Jayden's office. The walls are dark, but the furniture is white. Two industrial-sized matching desks occupy the centre of the room, each housing an iMac and a stack of paperwork.

Further along the corridor, I find the last room has been decorated in pastel pink, with cream embroidered bedding and a vanity station, in contrast to the dark, masculine colours lining every other wall in Jayden's mansion.

'Chloe?' Jayden's voice from along the hallway makes me jump.

'Just grabbing some water.'

With a million questions swirling around my head, I run down the stairs and back up again as fast as my legs will carry me, returning to Jayden's bedroom with my water. I deliberately don't look in the pink room again. It stirs questions that I'm not sure I want answered.

I place my glass on a bedside locker and snuggle back into the comfort of Jayden's arms. His bedroom is every bit as masculine as him. I feel safe, protected here in a way I didn't realise I yearned to be.

'That's better,' he murmurs, gripping my waist and grinding himself against me.

'Does that thing ever go down?' It's me who's feeling smug now.

'Not when you're around.'

My phone vibrates next to the water.

Warm hands slide around my chest to cup my breasts. The man is insatiable. It's not a complaint. 'Ugh. Who is that?' he groans.

'My sister. Payback's a bitch. I normally ring her every morning and wake her, but I've been preoccupied lately.' I reject the call and inch back onto Jayden's ever ready erection. A low moan of approval brushes my ear and a wave of contentment washes over me.

My phone buzzes again. When I reach out to grab it, Jayden grips my hips and growls, 'Don't you dare, Princess. Take the call, by all means, but don't even think about sliding off me.'

I mentally apologise to my sister before accepting her call.

'Chloe, where are you? Izzy said you've gone AWOL. You didn't check into the hotel yesterday and Ruby said she hasn't seen you in weeks.'

'I'm fine. Sorry, I'm catching up with... an old colleague.'

'What colleague?' She breathes a brief sigh of exasperation and then her voice returns to her initial high-pitched squeal. 'Never mind! I've got some exciting news. You'll never believe it. Adam Draker wants you to organise his next tour. He was so impressed with the stage set up for *It's Always Been You,* he reached out to Ryan yesterday. Ryan can't actually stand him, by the way. He's supposed to be a total womaniser, but I don't need to tell you how big this is.'

Jayden pumps me low and slow from behind, as if to demonstrate the precise definition of big.

'That's amazing,' I purr to him, not to her.

Sasha babbles on excitedly. 'It *is* amazing! It's exactly what you wanted. Liberty Events Management is going global, honey!'

'Uh, huh. It's exactly what I need.' I bite my lip to stop my moan as Jayden relentlessly drives into me, delivering me straight to heaven.

'When are you viewing the offices? I'll meet you there. Oh my god, this is so exciting.'

It really is. If I'm mixing in the music industry circles, I'm bound to cross paths with Jayden, even after our fling has ended.

What the fuck? Rein it in, Chloe. That wasn't part of the deal.

'I'm not sure. I'll call you back this afternoon.' I throw the phone across the room and grind back against the god-like creature behind me.

He flips me onto my front, face down onto the pillow.

I was only joking when I told Jayden I was a screamer. But it turns out, it was true. I just needed the right man to tip me over the edge.

Chapter Twenty-Two

JAYDEN

'You're looking at offices in Los Angeles?' It's an effort to keep the panic from my voice.

It's one thing enjoying incredible sex, intimacy and laughter with a woman who lives on the other side of the world, and another to allow myself to get so comfortable with her working in the same city as me.

I'm playing with fire and the flames are fanning higher with each passing day.

'Of course. I told you I wanted to bring my company global.' Chloe slides towards the edge of my bed and I instinctively catch her by the wrist, my thumb rubbing over her ever-present elastic band.

Somehow, over five weekends and approximately five hundred calls and texts, Chloe Sexton has done what no other woman has come close to. Bar one. And that was a long time ago and in very different circumstances.

She's gotten under my skin, as thick as it may be.

I think about her every waking second of the day and actually mark the days off my calendar until we're together again.

This is bad. Really bad.

Apart from the fact she doesn't do relationships, I am in no position to start one.

Chloe pensively stares at me. 'What's up? You look like you've seen a ghost.'

With images of Sofia bombarding my brain lately, I feel like I've seen one too. She was the only other woman I had romantic feelings for. Feelings I never got to explore. Perhaps in different circumstances, I wouldn't have even wanted to. But back then, she was my safe place. She lit my soul on the darkest of nights. Those huge brown eyes will haunt me forever. *If you ever escape this life, please drag my sister with you.*

I won't let her down.

'When you said you wanted to take your company global, I didn't realise you meant you'd be basing yourself in LA,' I say.

Chloe swallows thickly. 'I never planned to stay in Dubai long term. LA's the perfect place to base my new headquarters, given the ratio of celebrities to square footage.' She yanks her wrist from my hand. 'It has nothing to do with you, or us. In fact, there is no us. It's just a fling, Jayden, don't panic.'

A stabbing pain pierces my chest as she struts naked and glorious towards my en-suite. The sound of running water does nothing to soothe the jittery feeling inside my ribs.

I don't follow her in.

My phone vibrates with a text. It's Lula.

I've got all the paperwork. The interview's been scheduled for next month. The home visit should be 3-4 weeks after that. See you soon

And that's precisely why I can't afford to entertain romantic notions about Chloe. Even if I could coax myself over my own fear of commitment, this thing between me and Chloe can only ever be a fling.

The following week, a frustrating niggle is still eating my stomach. Having Chloe back on the other side of the world should theoretically ease my worries, but it only seems to amplify them.

The Vegas concert was amazing. It dominated every news station in the country, every paper and every social media site for days. After the drama with my other artists, I should be ecstatic it's going well, but an odd sense of restlessness creeps into my bones that I can't shake. Work doesn't take my mind off it, and exercise doesn't distract me.

So when my old friend, Gareth, arrives at my downtown office out of the blue, I'm grateful for the excuse to knock back a few strong ones.

We head out to one of Hollywood's most exclusive cocktail bars where blonde, waif-like models and actresses flood the place looking to make connections anyway and everyway. I take a deep breath and exhale slowly. It used to be one of my favourite pick up joints.

I glance at my watch, calculating the time in Dubai, imagining where Chloe might be. The woman possesses witch-like qualities. I'm sickeningly obsessed with her, counting down the days until I see her again.

It's another eight days. Another eight long Chloe-less days.

She'll be at her desk now, overlooking those skyscrapers, while I'm on the other side of the world, mooning around like a lovesick puppy. It's so bad I'm even starting to relate to my brother's soppy song lyrics. How did this happen to me? It wasn't part of the plan.

Unless I can come up with another one.

There has to be another way.

Though why rock the boat and jeopardise everything when Chloe made it clear this is only going to be a short-term fling?

Gareth nudges me. We're sitting at the bar where he's watching all the women with the keenness of a hawk hovering above a hapless rabbit. 'Five o'clock, pink dress,' he says.

From the devilish dart of his eyes, he's made his choice for tonight. Clearly, he hasn't worked up the balls to ask out Kim yet.

Normally I'd be right with him, scanning the crowd for my next conquest.

Tonight, all I want to do is curl up in my bed, inhale the pillow that Chloe's head rested on, and soak in the smell of her exotic shampoo.

Holy fuck, if anyone could see me now. I'm a mess. And these strange and unnerving feelings only seem to grow stronger every time we're together.

Maybe we could push out the end date? If we let it run on further, perhaps it'll eventually burn itself out.

Who am I kidding? The longer we let this thing run, the deeper I'm going to fall for her. I should stop it right now, but I'm not strong enough.

Like an addict, I keep promising I'll give up tomorrow. But tomorrow never comes.

There's not a woman in this entire bar who can hold a match to Chloe Sexton.

Across the room, a couple perch on high chrome stools, each clutching a glass of white wine. She's typical LA. Immaculate blonde highlights cut in a stylish bob, with a forehead too tight and bright to reveal any sign of ageing, although the weathered skin of her hands doesn't lie. She has to be mid-fifties.

He's tanned with an athletic build, like most people in this city. A slight paunch punctuates his middle, but otherwise he looks in good shape. His dark hair's peppered grey, the same shade as his high-end designer suit. Sharp and successful, they reek of old money. But the sharpest thing is his glare, which is aimed directly at me.

I recognise them, but it takes me a minute to place them. He's a politician. She's a former model. I remember now, I auditioned their daughter. She'd been hyped up as the next Brittney. Sadly, it was a waste of both of our time.

Johnson. Chardonnay Johnson. That was her name. I haven't thought about her since, but the way her parents are glaring across the bar, they clearly haven't forgotten. This is the type of Hollywood politics I can't stand.

'You ok, man?' Gareth taps my shoulder.

'Just a bit distracted with work.' I take a mouthful of whiskey, revelling in the burn in my throat.

Gareth gives me a knowing look. 'Come on, buddy. I've known you long enough to know you're putting on a show.'

'This is Hollywood. Everyone's an actor here.' I raise my glass to clink against his.

'What's her name?'

My head snaps up and my heart quickens in my chest. 'Who's name?'

'The woman who's been occupying your thoughts all night. Who is she? She must be something really special to have your shoulders slumping into your shot glass.' He grins and pokes me with his index finger.

There's no point lying. Gareth knows me almost as well as my brother. A weighted sigh slips from my lips and my shoulders sag. It's actually a relief to admit it to someone who won't murder me for overstepping a line. 'How did you know?'

He snorts and shakes his head. 'You haven't so much as looked at a woman since we got here.'

'I don't even have the energy to deny it.' I take another sip of my drink. 'For the first time in my life, I think I've found someone special, although the timing couldn't be any worse.'

Gareth sits straighter in his chair, closing the distance between us. 'So who is she, this mystery woman?'

'Someone I can't have, for a million reasons.'

'Ah, I see.' He cocks his head, tapping his finger on the side of his glass. 'Are you sure that's not the whole appeal? Jayden Cooper finally finds a woman who says no to him. This must be a first. No wonder you don't like it.'

A smirk lifts my lips as an image of us in bed invades my brain. 'She didn't say no exactly.'

'Uh-oh. How long exactly has this been going on?'

'A couple of months.'

'What? That's a record! I know you've been trying to be discreet lately, but I haven't seen a single picture of you with any woman in the tabloids all year.'

I mutter between gritted teeth, 'She's embarrassed to be seen with me.'

Laughter bursts ferociously from Gareth's chest. Every time he thinks he's finished, he opens his mouth to say something, then starts again.

He finally composes himself. 'Sorry, man. That's too funny. What is she? Fucking royalty or something?'

'Something like that.' I shrug and order two more drinks.

'Don't worry. It'll burn itself out, behind closed doors, of course.' He sniggers again.

'It would want to. The interview with Lula's been scheduled for next month. I can't fuck it up now.'

'Ah.' Gareth's expression turns serious. He's the only

person, other than Ryan, Declan and Kim, who knows what I promised I'd do for her. I'd prefer it to stay that way.

'It's probably a blessing in disguise that Chloe is allergic to anything serious, because I'm in no position to give it to her.'

'Chloe? As in Chloe Sexton? The woman you hate.'

I might have mentioned as much a couple of months ago over one too many drinks. 'The very one.'

Gareth snorts again. Tears of laughter roll down his face and his whiskey catches in his throat. He splutters, thumping his chest with a fisted palm. I hope he chokes on it.

Across the bar, the Johnsons stand to leave. The senator shoots me a look of pure disgust as he ushers his wife out of the door.

I can appreciate the sentiment.

I'm pretty disgusted with myself. It's just for very different reasons.

Chapter Twenty-Three

CHLOE

Dubai

'Are Sasha and Ryan staying with you?' Ruby approaches my desk and hands me a coffee.

I'm knee deep planning the wrap party. If I can crack London, I'll have a good shot at the British market. Who knows what opportunities that might bring. And the way I'm feeling lately, it might be safer to shack up there than LA.

In my wildest dreams, I imagine Liberty Events organising a lavish royal wedding, maybe one of Harry or William's cousins. I'm obsessed with The Crown and Downton Abbey. Netflix and work are the only ways to pass the days apart from Jayden.

I've got it bad. But if his panicked tone was anything to go by last month, he doesn't feel the same.

'Hello? Earth to Chloe.' Ruby's red-tipped fingers click in front of my face.

'Sorry. They're staying in the Burj Al Arab, of course, along with Ryan's security, PAs and the rest of the entourage. Not that I mind. The last thing I want is to listen to the guest room headboard banging against my wall all night.'

Ruby smiles dreamily into space. 'What I wouldn't do to find out what Ryan Cooper's like in bed!'

'Yuck. Ask my sister. She'll tell you all about it, trust me.' It used to be me regaling her with tales of the night before. Now I have to suffer hers. Gross.

I take a sip of coffee and wait for the caffeine to course through my blood. I've not been sleeping well, my mind overactive, analysing the escalating feelings I'm harbouring for a man who clearly doesn't feel the same.

If somewhere deep down I was secretly entertaining any daft notions of extending our agreement, the astronomic horror he expressed at me working on his doorstep rapidly shattered any illusions I'd imagined about a growing intimacy between us.

And yet, I could have sworn he felt the same. The signs were all there. The way his body moulds against mine, sheltering and protecting me each time we fall into an exhausted, satiated sleep together. How he insists I look at him while he pleasures me, like he needs to feel what I'm feeling.

Clearly my sleep deprivation's making me delusional as well as drained.

Thoughts of him perpetually spill into my brain. He's the one habit I can't even begin to contemplate kicking, but with only four tour dates left in the diary, eventually I'm going to have to go cold turkey.

Ruby perches on the edge of her desk, her voice dropping to barely more than a whisper. 'I suppose I don't have to ask where Jayden's staying?'

I might be tired and confused, but the prospect of scoring my next fix sets my tummy tingling. My lips part in a grin, despite myself.

'He has a room booked at the Burj.' I shoot a knowing glance at my friend, 'But he won't be using it.'

Ruby rolls her eyes skywards. 'Such a waste.'

'Trust me, it's not. Not when you know what I've got planned for him.'

Handcuffs aren't easy to source in the Middle East, so I plan on securing Jayden to my bed with my dressing gown tie instead. Just as soon as I get Sasha's customary dinner over with.

It's torture sitting through hours of small talk after a week apart. How Sasha and Ryan haven't spotted the energy thrumming between us is a miracle. It swirls so thickly, weighted with a promise that blurs my ability to focus on anything else.

'I'm green with envy. Brad and I are off again.' Ruby's head drops and she gnaws on her lower lip.

I pat the back of her hand affectionately. 'I don't know why you bother, Rubes. If he won't commit, what's the point?'

Neat black eyebrows arch skywards. 'Hello? Pot? Kettle?'

A blush heats my cheeks. She's right. Of course she's right. But for the first time in a long time, I might actually consider committing. It's just a shame Jayden doesn't feel the same.

'You're right, sorry. What do I know? Why don't you use the room at the Burj for the weekend? Order room service. Use the spa. Pamper yourself.'

'Oh, Chloe, I couldn't.'

'Why not? It's paid for, anyway. Use it, please.'

'Seriously? You're the best boss ever.' Ruby squeezes my shoulder before returning to her desk, thankfully happier than when she left it.

Jayden's flight from LA arrives six hours before Sasha and Ryan's touches down from Dublin. I wait at the airport, pushing away all thoughts of what might happen when this is over, determined to make the most of our last few weekends together.

Wearing a cream tailored dress, a sultry smile, and new La Perla lingerie, I answer a couple of last-minute calls about tomorrow night's concert, and one from my doctor's surgery reminding me my contraceptive shot is due.

I don't need to look up to know when Jayden enters the arrivals hall. Every single cell of my body instinctively zings to life. He shoots me his signature smirk as he stalks across the room, leaving a trail of gawping women in his wake.

For the first time, he substitutes his French double peck greeting for a full on panty-melting French kiss. And when his tongue slips inside my mouth, dangerously, I feel like I've come home.

'Excuse me.' An airport security guard interrupts us, frowning and pointing towards the exit.

I might not have been able to source handcuffs for the bedroom, but I don't intend to be restrained in real ones.

'Sorry.' Jayden apologises for both of us, ushering me out of the door.

'Are you wearing any knickers under that dress, Sexton?' he murmurs in my ear. Any awkwardness from Vegas has evaporated, thankfully.

'Play your cards right and you might just find out.' We step out into the humidity, but nothing makes me as hot as Jayden's filthy mouth.

I unlock the car and he places his small case in the boot.

'Want me to drive?' he offers, but there's no smugness in his tone this time.

I shrug and throw him the keys.

I think Jayden Cooper might have shagged me into submission. Surprisingly, it feels pretty good to hand over the reins, even if it is only for a short while longer.

Maybe there's hope for me yet?

'Are you hungry?' I slip into the passenger side and adjust the air-con to full. My dress hitches up, drawing his attention.

'I'm always hungry around you.'

Saliva pools in my mouth as he drops his free hand to my thigh.

'If you're not still embarrassed to be seen in public with me, we could stop for lunch somewhere? At least this side of the world we won't be hounded by the paps.'

I swallow hard. 'I told you before, I wasn't embarrassed of you before, I was embarrassed of me.'

Huge grey eyes slant sideways at me. 'And now?'

Now I'm stupidly enamoured. Thankfully, I don't say it out loud.

I shrug. 'Sushi?'

'Sure.'

'Take the next exit. I know a great place for lunch.'

He squeezes my thigh, and that smirk reappears. 'It's a date.' Ever the joker.

I wish.

Sunset Sushi used to be my favourite restaurant in the entire emirate. With a huge double-height dining area hovering over the ocean, both the food and views are to die for.

Ethan and I used to come here most Thursdays when we'd finished the working week, toasting whatever we'd accomplished in the previous few days. Back then, the business was growing at an alarming rate, but I didn't have the experience I have now. If I'd have been more savvy, I might have seen it coming.

I've only heard from him once since he left, when news broke at Christmas of my sister's engagement to Ryan Cooper.

Obviously, I didn't dignify it with a reply.

'What are you thinking?' Jayden asks when we're left with the menu.

'Nothing.'

A warm finger traces the back of my hand where it rests on the brilliant white linen tablecloth.

'Are you sure?'

'We agreed to embark on a fling, Jayden, not a friendship.' I yank my hand back and hide it under the table.

'Wow. Excuse me while I recover from whiplash.' All trace of his usual humour is gone. 'Is there a reason we can't do both?'

I'm being a bitch. It's not fair to take out my frustration on him. It's not his fault I want more than he wants to give.

'Sorry.' I place my hand back on the linen and reach for his. 'It's not you...'

His familiar smirk inches onto his lips. 'Don't tell me. It's not you, it's me.'

'My head's all over the show right now.'

'Is it the tour? All the American tabloids are saying it's the best in years. You've done an amazing job.'

I pause, revelling in his praise for a few seconds. 'It's not that, it's everything,' I sigh, taking a sip from a glass of water. 'I'm interviewing for staff. My phone's vibrating so much my battery barely lasts an hour these days. I've got more work than I can keep up with and I still can't turn any of it down.'

It's all true, but it's not the crux of what's really bothering me.

He leans forward, a look of concern carved on his face. 'Is there anything I can help with?'

Aurelia Arlington was right, Jayden definitely has a hero complex. He'd have to save himself first before he can save me, because I'd bet my life there's a reason he can't commit. And until he gets over that, how can he commit to me?

Stop, Chloe. Stop it. Never going to happen.

'No, but thank you.' I squeeze Jayden's fingers as a familiar voice booms behind me.

'Well, well, well... Chloe Sexton. It's been a while.'

My head whips around. Ethan's the last person I expected to see. His eyes dart between Jayden and me before finally landing on our joined hands on the table.

'Not interrupting, am I?'

Chapter Twenty-Four

JAYDEN

Chloe's interlaced fingers squeeze mine in a warning. It's unnecessary. I've spent hours worshipping every inch of her body over the past couple of months. I know her subtle tells better than my own.

This guy obviously makes her uncomfortable.

Dressed in a flashy designer suit and with more gold than any self-respecting man should wear, he's clearly trying to impress someone, possibly himself.

'Ethan.' Chloe greets him coolly.

'You're looking well.' His eyes scour her in silent assessment before returning to me. 'And who is this?'

'I'm her boyfriend.' It's out of my mouth before I can help it. 'Jayden Cooper.'

Stupid, stupid, stupid.

Chloe specifically swore me to secrecy, and I shoot my mouth off in front of the first guy who asks the question.

Not to mention if this idiot takes out his phone and takes a picture, he could jeopardise everything for Lula, and the vow I made to Sofia.

He extends a hand, but I deliberately leave mine interlocked with Chloe's in a show of support.

His narrow eyes widen and light simultaneously. 'Ah.' He clicks his fingers like everything finally makes sense. 'Agent and brother to Ryan Cooper, and one of LA's biggest players, if you believe the tabloids.'

'Huh.' I snort. And Chloe calls *me* smug. If that's the case, she has a type.

He waves his fingers between the two of us and sneers. 'Isn't this practically incest? Oh wait, you're not family yet, are you?'

It's a battle to hold my fist back from punching him in the face.

'And you are?' Not that I particularly care, other than something about him incenses my woman.

My woman. If only.

'Ethan Harte. Chloe's ex-boyfriend. I'm sure she's mentioned me.'

So, he's the one who almost ruined it for the rest of us.

Whatever he did, it must have been really bad for her to make her famous one date only rule. My jaw locks, imagining his smarmy hands on her. Kissing her. Touching her.

Even as the blood boils beneath my skin, I adopt an air of indifference. 'No, funnily enough, she never mentioned you.'

Ethan leers, finally retracting his hand.

'This is an interesting development.' He nods between the two of us, shoving his hands into his pockets. 'I assumed it was Ryan throwing you a bone with the tour, but clearly it's a different bone you've been working on this entire time.'

It's one thing trying to find a weak spot with me and entirely another to poke Chloe's.

Leaping from my seat, I tower inches above Ethan. 'Watch your mouth.'

Chloe stands, inserting herself between us. 'Jayden.' The

warning in her tone reminds me we're in a public place, but my fists clench with a rage I haven't felt in years.

Ethan chuckles and shakes his head as he places a hand on Chloe's arm. 'When he tires of you, call me. I want to discuss a merger.'

With that, he turns and leaves. Only when he's gone do I sit down again.

'Sorry about that,' Chloe says in barely more than a whisper.

'Why are you apologising for him? I'm sorry I spoke out of turn. I gave him the ammunition he needed.' I order a bottle of wine from a passing waitress while my heartbeat continues to pound in my chest.

'It's ok. It was really very satisfying.' A rare grin flashes across her face for a millisecond before she gathers herself. 'Seriously though, you didn't have to lie for me. I'm perfectly capable of fighting my own battles.'

'Princess, when you're with me, you'll never have to.'

She swallows hard and her mouth opens like she's going to say something before thinking better of it.

The waitress returns with the wine. She pours us each a glass half the size of what we might actually need to get through this conversation. I shouldn't ask Chloe about her past when I have no place in her future, but I can't help it.

'So, he's the one who nearly ruined it for all of us...'

Chloe swallows a large mouthful of wine and sets her glass down. 'I hired him to manage my office. We were together for almost two years.'

I have an insatiable urge to slam my fist on the table, or through Ethan's jaw, but Chloe's normally so reticent when it comes to her personal life, I let her speak.

'He left me for an office junior and I never saw it coming. It ripped open every barely closed wound in my heart. I'd survived my parents' deaths, but never truly grieved them. Then when I lost Ethan, that grief hit me like a tsunami.'

'Chloe, you should probably take some time with your sisters. Let them help you through the grief. It's something that never goes away, but you can't learn to live with it if you're constantly running from it.'

'You speak like someone speaking from experience.'

I lower my gaze and squeeze Chloe's hand tightly. 'My mother left us when I was three. It took me a ridiculously long time to grieve for her because I spent most of my childhood thinking she'd magically return.'

'Oh, Jayden, I'm so sorry.'

'I know your parents are gone, but they didn't choose to leave you. Mine did. Both of them, though in very different circumstances.' I take a sip from my drink and hold Chloe's gaze. While I have her undivided attention and her shield is lowered, there's something I need her to hear.

'I'm so sorry about your parents, Princess. I do feel responsible, even though we had no idea.'

Chloe straightens her back and leans across the table. 'You listen to me this second, Jayden. Just like my parents didn't choose to leave me, you didn't choose for your father to get into that car.'

No matter how either of us feels about it, it doesn't change the outcome. 'I'm sorry Ethan hurt you when you were already hurting.'

'To be honest, it was my pride he hurt the most. In the weeks I wasted nursing my broken heart, I took my eye off my business. Ethan took half of my clients. If it wasn't for Ruby's diligent eye, he might have taken them all. His company is my biggest rival. Or should I say, *was* my biggest rival before I landed Ryan's farewell tour.'

'Wow.' It's one thing being dumped, but being dumped and fucked over takes things to another level.

'I know, right?'

'We're not all like him, you know.' Who am I kidding? I'm no better. Not really. If I was, I'd stay well away from Chloe, instead of letting this thing between us bloom like a rose in a field full of strangling poison ivy.

Her gaze rises to meet mine. 'I'm finally realising it.'

'About the boyfriend remark. I didn't mean to make things worse. Ryan hired you because you were the best woman for the job.'

'Don't worry, I didn't for a second think you meant it.' For a millisecond, something like regret flashes across her face.

She feels it too.

Maybe this growing affection between us isn't entirely one-sided.

Did she also feel the panic I felt when she mentioned her LA office? Because she hasn't brought it up since. It's clearly another elephant that needs addressing, but not today. Not when I'm sitting in front of her. Because if she knows my body half as well as I know hers, she'll realise I wasn't panicking because I don't want her there. I was panicking because I do.

Chapter Twenty-Five

CHLOE

Last night's concert was my favourite so far, namely because I got to meet Aurelia Arlington again.

'You're still suffering him, I see,' she said to me. Those exact words. Thankfully, Sasha was nowhere near to hear.

Aurelia's right in some ways. Suffering is the word for it.

The feelings ripping through me right now are agonising. Every tremulous smile, every fevered kiss, grabs my rapidly swelling heart and twists it upside down. I'm falling in love with the man who's currently sprawled like a starfish across my bed. The same one who has been exceptionally open that he unequivocally can't commit.

Seeing Ethan only confirmed it. When Jayden said, "I'm her boyfriend," in that panty-melting possessive tone, I swear my heart rate cantered like a racehorse.

I thought I loved Ethan.

I didn't. Not really. I loved the security of being together and that we shared the same drive for business. At least, I thought we did.

And when Jayden stuck up for me, a warm honeyed sensation spread through my veins and heart, plugging the hole in my chest.

My escalating feelings for him are utterly stupid, inappropriate, and futile. He's leaving tomorrow and we only have three more dates left. I need to get my head together.

Jayden made it clear he's unavailable. He's never messed me around. In fact, he treats me better than Ethan ever did, and we were *supposed* to be in a committed relationship. Beneath his smart quips and frequent smirks, Jayden Cooper has an underlying honour I'd never have thought he possessed. And when he peels back his mask, and drops the ruthless act, he's actually very sweet.

Lying on my side, resting my head on my elbow, I stare at him while he sleeps. Sleeping Jayden is so different to awake Jayden. Sleeping Jayden has an endearing vulnerability that awake Jayden wouldn't dream of revealing.

Thick masculine stubble dots his square jaw, and it's a battle not to rub my fingers over it. Long black lashes occasionally flutter like he's dreaming. Is he dreaming of me?

No. That's a stupid romantic notion.

Ethan might have been right, Jayden is notoriously one of LA's biggest players, but he's never made a secret of it. It's probably why he's so damn good in bed, with all that experience he's gained over the years. Unlike Ethan, he doesn't pretend to be something he's not.

The call to prayer sounds. Jayden groans, pulling a pillow over his head. 'I don't know how you stick that five times a day.'

'You get used to it. I barely hear it anymore.'

His hand fumbles under the sheets until it lands on my bare hip. A moan of something like approval emerges from his lips and he pulls my body closer, flinging the pillow to the floor. Enormous steely eyes capture mine.

'Hey.' He brushes my hair back from my face. It's a

gesture that feels way too loving for people who are merely having casual sex.

A slow smile parts my lips. 'Hey.'

With a rare serious expression, his finger traces the side of my face and my heart lodges in my throat. 'I was dreaming about you.'

'Really? And what was I doing in this dream of yours, exactly?'

'You were...' His low voice is weighted with the same sadness that curls around my heart when I think of this thing between us ending.

I'd almost swear he's on the verge of admitting he feels something similar.

The need to tell him I have feelings for him consumes me, but so does a fear of his rejection, especially given his reaction to my setting up in LA. I kiss my index finger and press it to his lips, silencing him in the gentlest way.

I reach under the bed and pat around the floor for the dressing gown I deliberately left there last night. Then I unhook its velvet belt and dangle it in front of Jayden's amused features.

'Ah, I see. Back to the list,' he muses, snatching it through my fingers.

He flips me onto my back, pouncing on me like a ravenous predator about to devour his first meal in months.

'You didn't seriously think *you'd* be tying *me* up, did you?' He works quickly, securing my wrists to the bedposts with a secure army-like knot, and tugs the material to test its strength. He needn't have bothered. There's no way in a million years I'd move from this spot.

A shiver of excitement tinged with mild apprehension tingles the lengths of my spine.

Who would have guessed the woman who normally

relishes taking control would so easily surrender it? And for Jayden Cooper, no less.

He hovers over me, effortlessly eye-fucking me like he's a goddamn porn star.

'Cat got your tongue?' Twin pools of lust feast on my nakedness as he parts my legs without breaking eye contact. 'Don't worry Princess, it hasn't got mine. I'm going to lick every single inch of you until you're unable to bear it for a single second longer.'

'I suppose I'll put up with it for a while.' My faux reluctance is fooling no one. One swift seductive swipe of his finger across my entrance and my accompanying gasp proves it.

The signature Jayden smirk is back in full force as he grabs my ankles, pinning them to the bottom of the bed. His tongue treats my inner thigh to maddeningly languorous licks. Each time he gets near my centre, it dips again, moving onto the other leg.

My vision clouds and blurs, and a fiery longing burns through my stomach and lower. I squirm as he eyes me with a mocking semi-smile, continuing to torment me with that expert tongue.

'Can I help you, Princess?'

'You're driving me demented. I didn't realise until today it was possible to go blind with lust. I thought that's just something they wrote in romance novels.'

He sniggers and his hot breath sends goosebumps rippling across my skin.

'You know what you have to do then, don't you?' Hovering at my core, he's so close, but so goddamn far.

Whichever way we do it, whatever we're ticking off the bucket list, it always comes back to this. His filthy mouth. It's his kink. And I love it.

Ethan was always super polite in bed and predictably vanilla. Nice. Satisfying occasionally. But memorable? Never.

The man currently between my legs thrives on possession. Ownership. He gets off on making me beg him with the filthiest words in the English language. Which is precisely why I'm going to give them to him. Using those sorts of words is something I wouldn't have dreamed of with anyone before him. Secretly, it thrills me as much as it thrills him.

'Jayden, I need you to stop teasing me and fuck me with your tongue.'

His mouth anchors to my sex. Within seconds, my thighs are trembling so hard he has to hold them still. My release builds hard and fast. Instinctively, I reach for his hair, but my arms are yanked back by the velvet cord and army-style knots.

A moan gurgles in my throat as my eyes dart between my secured wrists and the man between my legs, who's absorbing me through hooded eyes while his tongue relentlessly rakes over the length of me.

He treats me like a goddess. Like he's getting as much pleasure out of this as I am. I'm luxuriating in the sheer indulgence of his intensity.

My pelvis arches greedily to meet his mouth. 'Jayden, I'm going to...'

Convulsions rip through me, shuddering and rocking the world as I know it. Wave after wave of pleasure cascades through every inch of me as stars shoot and soar behind my eyes.

He plants a final kiss there before wriggling up the bed on three solid legs. Slinging my dead legs over his powerful shoulders, he inches into me slowly, filling me up bit by bit, until I take in every inch of him.

He sweeps my hair from my brow, pausing for a second. 'You okay, Princess?'

There it is again. That tenderness we're not supposed to share.

I nod, emotionally and physically wrung out. For some reason, tears are threatening beneath my closed eyelids.

'Look at me,' he commands and I obey. Neither of us is under any illusion he's in complete control.

'Am I hurting you?' He withdraws an inch, resting his weight on his elbows on either side of me.

'No.'

Not physically, anyway. But when this thing eventually runs its course, I fear I'll encounter a more severe pain.

'Jayden. I need to feel you.' What I need is for him to distract me enough to take my pain away.

When we finish, he holds me like I'm the most precious jewel in the world.

And it's precisely what I've been unintentionally searching for these last few years. And the reason no one was afforded a second date was because not one of them came close to making me feel like this.

When this thing between us is over, the only date I'm going on is one with myself to a therapist.

Three hours later, I'm in a much brighter place. The Hilton Jumeirah has a private beach with an à la carte restaurant. The cocktails are so colourful you need sunglasses to look at them, while huge swaying palm trees flank us in a man-made semi-circle offering guests that bit more privacy.

Jayden heads to the bar while I bag us two sunloungers under a huge cream parasol. His shirtless broad back and short-clad backside could have been sculpted by an artist. A mad rush of emotions floods my body. What is that?

Contentment?

Is that it?

It should hardly be a surprise. I've just experienced wave after wave of the most intense orgasms with the most gorgeous man I've ever clapped eyes on. And my business is thriving. I'm so close to going global, just like I dreamed. And if the end of tour party goes as well as the rest of the tour, I'll get London too.

Why wouldn't I be content?

I usually spend Saturdays by myself in the office, prepping for the week ahead. Ordering, checking, triple checking venues, prices, numbers. Or hung-over alone after a Friday brunch with Ruby.

This thing with Jayden is giving me the warm and fuzzies. Dare I admit it, but I think I'm enjoying dating again. I know it's not real. We're just fulfilling our respective sides of a bargain we made all those weeks ago. But, no, it's more than that. This fling with Jayden has shown me enough time's passed and that I'm finally ready to move on from Ethan's cheating and trust someone enough to let them in. To put myself out there again.

Although, where will I ever find a man who's able to compare to the pure perfection that's strutting towards me?

Jayden carries two hot pink frozen daiquiris over. I'm blessed with a view of his rippling torso as he bends to place one in my hand before flopping onto the thick cream sunbed next to me.

'You ok?' He cocks his head to the side, checking on me for the hundredth time today. I think I might have weirded him out earlier. Almost crying during sex wasn't on the bucket list.

'I'm good. Thank you.' He's so attentive. Imagine what it would be like being married to a man like him?

Wow! Where did that come from?

What a ridiculous and dangerous thought to entertain.

But, oh, my god, what a fantasy to store for later. Imagine the wedding night.

Stop it, Chloe! You're morphing into one of those women you hate!

'What are you grinning about?' Jayden lifts his Ray Bans and perches them on top of his head. His hair's longer than normal. Shaggier. I like it. More to run my fingers through while he's...

Chloe!

'Nothing. Just another fantasy.'

His gaze narrows and sharpens, and those full lips lift into another crooked grin. 'I think I like the sound of that. Enlighten me.'

'I think this one might be a bit much, even for you.' I snort at my private joke before taking a sip of my cocktail.

'Now there's a challenge, if ever I heard one.' He inches closer, resting on his elbow to tower over me, and my core clenches.

'Ah, come on! It's a bit too late to pretend you're shy now.'

'Trust me. This is a step too far for both of us. It could only ever be a fantasy.'

Curiosity flashes behind those beautiful, cool eyes. 'Tell me, you're always so reticent, but you don't need to be with me...'

'I can't help it. I don't know how to be any other way.'

The shrill ring of his phone interrupts us before he can probe further. He tuts as he glances at the screen.

'It's Ryan.'

Sometimes, when I'm with Jayden, I forget there are other people on the planet. Other people we're obliged to act normally around. He rejects the call and slips the phone back into the pocket of his shorts.

Steely irises glint with devilment and his fingers trace my inner thigh. 'Where were we?'

His phone rings again and he tuts, shaking his head. 'Once is okay. Twice means we have a problem.'

My own phone rings in my beachbag, and I scratch around to silence it. A quick glance at the screen shows it's Sasha. Shit. Maybe we've been busted?

I hold the phone up to show Jayden the caller ID. He presses the red button and flicks it onto vibrate. Pressing his index finger to my lips, he answers his own phone with the other hand.

'Hello?'

'Where are you?' Ryan's distressed tone carries over the speakerphone on the balmy breeze.

'On the beach.' Jayden shoots a tentative gaze around to see if we've been busted.

Would it really be so bad if we have? The urge to confide in my sister is growing by the day. Even Ethan saying I'd only got the contract because of who I was sleeping with didn't bother me nearly as much as I thought it would. Is there any need for all this secrecy at all?

'We have a problem. The stories out. All of it.' Ryan's voice cracks with emotion.

'What story?' Jayden shoves his hand through his hair and leaps off his lounger.

I know exactly what story.

It's the one we've been trying to keep out of the papers for months. The one that necessitated everyone involved to sign a non-disclosure agreement at Christmas. The one that's going to force us all to face the enormity of the past again. The one we've been trying to protect our little sister from reliving during her final exams.

The one where the world discovers Ryan's father killed his fiancée's parents.

Chapter Twenty-Six

JAYDEN

My heart plummets.

I promised Sofia I'd take care of Lula. It looks like I've fucked up on the final hurdle.

'Who is doing this to us?' My voice is so low it's a fucking growl.

'I don't know, but the timing couldn't be any worse.' Ryan's tone is weighted with despair. 'Victoria's in the middle of her final exams. Sasha is devastated, obviously. The girls have to relive the entire thing again. I'm royally fucked off that someone broke not only the NDA but our personal trust. What does anyone have to gain by dragging Dad through the media now?'

'Dad?' Realisation dawns, along with sweet relief. He's talking about Dad's crash, not my relationship with Chloe, the one thing that could jeopardise everything for Lula.

Dad can't be saved. He doesn't want to be. But it's not too late for Lula.

'Yes, Dad. What did you think I was talking about?'

'Never mind.' As terrible as it is on the Sexton sisters, the publicity will draw even more attention to Ryan's farewell tour. Scandal sells.

'It has to be someone on the inside. How else would they know?' My little brother's frustrated sigh echoes down the phone line. The urge to swoop in and sweep this under the carpet is primal, but realistically, this story was always going to break one day.

'It's all over every single news channel. Sasha is beside herself. She can't believe it. Of course, she's worried about the impact on Victoria. She's asked Megan to keep her away from her phone, the TV and radio until we get back tonight, and you can imagine how hard that's going to be.'

'Shit.' I shoot a glance at Chloe. To a passer-by, she looks relaxed but the pressure her pursed lips are applying around her straw hints that she heard everything.

'They're saying we knew, Jay. That we fled the country that night because we knew Dad had run Sasha's parents off the road.' Despite the brave face he puts on for Sasha and the rest of the world, I know he feels responsible, the same way I do.

'You know how the media works, Ryan. They're going to take this story and spin it fifty different shades of fucked up. That's just what they do. Sasha knows the truth. You know the truth. I know the truth. That's all that matters.'

Ryan sighs again. 'I'll ring Declan and see what damage limitation we can do. I assume he's still running his lucrative business helping the celeb's of LA?'

'Of course. He found Lula, didn't he? Look, why don't you leave it to me? You take care of Sasha. I'll call him now.' It's something I should have done weeks ago, because I suspect whoever is targeting us is actually targeting me.

This has to be connected to what's happened with my acts, Mia and Naomi. I don't believe in coincidences.

My biggest fear now is that it's only a matter of time

before a story breaks about me and Chloe. Or me and Lula. Right now, I'm not sure which would be worse.

I'm asking for trouble appearing in public with Chloe. It would only take for a photographer with a long lens hidden in the bushes and our secret would be destroyed. Chloe's career will be a laughing stock. All that I've promised Lula will blow up in smoke. Everyone I care about let down or disappointed, as usual.

This fling with Chloe has me uncharacteristically distracted. I've taken my eye off the game, something I never do.

Declan answers on the second ring. 'Jayden, I was expecting your call.' His thick, familiar Irish accent is as reassuring as the morning sun. He'll find who's responsible. I trust him. Have done since he had my back in the playground. His methods aren't always strictly legit, but he always gets the job done.

He'll find who's responsible and I'll make sure they pay.

'It's a shitshow, Dec. Ryan's going off his head. You know as well as I do there's no such thing as bad publicity, but apart from the horrific timing, someone broke their NDA, and that's something I refuse to ignore.'

'I'm already on it. I'm doing a background check on every single one of Huxley Castle's staff. But other than an ancient Driving Under the Influence, I've got nothing yet.'

I survey the white sandy beach, taking in the turquoise waves gently cresting at the shoreline. The heat of the Dubai summer sun scalds my skin, but I can't shake the icy shiver shuddering down my spine. Chloe stares silently into space, listening to every word. What is she thinking? None of us will escape the repercussions of this story where the media's concerned.

'I think you're starting in the wrong place, Dec.' I scratch the rough stubble of my jawline. Who else would be close enough to our families with the motive to try to take me down?

'How so?

'Two of the girls I signed have been targeted over the last few weeks. One with drugs and the other with a sex tape. I don't think Ryan's the target here. I think I am.'

Declan lets out a low whistle. 'Send me everything you have on your artists. Who was near them? Who had access to them? No matter how irrelevant, I need it.'

'I'll get Kim on it.'

'Let me check her out first,' Declan says grimly.

'Seriously?' Kim's been with me for years. I've come to rely on her friendship and loyalty almost as much as Declan's.

'If she checks out, make use of her. I'll get back to you.'

'I don't need to tell you how urgent this is, Dec,' I remind him.

'I know. Trust me. I'm all over it.'

'Another thing, I need you to see if there's another way...'

'For....?'

'Lula's visa.'

'Oh.' He clears his throat. 'I'll look into it.' He hangs up without saying goodbye.

Chloe's huge oceanic eyes pensively meet mine behind her giant oversized sunglasses. Her plump inviting lips flatten into a subdued line, but it does nothing to diminish her beauty. Is it any wonder I'm struggling to uphold the promises I made to Lula?

Beneath Chloe's hard but stunning exterior is a heart so full and so fragile I want to hang onto her forever. Fix her.

Love her back to life. Because whatever she's been doing out here the last few years post Ethan, definitely isn't that.

Ethan.

Would he be responsible for this shitshow?

No.

It started before we were introduced. There's no way he could have known, is there? I'll get Declan to check him out, nevertheless.

I perch on the edge of the lounger and sip my own melted daiquiri. But my mind's on other things. Ten minutes ago, everything was grand. Rosy even. At least on the surface. Now, everything's turning to dust around me.

Was it grand really, though? Or was I deluding myself? Someone's been targeting my artists for weeks.

I'm doing something unthinkable, falling in love with someone I can never have. Although lately, I could swear...

Chloe sits up, straightening her spine as if she's preparing for battle. 'I take it the shit's hitting the fan?'

'I'm afraid so.'

Her slim fingers reach out to take mine, but I pat the back of her hand and pull away. The situation I'm currently in is too precarious.

A flicker of hurt crosses her face and she leaps from the lounger.

In a split second, whatever intimacy we shared this morning has evaporated. Blown into oblivion.

Mrs Silver Spoon is back, and I don't know if it's because of the parent thing, or because I pulled away from her.

She grabs her beachbag, throws on her kaftan and stomps back towards the hotel car park. 'I guess it's finally time for all of us to face the music.'

'Chloe wait. There are things you don't know...' Maybe I should just come clean about Lula. But how would that sound?

By the way, I want to date you properly, but I actually have to marry someone else.

No woman would go for it, let alone Chloe.

Her long, slim legs are no match for mine. I catch up with her in four deft strides.

'Chloe, there's' so much more at play here. If you'd just let me explain...' Her coldness chills me to the bone. The sudden urge to tell her about everything that's happened this year is bursting in my chest.

Her head whips around to look up at me. 'There's nothing to say. We have a mutual problem. I need to go to Ireland. Sasha will need all the help with Victoria she can get right now. You need to set your reputation straight. And Ryan's for that matter.'

'And we'll continue this,' I motion between the two of us, 'in Ireland?'

We're both scheduled to be there in ten days anyway for Ryan's Irish leg of the tour. And after that we just have Edinburgh and London, and that's it.

Her features pinch into a frown as she assesses me from behind her huge Gucci glasses. Finally, what feels like minutes later, she offers a curt nod. The breath I'd been unwittingly holding soars from my chest.

I drive her car back to her villa and hop into a taxi back to the hotel I'm supposed to be staying in to sort out the shit-show that's my life right now.

Chapter Twenty-Seven

CHLOE

Ireland

Returning to Huxley Castle is never easy. Pushing through hundreds of frenzied paps desperate to get a story from outside the front gate doesn't help. The concert isn't for another twelve days and the prospect of spending two weeks here, in the place I've avoided for the last ten years, is about as appealing as getting back into bed with Ethan-Has-No-Harte.

The absence of my parents is always painfully more acute here. At least when I'm away, I can pretend they're all still alive and well, running the castle.

As I walk through the wrought iron front doors and into the ginormous atrium, my sternum tightens. The hole in my chest is back, bigger than ever.

My Louboutins click across the mosaic tiles, the sound echoing through the spacious reception area. Louise, the bubbly blonde head receptionist, cradles a phone between her neck and ear. When she finally glances up, her face lights up with an effusive welcome.

I raise a hand, fighting an overwhelming surge of nostalgia.

Flames crackle from a roaring open fire which the porters light daily, not only to create a welcoming ambience, but because the weather in this part of the world leaves a lot to be desired most of the year. The familiar smoky scent of burnt kindling assaults my nostrils while a million childhood memories flood my brain.

Returning to the long days of an unpredictable Irish summer, the weak sun shines a surprisingly powerful light on everything that's missing in my life. It's impossible to pretend anything here. It's impossible to hide. Especially from myself.

It's why I don't come home often. Selfish, I know. My sisters probably need me more than they let on, but it's self-preservation.

It's been ten years since the night that turned our lives upside down. Perhaps this time I might finally be able to put on my big girl's pants? After all, if I can get over my fear of sort of dating again after Ethan, surely I can come to terms with something that happened ten years ago and find a way to be present in both my sisters' lives without spiralling into a hot grieving mess.

The night Mam and Dad died, Ryan and Jayden disappeared to the States with their father. We had no idea the two events were connected at the time. Sasha paced the castle day and night, mourning the loss of our parents, and her first love. Five months later, when I thought things couldn't get any worse, Sasha lost a baby she'd never planned on having.

If she can get through all of that, surely I can get through a couple of weeks here?

The hotel manager, our dear school friend, Megan Harper, bounds down the intricately carved walnut staircase, greeting me with a grin bright enough to illuminate Blackpool.

'Well, well, well… the wanderer's returned!' Her warm arms envelope me into a hug I hadn't realised I needed. My shoulders sag and I squeeze every drop of comfort from this exchange because shortly it'll be me who has to be the strong one.

I can't return to help and be anything less.

Burying my face in her red spiralling curls, I tell her honestly, 'It's so good to see you, Megan.'

'Your sisters are beyond excited about your arrival. They weren't expecting you until tonight.'

'I caught an earlier flight. I wanted to surprise them.' I don't admit it's because I still can't bear anyone driving to the airport for me. I mean, what if something happened to them on the road, and the only reason they were in the car in the first place was to collect me?

I would lose everything and everyone precious to me and it would be all my fault. I care about them too much to risk it. They say lightning doesn't strike twice, but why take the chance?

'I thought I heard your voice!' Victoria, my not-so-little sister, shrieks from the top of the staircase before bounding down them, two at a time.

'No need to run!' I caution. 'I'm here for two weeks.'

Gone is the gangly teenager from Christmas. The girl who lunges for me is all woman these days, her full chest squashing against mine.

I press a kiss to her cheek and squeeze her like she's the most precious thing in the entire universe, because to me, she is. I might not be here nearly enough as I should, but not a day goes by I don't miss her.

'I can't believe you're actually here!' Bright hazel eyes twinkle from behind thick, quirky, black-rimmed glasses. Chanel, no less. Apparently, she's developed an interest in fashion in the last six months.

'Of course I'm here. I had to see you're okay. It's like a fucking zoo out there.' I gesture to the madness behind the gates.

'Language,' my older sister chastises from the bottom of the staircase. I'm so wrapped up in the growth of our little sister, I didn't notice Sasha descend. Elegant as always in a pencil skirt and silk blouse, she mockingly wags a finger in our direction.

'I'll be eighteen this weekend! And there's no law that states under eighteens can't say "fuck" anyway.'

'Mammy and Daddy would turn in their graves if they could hear their baby spouting such foul language.' Sasha's full lips are poised into a firm line she can't hold straight for more than three seconds. An infectious burst of laughter tumbles out as she and Victoria cackle, clinging on to each other's arms.

'As if!' Victoria snorts.

She might have only been seven years old when our parents passed, but she clearly remembers our father's propensity for swearing like a sailor.

My attention darts between the two of them, dumbfounded they can joke about Mam and Dad so easily.

To hide my shock, I reach into my oversized handbag for the gifts I brought. Pristinely wrapped perfume from an exclusive Dubai boutique.

'Here.' I press them into each of their hands as they squeal with excitement. Passing guests stop and stare, grinning at the excitement bouncing between them. I feel like an outsider. I guess I only have myself to blame.

I expected to return to a sombre, sorry affair of continued mourning, but my sisters are carrying on like normal, even amongst the despicable media frenzy at the gates, as if the deepest, darkest secrets of our private lives, and a thousand rumours about each of us haven't been splashed over every trashy tabloid over the past three days.

James, one of the porters, arrives with the suitcase I'd abandoned in the boot of my hire car. He's been here for as long as I can remember and is practically a Huxley Castle national treasure.

'Miss Sexton, welcome home.' His smile mirrors the welcoming warmth of his words.

The uneasy feeling in the pit of my stomach ebbs slightly. Instead of reliving the loss of my parents, all I've felt since I walked through the door is what I've gained. The unwavering love of my sisters, bound by not only blood but the bond of our shared experience.

It's a little overwhelming.

Things have changed.

Or maybe I've changed?

'Is it drink o'clock yet?' I ask, turning to Sasha, but it's Victoria who answers.

'It most certainly is.'

Sasha rolls her eyes and shakes her head. 'This one's got a taste for the good stuff.' She ushers us into one of the private drawing rooms reserved for family.

'What, lemonade?' My elbow nudges her playfully, and she snorts again.

The double-height drawing room has been decorated in a vibrant shade of teal, a far cry from the traditional navy and dove grey it was painted when I was last here. A plush-looking pastel pink suite of furniture matches trendy transparent drapes that replace the old drab curtains that used to hang across the sash windows.

It's a reminder that at Christmas we agreed Sasha would no longer preserve the castle as a relic to Mam and Dad's reign and to introduce a more modern, fashionable colour palate.

'Wow.' My gaze wanders to the art on the walls. Landscape paintings of our favourite beach have been replaced with a hundred photos of our family, each hung in similar thick, gilded frames.

My throat thickens, making it hard to swallow as my emotions surge like a spring tide in my chest.

How can they bear to look at our young, carefree, smiling faces of the past every day, knowing we had such a traumatic ordeal ahead of us?

I ping the elastic band on my wrist, forcing myself not to revisit the horror of years gone by.

'You've certainly changed things up around here. Good for you.' It's the best I can muster, and it doesn't go unnoticed.

Victoria eyes Sasha warily, like *I'm* the baby. I ignore it, like I do most things that make me uncomfortable. 'Where's that drink you promised?' I ask.

Ryan strides into the drawing room with a bottle of the castle's finest champagne tucked beneath his burly left bicep. A huge hand precariously clutches three crystal champagne flutes.

His resemblance to Jayden is subtle, yet striking. Jayden's at least an inch taller, but the ebony shade of their hair is almost identical. They're both blessed with the same thick, luscious eyelashes most women would kill for, and lips so perfectly plump and kissable that cupid himself couldn't compete.

But Ryan's big, brown eyes are missing something Jayden's steely ones never fail to deliver. A lust-fuelled promise and a drive to do whatever it takes to fulfil it.

My cheeks flush as the memories flood through my mind.

Sasha's elbow connects with my side. 'Would you stop ogling my fiancé? It's bad enough every other woman on the planet wants a taste of him without having to compete with you.' She sticks her tongue out to show she's messing.

She needn't worry. It's not him I'm picturing.

Victoria pipes up with an exaggerated eye roll. 'Not quite every woman.'

'Woman being the key word in that sentence.' Ryan

shoots her a playful wink. 'You're not there yet, pipsqueak.' He pours us each a glass of champagne, and half a glass for Victoria as she's bang in the middle of her exams.

'Four days and counting.' Victoria's eyes light up at the prospect of legally coming of age. Oh god, is the sweet girl before me about to morph into a pheromone-driven monster? Her teenage years have been pretty tame to this point. Surely at some point she'll have to do something wild?

My eyebrows draw together. 'What will she be like when she gets to college?' I address the actual adults in the room.

'Hopefully, nothing like you,' Sasha jokes, but it stings like a barbed spear in my side.

Am I that bad?

The three of them squawk, snorting at their own joke. A pang of envy pierces my chest. While I've been away, the bond between them has grown strong.

I'm just not sure now where I fit in.

Chapter Twenty-Eight

JAYDEN

I pace the plush polished floor of Richard Lambert's office at Diamond Records. When I was summoned by the CEO, I wasn't stupid enough to think it was because he missed me while I've been on tour.

'Jayden, I hate to say it, but you're attracting a lot of attention and none of it positive.' His thin pale lips wrap around a three-hundred-dollar cigar before sucking deeply.

My gaze casts over the bustling, circus-like city below. 'Believe me, I know.'

Richard blows out a long, slow breath before stubbing out the remainder of the cigar in a crystal ashtray on his humongous desk. 'I've always had a soft spot for you and your brother, you know that.'

'I do, sir. And we both appreciate what you've done for us over the years.' If Richard hadn't dragged us out of the gutter, god only knows where we'd be now. One of his scouts saw Ryan and insisted Richard take him on, and me, in the process.

'You know we prize our reputation here at Diamond

Records above everything. Without our reputation, we're nothing. That's why we only sign the best and we expect their people to keep them on the straight and narrow and out of the headlines for the wrong reasons. But now we've got a cowgirl virgin turned porn star and a Disney drug addict. That's before we even get to your family situation.'

I pinch the bridge of my nose and close my eyes as I attempt to summon something, anything, to make this better.

The truth is, there isn't anything. I've been back in LA for three days and I'm no closer to finding out who's responsible for this apparent vendetta against me.

Thankfully, Mia's back to full health and has been cleared of all charges. A CCTV tape showed two men breaking and entering her apartment with suspicious looking packages. But if Diamond Records drops her, no one else on this earth is going to take the risk of signing her.

Meanwhile, Gareth pulled off Naomi's PR stunt seamlessly, and her team has offered access to the media of her recently announced wedding to turn the focus of her story around.

And Ryan and I are still navigating our way around the drama our father's caused, but at least we persuaded him to release a statement from prison, clarifying that we knew nothing about the car crash that killed Chloe's parents.

'The tragic thing is none of it is true. Mia and Naomi were framed.'

'Both of them?' Richard arches a wild, bushy eyebrow.

'Come on, they're great artists. You've seen how talented they are.'

'They're a liability to the company. It kills me to say it, but you're on your final warning, Jayden. If I so much as hear a whisper of another scandal surrounding you, or any of the artists you represent, I'll have no choice but to drop them.'

He pours himself a scotch from a decanter on his desk and sniffs it before adding, 'And you.'

'It won't happen again.' I nod before excusing myself, hating that once again, I just made a promise that I might not be able to keep.

With my phone pressed to my ear, I sling a few outfits into my Samsonite suitcase.

I'm not due in Ireland until next week, but I'm gate-crashing Victoria Sexton's eighteenth birthday party, purely because I can't sleep straight for thinking about Chloe. Apart from the scandal circling both our families, I have a feeling she might need a bit of moral support returning to the home she's avoided for years.

Our usual flirty phone calls have been subdued. She's distant. I don't know if it's being there or if she's mentally withdrawing from me because our secret arrangement's approaching its inevitable end.

Either way, I don't like it. I didn't mean to get involved. I'm not supposed to care.

How am I supposed to save both Lula and Chloe?

The pile of untouched documents sitting on my bedside locker glares at me.

'Are you there?' Declan's voice resounds through the receiver.

'Yes.' Physically I am, anyway. Mentally, I'm all over the shop. Lula is due back from Mexico today. Another reason I wanted to hop on the first flight to Ireland. I can't face her right now. It's not her fault that the promises I made to her to keep her in this country are jeopardising my one true shot at happiness. I'm so relieved I found her, but I'm not sure I can pretend it's not costing me something I never even believed in until I got to know Chloe, anyway.

'I have a few more questions for you.' Declan drags me back into the moment. 'I'm aware of each and every threat to Ryan over the previous ten years, but has anyone ever threatened you specifically before?'

It's an obvious question, one I've asked myself a hundred times over the past week.

'Yes, and no.' My bottom lip catches between my teeth as I try to think of the right words to explain. 'My line of business has always been cutthroat. LA is not for the thin-skinned. I must have rejected a thousand wannabe artists. None of them have ever taken kindly to me shattering their dreams, and it's not unusual to get threatened. I mean, it's usually low-level stuff. People saying things in the heat of the moment, like "you'll regret this" or "you'll pay for that." You know what I mean?'

I hear Declan tapping loudly on a keyboard. 'I need names and numbers for all of them.'

'Seriously? All of them? Most of them are barely memorable, which is why I didn't sign them in the first place.'

'Unfortunately, someone remembers you, because it seems to me that you are the centre of this whole thing. Not Ryan. Not Mia Sweet. Not Naomi Carden. They're all collateral damage. You're the common denominator.'

'I'll get Kim to go through the diary.'

'*All* the diaries,' he corrects me. 'Not just this year, or last. Someone has a vendetta against you, Jayden. Someone wants to bring you, and your artists down. And whoever it is either has a lot of power or a lot of cash. Probably both.'

He's only voicing what I've already concluded.

But who? And why? I've always done my best to help people, albeit in a roundabout way.

'What about the women I've slept with over the years? Do you want their details too?'

'Absolutely.' Declan's fingers continue to pound a keyboard.

My expression screws into a wince. 'Even the married ones?'

'Seriously, Jayden?' His tone rachets up several decibels. '*Especially* the married ones.'

A weighted sigh whooshes from my chest. 'They were separated, to be fair. I'll have Kim compile a list and email it to you.' Thank god she's not on the list. A small mercy at this stage.

'Keep your security detail with you at all times until we get on top of this. It might take a few days.' Declan sniggers. 'If your reputation's anything to go by, that could be one hell of a long list.'

'Fuck you, Declan.' I can't even bring myself to smile.

'No, thanks. I'm on enough lists as it is.' A throaty chuckle sounds again. 'I think I'm onto something with the visa, by the way.'

'Seriously?' A spark of hope ignites inside me.

'Now Lula's not in immediate danger of being deported, we have a small window of opportunity. I'll get back to you. Try not to worry. I know you've got a lot on your plate, but we'll get to the bottom of it and sort it out.'

'Thanks, Dec.'

I throw the phone onto the bed, gazing out across my pristinely manicured lawns.

Who have I pissed off enough to start a war? If I wanted to take someone out, I'd bulldoze down their front door, yet someone is trying to bring my house down pillar by pillar while I'm still living in it.

I'm going around and around and circles here, driving myself demented.

Is it possible I'm doing a Chloe? Fleeing the country to

escape my problems. Only instead of running *away* from Huxley Castle, I'm running *to* it.

No. Who am I kidding? What I'm really doing is running to *her*. Because some time over the past few weeks, she's become more important than anything else in my life.

Chapter Twenty-Nine

CHLOE

Being at the castle isn't nearly as hard as I'd anticipated.
Cocooned behind the safety of its majestic walls, my sisters
and I are sheltered from the media frenzy outside the gates.

I work on my laptop from eight until six each day, final-
ising the Irish leg of the tour next week, and planning a ruby
wedding anniversary party for two A-list celebrities in LA -
my first job there - and organising the catering for the epic
London finale.

I'm too busy to worry about what the papers are printing
about the weird way Ryan, Jayden, and us Sextons are all intricately entwined.

And as for Victoria, she's knuckling down hard, cramming
for her final exams.

She's hoping to secure enough points to study medicine.

Sasha hired a private tutor who arrives like clockwork
each day at four o'clock and doesn't leave until eight. By the
time Victoria emerges from her study, she's not nearly as
chirpy as she was three days earlier.

Tonight, the four of us are dining together in our private
quarters on the top floor. Conor, the castle's talented chef,

has prepared a feast of succulent pink juicy beef, Yorkshire puddings as big as our heads, and the richest red wine infused gravy.

'More wine?' Ryan tops up Sasha's glass, then mine, before excusing himself to the recording studio they've built in the basement.

'Vic?' I offer her a glass, but she shakes her head with a small, languid smile. I don't blame her. Her final exam is in the morning.

'Take tomorrow off, Chloe, please? You've done nothing but work since you arrived,' Sasha complains good-naturedly.

'I'm ridiculously busy.' It's no lie. Ruby emailed me sixty-eight times alone today, not to mention all the messages from the other forty-eight staff I've acquired over four different countries.

I'm still not busy enough to forgo thoughts of Jayden Cooper. He lingers in every corner of my mind, bursting to the forefront at every opportunity. I'm like a teenager with an all-consuming crush, but instead of crushing on the stereo-typical famous rock star, I'm crushing on his bad boy older brother.

And like every crush, it's an agonising double-edged sword. The highs are transcendent. The low I know I'm going to feel when it's over may just be lethal.

As usual, I bury my head, refusing to think about it even though it ticks like a time bomb, growing louder with each passing day.

'Too busy to spend the afternoon at our brand-new state-of-the-art spa with your two sisters? We ought to mark Victoria's final exam being over.' Sasha flicks a bouncy curl from her shoulder, pretending to pout.

Victoria yawns. 'I might fall asleep in the jacuzzi, but count me in. On that note, I'm going to bed.'

I pull her into an affectionate squeeze as she rises from the huge oakwood table. 'I'm so proud of you, Vic.'

Her index finger nudges her glasses up her nose, something she does when she's uneasy. Compliments render her uncomfortable. She might be the image of our mother, but she's clearly inherited that from our father.

'Night, Vic.' Sasha blows her a kiss. She's been the only mother Victoria has really known. Another sliver of guilt cuts me in two. I should have been here for her, to support her when she needed me most. I shouldn't have left. But staying would have been detrimental to my own mental health. So much sadness, so much loss within these castle walls.

My phone vibrates on the table with an incoming text. I snatch it up quicker than lightning before Sasha can see, but it only rouses her suspicions.

Her perfectly preened eyebrow arches. 'Who's that?'

'Nobody.' The irrepressible grin on my face says otherwise.

Jayden's calls and texts have been the highlight of my day for months. Where his smirk used to infuriate me, now it invigorates me. His flirtatious banter used to turn my stomach. Now it floods it with a thousand butterflies. He's scarily good at judging my mood before we've even spoken. We've only spent a few weekends together, but we've known each other for a hell of a lot longer.

Between my secrecy, my mood swings, and the heat creeping into my cheeks under my big sister's scrutiny, it wouldn't take a genius to work out I'm battling the highs and lows of being in love.

There, I admitted it. Not out loud, of course, but even to myself is a start. Not a particularly healthy start, given we're both commitment-phobes and even if I'm willing to try to get over that, he clearly isn't given his reaction to me potentially moving to LA.

Which room are you in?

My fingers go to my mouth, covering it because it's physically impossible to restrain my lips into a normal expression.

He's here! Or at least near! And he's early. The possibility of spending an entire week or more with him sets my heart soaring. Never mind the spa tomorrow, I need to get there now. I thought I had at least a few days to prepare.

Sasha's hand sweeps across the table, her fingers sliding through mine, attempting to wrestle the phone from me. She's got more chance of winning the lottery. There's no way I'll part with it.

She eventually relents, retracting her fingers, impatiently rapping long manicured nails on the table between us. 'Well, well, well. Who is he?' Her pitch is three octaves higher than usual and her jade eyes glitter with excitement.

'Who's who?' My lips defy gravity, still refusing to behave.

'The man that has you beaming from ear to ear! Don't even try to deny it. I can feel it through our freaky, sisterly bond.'

Our sisterly bond has always been strong. It's nearly impossible to lie to her. And I actually don't want to anymore. The urge to blurt out that I'm sleeping with her brother-in-law is bursting through my core.

But how can I?

She knows better than I do he doesn't commit and that it will end in disaster. And then she'll be worried about tension at her wedding in October.

No, I can't tell her.

'Jesus, Chloe, when have you ever spared the details? I'm

intrigued!' She tops up my wine glass as if that's going to help loosen my tongue.

Another text pings on my phone. Sasha sits back, watching me, trying to read my every single micro-facial expression.

> What room? I need to make sure I'm next door. Not because I'm going to occupy it, but because no paying castle guest should be subjected to your screaming ;)

Laughter splutters from my chest as I tap out the quickest reply.

> Behave.

Before I can even exit the screen, another text flies in.

> Room? Don't make me tear down your castle, Princess.

A memory of the last time he came looking for me springs to mind.

> 102. Top floor.

> Good girl x

Shoving my phone under my backside, out of sight of Sasha's beady but beautiful eyes, I finally raise my gaze to meet hers.

'Spill. You know you want to!' she screams.

'It's nothing, really.' My fingers circle the stem of my glass, back and forth rhythmically. It offers a modicum of comfort. Or is the comfort I feel simply because my man is on his way?

My man? I wish. But he's mine for a while longer, at least.

Sasha peers coyly over the rim of her own glass. 'Have you slept with him?'

I knew this was coming. I swallow hard. 'Yes.' It's barely a whisper.

The side of her mouth tugs upwards in a knowing smirk. 'More than once?'

I nod, unable to quite meet her gaze.

'Oh. My. God. Who is he, Chloe? He must be something exceptional for you to break your one date rule.'

Other than Ruby, who I trust with my life, I haven't told a soul about Jayden. I'm dying to talk about it with someone, especially Sasha, but I can't.

'He is exceptional,' I admit with a shrug.

'This is amazing! I knew you'd finally get over that twat Ethan-Has-No-Harte! Come here!' Sasha rushes around the table and yanks me into a sisterly squeeze, which I reciprocate with only half of her enthusiasm.

I might have finally gotten over what Ethan did, but am I really any better off? I'm in love with a man who is emotionally unavailable.

Sasha guides me by the hand towards a huge velvet couch and urges me to sit.

'Come on, tell me everything. I'm dying to hear about the man who's melted my hard-ass sister.'

'There's not much to tell.' More like there's not much I *can* tell. 'Apart from he's everything I thought I didn't want.'

'What's his name? What does he do?' Bright eyes gleam at me through the twilight.

I swallow hard. 'You know, I'd rather not say. It's early days. It probably won't go anywhere.'

She pats my forearm. 'Oh, sweetie, not every man is like Ethan.'

I meet her gaze. 'I know, believe me, he's nothing like Ethan.'

'Why are you being so negative about it, then? Especially when clearly he makes you happy.' She tucks a curl of hair behind her ear as if it might help her hear better. Help her understand.

A sigh slips from my lips as I struggle to find the right words. I don't want to reveal too much. 'We're too alike,' I say. It's the best I can come up with.

'That's no bad thing.'

'He's a commitment-phobe.' There, I've said it.

Sasha laughs. 'That's the problem?' She swats the air in front of her face dismissively. 'You were a commitment-phobe too. We all change. It'll work out, trust me.'

She's wrong. Jayden's not your average commitment-phobe. The man's a world-class player with his pick of an extensive crop. Why would he commit to anyone, let alone me?

Although he hinted that if things were different... What things though?

Oh god, he's so reticent about everything as well. We really are two peas in a pod. Mirror images. Soulmates.

Stop it, Chloe. Don't go there. Unrequited love isn't a good look on you.

'This is different. I'll enjoy it while it lasts,' I say. 'And maybe, just maybe, it's given me the kick-start I need to actually try dating properly again.'

'Don't write him off before you've given him a chance.' A frown flickers across Sasha's forehead. 'Will you at least tell me his name?'

The thick walnut door of our private family quarters bangs closed.

'Who's name?' Jayden arrives in all his panty-melting glory.

'Jayden! Welcome!' Sasha stands to greet her brother-in-law, wrapping him in a warm embrace.

He pats her on the back as she squeezes him, and his eyes lock with mine over her shoulder with a heat so intense it's smouldering.

'I hope I'm not interrupting anything. I just arrived and couldn't find Ryan, so I came straight up.'

He crosses the room in four huge strides. I stand to greet him, praying I can control my facial muscles more than I did five minutes earlier. With his back to Sasha, he kisses my right cheek, but before his lips reach my left cheek, his tongue flicks decadently over my parted mouth.

'Not at all.' Sasha busies herself fetching another wine glass. 'Ryan's in the recording studio, so you'll have to make do with us for a while. Chloe was just telling me about this "exceptional" guy she's been seeing.'

Jayden's lip curls and amusement twinkles in those amorous eyes. 'Is that right?'

'Well, Chloe being Chloe, she's hardly said anything, but look at her.' Sasha points an accusatory index finger straight at my chest. 'Doesn't she have that "just fucked" luminous glow about her? And you should have seen her face a minute ago when he texted. She was purple with pleasure!'

'Is that so?' Glittering steel slices straight through me, as if he can see directly into my soul. 'Tell me more.'

Ground, swallow me whole, please.

My intention was to come here and comfort Chloe, yet here I am teasing her again. I'm dying to hear what she's been saying to Sasha about me. Is she as reticent with her sister as she is with me?

'Exceptional, huh? Tell me, Chloe, does he make you scream?' My dick twitches in my pants at the memories. All. The. Memories.

I drop onto the couch next to her and she swats my arm. 'Stop it, Jayden, please.'

'You won't say that later,' I whisper, barely out of Sasha's earshot, as she returns from the table with a glass of red wine for me.

'Don't be teasing her now, Jayden,' she warns me jovially.

Oh Sasha, I'm going to spend all night teasing your sister. If only I could steal her away from here.

If Chloe's pinched thighs are anything to go by, she feels exactly the same.

Sasha flops into the velvet armchair opposite and continues to pry. 'So, what's his name?'

'Okay, okay.' Chloe lifts her arms up in resignation. 'It's Pedro.'

'Pedro?' Sasha and I shriek in unison.

'The pool boy!' She winks at me. 'He just loves my teeny-tiny bikinis. You wouldn't believe the stuff he's capable of, alfresco, under the sun. That man has no shame. He's got *all* the equipment, if you know what I mean.'

Sasha removes a cushion from behind her back and chucks it unceremoniously at her sister. My future sister-in-law is growing on me by the day.

Chloe sniggers, slanting a sidewards glance in my direction.

Sasha's undeterred. 'So, does "Pedro" live in Dubai?'

'He travels.' Chloe squirms, all trace of amusement gone from her face. 'That's all you're getting. I don't want to talk about him anymore.'

Sasha points at me and for a split second, my heart plummets in my chest.

We've been busted.

'Don't let Jayden put you off. He's heard worse, and I'm pretty sure he's done worse. Besides... we're practically family, right?'

Phew. I can't bring myself to look at either of them for fear of laughing at the absurdity of it or crying at the injustice of the entire situation. Because the longer this fling with Chloe goes on, the more I want us to be a family. Just not quite the same way Sasha means.

Thankfully, Declan's found a workaround that means I won't have to marry Lula to save her from deportation after all. And that opens up a terrifying new possibility with Chloe.

'I'm not saying another word, and especially not in front of *him*.'

'Okay, okay, but this isn't the end of this conversation,'

Sasha warns Chloe. 'Tomorrow, in the spa. I want every single minute detail.'

'We can't do that to poor Victoria.' Chloe's blue eyes widen, feigning horror.

I shrug. 'She's off to college soon. We might as well start her education sooner rather than later.'

'Don't remind me.' Sasha shakes her head.

I don't mind Chloe sharing details with them, as long as one of those details isn't my name. At least not until Declan amends Lula's visa application.

By the time Ryan emerges from the studio, it's late. I've had three glasses of wine and I'm absolutely exhausted from the stress of my meeting with Diamond Records, and from months of flying round the world.

Chloe excuses herself first, placing her empty wine glass on the coffee table beside her.

As she stands, she sways unsteadily in her four-inch stilettos. I can only assume the girls started early on the vino.

'Want me to walk you to your room?' I offer, catching her elbow as she wobbles.

'Make sure you lock the door behind him. He's an animal,' Ryan calls over my shoulder.

'Damn right. I'll double lock it and bolt it to be sure,' she sniggers.

Ryan snorts. 'You know him well.'

'Huh, you guys know better than anyone you shouldn't believe everything you read in the tabloids.'

He's right though. Once upon a time, I was an animal. But now I'm practically Chloe's pet. And the worst thing about it, I fucking love it. Who even am I?

Chloe and I stroll a wide corridor lined with huge gilt-framed paintings of picturesque beaches. Thick crushed velvet curtains remain open, secured with rope tiebacks. An open sash window offers a gust of fresh, lavender-scented air. I can see why Ryan and Sasha are so happy here.

When Ryan said he was retiring from the stage, I thought he was mad, but perhaps, if I had what he had, I'd take a step back, too. Without him in LA, what am I even doing there? Dodging someone who hates me enough to try to tear my empire down, corner by corner, and representing artists I barely see from one day to the next. I could do that from anywhere.

My phone vibrates in my pocket. I pause, gazing out at the lush, expansive scenery, manicured gardens and the Irish Sea way off on the horizon, a million lights dotting the landscape in between.

Chloe shoots me a quizzical glance. I accept the call before touching my lips against hers like I've been dying to do all night.

'Jayden?' Declan's familiar voice penetrates my ear.

I reluctantly drag my mouth from Chloe's. Slim fingers guiltily stroke her lips as she glances up and down the corridor. I checked. There's no one here but us.

'Any update?' I wrap my arm around Chloe's waist and pull her close, nuzzling into her neck to inhale her unique scent. I've missed her so much, it doesn't bear thinking about.

'I just wanted to check something. I know it's a delicate situation, but could this have anything to do with your father?'

'Dad? No way.'

Chloe looks up and I shake my head, hoping to convey it's not important.

'What about inadvertently? Could someone be trying to bring you down to hurt him? He was involved with some shady characters back in the day,' Declan reminds me.

'If someone had a beef with him, why would they go to all

the trouble with me when he's a much easier target? The man's a sitting duck in prison.'

'True,' Declan muses. 'By the way, is Colton with you?'

'No, why do you ask?'

'He's not at your house.' Fingers tap on a keyboard in the background.

'Good for him. Perhaps he's finally got himself a woman. He came back clean, didn't he?'

'Yes, he did.' Declan doesn't sound entirely convinced.

Chloe, leaning against me, yawns. Her beautiful blue eyes flutter in an effort to stay open. She's wrecked. No wonder. World domination comes at a price. She could do with a partner. An image of her slimy ex pops into my brain. *"I want to talk about a merger."*

I'll merge his face with my fist. How's that for a merger?

'I'll check in first thing in the morning,' Declan says. A can pops in the background. I hope he's drinking Coke and not lager, because I need answers, fast.

'Goodnight.' The phone line goes dead.

'Who's that?' Chloe asks, stifling another yawn.

'Jesus, you're sounding like a nagging girlfriend.' I press a kiss on her head and smile.

Her features rearrange into one of mock horror and I get a glimpse of her raspberry tongue, the one she knows exactly what to do with. 'You should be so lucky.'

I can't argue with that.

We continue the walk to her room. The castle's eerily quiet at this hour of the night.

'Seriously though, is everything ok with your dad? I didn't mean to eavesdrop.' Her bottom lip catches between her gleaming white teeth.

'Dad's fine, although I wouldn't have thought you cared.' This is the closest we've ever come to speaking about what happened that night my father's reckless driving killed Chloe's parents.

Is it the wine? Or is she finally opening up to me?

'Of course I care. He's your father. Ryan's father. He made a mistake. He's not the first and he won't be the last. He's paying for it now.'

'How can you be so forgiving, when, you know, he did what he did?"

'Because it's not entirely his fault.' Her eyes darken three shades and her fingers reach for the elastic band around her wrist. She snaps it against her skin.

And all this time, I thought it was for her hair.

She swallows hard. 'It's also partly mine.'

'Chloe, what are you talking about?' I halt her in her tracks, frightened if we move even a millimetre, she'll clam up on me again.

Tears spill across her cheeks, streaking her face with inky mascara. My thumb instinctively sweeps the smudges away while my left hand cups the back of her neck.

'You can tell me anything, Chloe. This thing between us... ' I swallow back my emotion because what she needs is strength and support right now. 'It turned into something else, didn't it? Something more.'

The air crackles between us as she nods.

'You can trust me with anything. We all have things we're ashamed of,' I say.

With the back of her hand, she wipes away the streaks, pausing for a few seconds to take some shaky breaths.

'Take your time. I'm here. I'm not going anywhere.' My palm traces lower across her spine, doing my utmost to soothe her.

Crying women do something to my insides. They always have done.

She swallows hard again. 'It's my fault my parents were on that coast road.'

'I thought they were on their way back from Victoria's school Christmas concert?'

'Yes, but when they rang to say they were leaving, I asked them to pick up takeout from that fancy Chinese restaurant on the coast road on their way back. They didn't want to, but I begged them.' Her voice cracks with emotion.

'If they'd have come straight home, they'd have taken the main road instead. I can hardly blame your father when it was my fault they were even on that road.'

'Oh, Chloe, it's not your fault.' I sweep her up into my arms. 'It's not your fault.' She nestles into my chest, shaking with silent sobs as I carry her down the length of the corridor.

Her room is vast, decorated with resplendent ruby drapes and shimmering golds. Nothing less for my Princess. A huge four-poster bed piled with plump, inviting pillows dominates the room. I place her on the bed and slip her stilettos from her feet before kicking off my own shoes.

Curling behind her, I pull a cashmere throw over both of us and wrap my arms around her waist, balancing my chin on top of her head as she cries out ten years' worth of hurt, guilt and sorrow.

'It's ok, Princess. It's not your fault.' I repeat the same words over and over, hoping eventually they'll sink in.

When her silent sobs finally slow, her breathing pattern changes. She's asleep. It's the first time we've gone to bed together and not had sex. Instead, we've done something far more intimate.

For a man who was exhausted an hour ago, I'm suddenly wide awake.

No wonder Chloe's the way she is. She doesn't shut people out because she thinks she's above them. She shuts them out to protect her secret, save herself, and save them from this pain she's been carrying around all this time.

I had no idea she blamed herself. Blame's so pointless. I spent years blaming myself for not being able to save Sofia. Even if I save Lula, it won't bring Sofia back. When your time's up, it's up.

And no matter how much time I have with Chloe Sexton, it's never going to be enough. But one thing's become crystal clear tonight. Whatever Declan does or doesn't work out, I can't go through with marrying Lula.

Not now. Not ever.

My heart belongs to this woman beside me. I never intended to give it away, yet somehow she took it anyway, stealing it straight from my chest.

Chapter Thirty-One

CHLOE

The bright early morning sun filters through the open curtains, but the memories of my tipsy confession last night trigger a darkness I can't shake.

I've never revealed the part I played in my parents' death to anyone before, not even Sasha. I was afraid she'd hate me, as much as I hate myself. I sent them onto that road. If I'd only kept my mouth closed, our lives would all have been so much different. And all for a fucking fortune cookie.

What if Jayden was simply being kind last night and secretly he's disgusted with me? Or did he take some relief that his father's not *entirely* to blame?

No, stop it.

He spent the whole night whispering soothing words into my ear. Tenderly smoothing my hair from my face, the same way Mam used to do when I was sick as a child. His sculpted body remains curled around me, heating me from the inside out, hanging onto me like I'm his most precious possession.

I wish.

We all have things we're ashamed of.

His words come back to me like a whisper on the wind, but he didn't elaborate.

During the night, I must have taken my dress off because when I wake up, I'm in my less than sexy white M&S cotton pants and a plain white bra. At least they match.

Clearly, I wasn't expecting company.

But if the tears didn't put him off last night, I doubt my comfy 'mom-derwear' will. Our "situationship" has been catapulted to a whole new level.

'Good morning, Princess,' he whispers into my ear. Strong hands squeeze my waist as he nuzzles into my neck.

'How did you know I was awake?'

'Your breathing changed.'

'Were you awake the whole night?' I wriggle out of his firm grip and roll over to face him.

'Not all of it.' Huge grey eyes bore into mine with an intensity so powerful you could be forgiven for mistaking it for love. Or maybe that's simply wishful thinking.

My eyes dart away from his, unable to bear the weight of them any longer. Of not knowing what he's thinking and too frightened to ask. 'I'm so sorry about last night.'

'You have nothing to be sorry for.' Thick fingers find my chin, drawing it up to meet his gaze again. 'Nothing. Do you understand? Nothing.'

'I didn't mean for all my baggage to tumble out.' My teeth worry my bottom lip until he brushes a thumb over my mouth to stop it.

'I'm glad it did. I wish you'd told me before. Or told Sasha. It's not your fault, Chloe. It was a tragic accident. There are a hundred tiny minute details that put your parents there at that specific split second that night.

'Suppose they reached the traffic lights a second later and got caught on a red? Or let someone else out of the school car park before them? Or stopped to talk to another parent? Any single variation could have resulted in a different ending. I honestly believe when your time's up, it's up.

'I'm so sorry for your loss, sweetheart, but the bigger loss is that you've not been able to come home and spend time with your sisters because your guilt is eating you alive. Don't lose any more of your life to it.' Hot lips touch a tender kiss to my temple.

Warmth blazes through my blood. I feel accepted. Cared for.

With his words, and that loving gesture, a fraction of the tension I've carried in my shoulders releases.

I won't get over it overnight, but his words make perfect sense. Any single subtle variation of events would have resulted in a different outcome. And coming from Mr-Ruthless himself, I don't doubt he means it.

'I think you should tell Sasha. I'm certain if you talk to her, she'll tell you the same thing. And hearing it from her will probably mean a lot more than hearing it from me. But hearing it from us both might make you more likely to believe it.'

Full, plump lips seek mine, tenderly pushing them open. For the first time in ten years, I feel safe. I feel loved. And I feel seen.

Ethan never saw me. Not really. Not like Jayden does.

And if I can open up about my parents' death, maybe I can open up about other things too? Learn how to voice my feelings like the adult I am, instead of shutting down and fleeing at the first sign of discomfort.

Starting with Jayden.

I don't want this thing between us to end. Before the week is out, I'm going to tell him.

Pushing my tongue into his mouth, I deepen our kiss, nudging his shoulder so he rolls backwards. The urge to straddle him is primal.

Curious eyes rake over my conservative underwear.

'I wasn't expecting company,' I explain sheepishly.

'I should hope not. I told you, I don't share.' Those lush lips move, but I'm barely listening, too busy memorising every single inch of him. Tracing the symmetrical lines across his taut, toned torso.

His body fits mine like a piece of art. My skin is slightly darker than his, but his hair is darker than mine. We're like the black and white yin and yang that fit together perfectly in their colour-coded glory.

'We never did get to the role play,' he reminds me, flipping me onto my back.

I yelp, then giggle as he grips my wrists, pressing his hardness between my legs. So last night definitely didn't put him off. Maybe I should wear my M&S underwear more often.

'Who do you want me to be?' he demands, a hungry glint in his piercing eyes.

I'm not sure he's ready for who I want him to be, because it's way more taboo than anything plucked from a sex bucket list.

It's the raw and honest truth. I said I'd try to open up. What better way to test the water?

'I want you to be mine.' I avert my eyes, looking everywhere and anywhere.

His silence is painful. Seconds feel like minutes. What's holding him back? We've already crossed so many lines, why not just get rid of them? I'm willing to try if he is.

He knows why I'm the way I am, but he's never revealed much about himself. Who damaged him enough to avoid a loving relationship? Did one of his many short-lived conquests inflict such pain on him? Or is it because his mother left when they were toddlers?

'I wasn't lying when I said I'm more unavailable than you

could imagine,' he whispers, with what sounds like regret. 'But I am working on it...'

'Work harder. If I can manage, so can you.'

His lips twitch into a smile. 'Wow, Chloe Sexton has finally found her tongue.'

'Yes, and I intend to use it a lot more from now on.'

I drag my eyes back to his. Huge pupils bore into mine with a smouldering intensity.

'So fucking hot,' he murmurs into my neck, all trace of regret or anything else melting quicker than an ice cream in mid-July.

'You know if I were yours, I'd lick and kiss every single inch of your body every day for the rest of my life?' Hot fingers trace my collar bone, skirting downwards to circle my breasts.

Game on. Except I'm not playing. I haven't been for a long time.

'I suppose I could live with that.' He pushes me back, assuming control.

His face dips, tongue following the same path as his fingers, licking my rippling skin as if I'm the most delectable thing he's ever sampled.

He sounds a hum of appreciation and his head lowers, settling between my legs. No matter how many times he does that to me, it feels like the first time. Stubble grazes my inner thighs as his tongue gets to work, rolling, sucking, teasing deliciously. Huge eyes gaze up at me and for the first time since we've been naked together, I feel almost shy.

Not because of what he's doing to me, but because of everything we've talked about. I've exposed way more than my body to him. And he's still worshipping it. It's an entirely novel experience. It's loving, reassuring, and empowering all at the same time.

My quads tighten as I brace myself for the escalating pleasure that's seconds away from exploding inside me. I'm waiting for him to stop, to tease me and make me beg him, but he doesn't. My fingers scrape through his hair as my pelvis arches with wave after wave of pleasure. He continues to lap at me long after I come undone.

Tugging his hands upwards, I draw him up the bed and on top of me. 'I need you.'

'You have me, Princess.' Something in his husky tone makes me think he doesn't just mean right now.

Assertive hands grip my wrists, securing them either side of my head as he guides himself into my core, inching inside, until I'm full of him. His hips roll and my body sings with every slow and powerful slam. A moan of satisfaction glides from my throat as my release builds again.

I'm in sensory overload. The scent of his raw masculinity. The weight of his ripped torso as his sweat-sheened skin slides over mine. The friction of his length as he slowly rocks inside me. He's rocking more than just my body. He's rocking the entire universe as I know it.

Startling eyes observe me from above, radiating a heat so explosive I'm in danger of combusting. His grip on my wrists softens. Firm fingers work the elastic band from my wrist, throwing it across the room. 'You don't need that anymore. You have me.'

I nod. There aren't words.

His hands go to my nipples, and he sighs a sound of pure satisfaction.

Lips part millimetres from mine. I'm certain he's going to kiss me. Instead, he says three words I never dreamed I'd hear from those smug lips.

'I love you.' It's barely more than a whisper. Earnest eyes blaze with heat and vulnerability.

My heart flips. Core clenches. Legs part further. Fingers

dig into his sculpted backside, dragging him deeper inside of me.

Still, I can't bring myself to say the words. It's like they're lodged so far inside of me I can't coax them out. Instead, I show him.

My lips crash on to his with a newfound urgency, devouring him.

We come together, literally and physically. If there's a heaven, I think I just found it.

Chapter Thirty-Two

JAYDEN

I wake naturally from a deep sex-induced coma with my cheek pressed against Chloe's magnificent tits.

I probably shouldn't have told her I loved her last night. It's not something I planned, but the words tripped off my tongue as easily as water flows from a brimming reservoir. I'm still not really in any position to declare my love for her, not until I can resolve the arrangement with Lula, at least. But I will do, soon. I'm going to make sure of it.

I've never told a woman I loved her before. I've never told anyone I loved them. I'm not sure I even knew what love was until I found it in the most unlikely place. I'm not bothered she didn't say it back. I feel it, even if she can't bring herself to say the words. I'm more concerned about her reluctance to trust anyone, and that's something I'm going to work on.

Three pounding knocks sound on the door, setting my heart rate spiking.

Chloe mumbles as I prise my cheek from her chest.

'Chloe?' Pressing my lips to her neck, I breathe on the sensitive skin below her ear and she wriggles with a giggle. 'Wake-up sleepyhead.'

The pounding starts again.

Thick lash-framed lids flutter open, treating me to a view of those huge oceanic blue eyes.

'Who is it?' I whisper, reluctant to move from my own personal heaven.

Chloe's hand swats my bare backside. 'It's probably only Jacinta from housekeeping.'

'Jacinta?' That's a name I wasn't expecting to hear. 'She still works here, then?'

Chloe's prolonged laughter rattles through her chest, shaking my comfortable foundation.

'Very funny.' She had me for a second there. The arrival of the chambermaid I had sex with all those years ago could be slightly awkward.

'Chloe?' Sasha calls from the other side of the door.

All traces of laughter vanish from Chloe's mouth. 'Quick. Get under the bed.' She shoves me unceremoniously from on top of her.

My belongings are scattered round the room and I have a monumental need to pee. 'What about my clothes?'

'Take them with you, Einstein,' she hisses.

To Sasha, she calls, 'One minute.'

After scrambling round for my belongings, I dart under the bed, seconds before the door opens. Sasha's pointed boots come into view, alongside Chloe's bare, tanned feet. God, even her feet are fantastic. So, this is what love feels like.

'Are you okay?' Sasha's voice rings with concern.

'Sure, why?' The bed springs squeak as Chloe sits down. It's so tempting to tickle her feet, but I daren't risk being caught.

One day maybe, if I sort my shit out, Ryan and Sasha might even be happy for us. Surely they'd prefer us to be together than at each other's throats?

'You missed breakfast.'

'I did?' Chloe feigns ignorance.

'It's the first time you've overslept since you were a teenager.'

Chloe sighs and I silently will her to tell Sasha what she told me last night. To open up to her sister. To strike while the iron's hot.

'A combination of too much red wine and work catching up with me.'

The bed dips again and Sasha's shoes hover next to Chloe's feet. 'We're worried about you, you know. You're working so hard. We thought we were doing a good thing asking you to take on this tour, but maybe we asked too much of you.'

'No, the tour's the best thing that ever happened to me. My business is booming. I met Pedro.' She sniggers and I can't help flicking her foot.

'You should take some time off. Relax. Have a break from it.'

'I can't take my foot off the pedal now, Sasha. You know better than anyone what it's like to run a business.'

'Well, get some help then. Hire some more managers and start delegating.' Concern weaves into her every word.

'I will, I promise, as soon as I've got the new branches up and running.' Chloe sounds so convincing, I almost believe her.

Someone else knocks on the door. I bite back my sigh. Doesn't anyone in Huxley Castle have work to do?

'Sash?' My brother's voice carries into the room a split second before I glimpse his trademark black Doc Martin boots.

'Come in,' Sasha calls like she owns the place. Oh wait, she does. The urge to pee is almost unbearable now.

'Has anyone seen Jayden? He's not in his room.' Irritation tinges Ryan's tone.

'Nope.'

'Megan's looking for you downstairs,' he says. I assume he's talking to Sasha. 'A guest's complaining the duck down pillows have triggered an allergic reaction.'

'Honest to god,' Sasha sighs, as her feet touch the thick wine-coloured carpet. 'Meet us in the spa at three o'clock, if I don't see you before. I'll have the girls bring up a breakfast tray for you. Divert your calls to Ruby. That's why you pay her six figures. Get some rest.'

'See you later,' Chloe calls.

It feels like years before the door clicks behind them. Rolling out ninja-style, I run to the bathroom. When I've finally relieved myself, I turn on the power shower and hop in.

'Mind if I join you?' Chloe's head peeps round the door. We've definitely progressed to the next stage of our relationship. She's never joined me in the shower before, but then she famously never did the-morning-after.

Beneath the cascading droplets, Chloe lathers that delicious smelling shampoo through her hair, beaming up at me. Taking her hands from her hair, I place them on my waist to steady her and take over the lathering, massaging her scalp. Her eyelids flutter closed as she moans appreciatively.

'I'll do yours in a sec,' she promises.

'But then I'll smell like you, and everyone will know we were together.' My fingers work over her head before dropping to her breasts. I can't seem to keep my hands off them. Inevitably, they always gravitate back.

Dubious eyes flick up to mine. 'Maybe we should just tell them?'

'What?'

'Unless it's actually *you* who's embarrassed to be seen with *me*?' She worries at her bottom lip with her teeth again.

It's tempting. It really is. But Ryan will want to know how I plan to keep Lula from being deported if I'm not going to marry her, and even though Declan has a plan, I haven't quite worked out the details. Until then, it needs to stay between us.

'I could never be embarrassed to be seen with you. You're way out of my league, Princess. You always have been. But if we come out, it'll be front page news by midday. I know you were worried about everyone thinking you only got this contract because of your connections, and I don't want to make that any worse. You know what the media are like.'

I hate myself for not being honest with her, but it's for the best. It's too complicated. All I need is a little time to work things out.

Chloe's gaze falls to the soapy shower floor. 'Oh, okay.'

'I meant it when I said I love you. I want to do things the right way.'

She nods, busying herself, rinsing out the suds from her luscious long hair. That's the second time I've told her I love her with no response.

Not that I'm counting.

Chapter Thirty-Three

CHLOE

The new spa is amazing. Modern, plush and dripping with enough crystal chandeliers to give any spa in Dubai a run for its money, with the added bonus of the view. The lush green landscape stretches all the way to the Irish Sea in the distance and the scent of lavender wafts on a gentle breeze as the hazy summer sun dodges in and out between fluffy clouds.

For the first time in a long time, I imagine what it might be like to live here again. To spend time with Sasha and Victoria like this regularly. Those sorts of thoughts used to suffocate me, but now heat spreads through my chest where the hole used to be, before Jayden Cooper plugged it with love.

I honestly didn't realise it was possible to be so happy.

Obviously there are a lot of details to be ironed out, but He Loves Me! I'm like a giddy schoolgirl, and that was before the champagne.

Victoria slips into the outdoor jacuzzi with shadows lingering under her eyes, but her lips lift into a grin.

'I take it the exam went well?' The water rises as the three of us shuffle to find a jet to lean our backs on.

'It's done,' is all Victoria says. 'Time will tell.'

'You'll have smashed it.' I offer her arm a reassuring squeeze.

'And even if you didn't, 'Sasha interjects, 'it's not the end of the world. Look at Ryan. He doesn't have a single qualification to his name and look what he's achieved.'

I stick my fingers in my mouth and make a vomiting motion at my little sister. 'It always comes back to Ryan, doesn't it?'

Victoria sniggers and winks. 'Speaking of boyfriends, tell us about Pedro.'

My head whips around in Sasha's direction. She's suddenly become engrossed fiddling with her engagement ring. 'Witch!'

'Sorry, was it a secret?' she gasps, mockingly.

'It's the biggest news of the century. Chloe's started dating again. Properly dating, not using and abusing more unsuspecting men before breaking their hearts,' Victoria exclaims.

'You've been watching too much teenage drama on Netflix. There were no broken hearts.' Apart from mine. Thankfully, it's stitched back together, beating in full force again. Jayden has breathed life into parts of me that have lain dormant for years.

Victoria flicks water in my direction and arches an eyebrow. She's like a mini-Sasha. 'Come on, tell us about him! It's not as if we're likely to bump into him in the street, is it? What's he like?'

I bite back the smile that springs to my lips at the mere thought of Jayden. 'Very well.'

It's almost impossible to articulate how amazing he is. How far we've come. A hundred images bombard my brain.

The time we had sex in the sea.

The time he snuck into my room in Sydney.

Last night, when he carried me along the corridor, his shirt soaked with my tears.

The way he held me all night.

The way we opened up to each other.

So many memories.

Sasha leaps into the air, reaching for the bottle of bubbles. 'Oh my god, Chloe! You're in love with him, aren't you?'

There's no biting it back any longer. The corners of my mouth extend to each ear.

I shrug, like it's not absolutely monumental.

'Ahhhhh!' Sasha does a jig around the jacuzzi, sending water flying in every direction. 'I'm so excited for you! Will you bring him to my wedding?'

'If he plays his cards right.'

And if he doesn't, he'll be there anyway, which doesn't bear thinking about if this thing between us goes tits up beforehand.

No. Don't go there, Chloe. He's not Ethan. Not everybody lies, cheats, and runs off with a younger woman.

'Look, it's early days, but yes, I'm in love with him,' I say, as my sisters stare at me like I've grown two heads, the two most wondrous heads they've ever seen. If I can say it to them, maybe I'll be brave enough to say it to Jayden. 'We both have commitment issues, but we're working through them.'

'Ahh. This is amazing!' Sasha whoops like a giddy child at a fairground. 'When can we meet him?'

'After the tour. If he doesn't break my heart first.'

'He won't.' She takes my hand and offers it a reassuring pat. 'He won't.'

I gulp down another mouthful of fizzing champagne before addressing an issue I've had on my mind all day, now that I've apparently found my tongue again. 'Speaking of which, you know, I thought I'd come here to find you broken-hearted, Victoria.'

'Me?' she shrieks.

'Yeah, not over a man, but with this circus parade outside the door, and the media raking up the past about Mam and Dad.'

'Why would I be broken-hearted? I know the truth. They can't print anything I don't already know.'

A lump catches in my throat. 'Isn't it hard? Going through it all again, though?'

'You tell me.' Victoria eyes me over her glass, sounding way wiser than her years.

'I'm not going through it again. I'm holed up here with you.'

'Exactly.' Sasha and Victoria clink their champagne flutes in a private toast.

'I don't follow.'

Sasha sits up straighter, readjusting her white bikini top. She's in full-on bride mode already. If I'd have known beforehand, I'd have bought her some of those white M&S bad boys.

Who knows, they might even have the same effect on Ryan as they did on his brother.

'I didn't drag you over here for Victoria's benefit,' Sasha says. 'I did it for you. Call it a "sister-friend-shen," if you like.'

'What?' My tone's loaded with incredulity. 'You thought I needed an inter-friend-shen? Why? I'm one of the most grounded, steady people I know.'

Sasha takes a deep breath, leaning forward like she's about to let me in on one of the greatest secrets of the world. 'Sis, you're one of the most closed up, workaholic, emotionally stilted people I know. Sorry, but it's true.'

'Wow, don't hold back or anything.' I down my drink and hold out my glass to Sasha for a refill.

'Seriously, Chloe. We were worried about you out there on your own.' Sasha says "out there" like I've been camping in the Wild West, instead of living the life of luxury and partying with Ruby every weekend.

Is it a luxury, though?

Waking up in Jayden's arms this morning, feeling safe and loved, was probably the biggest luxury I've ever been afforded in my ridiculously privileged life.

In a rare moment of honest reflection, before I can over-think it, I confess, 'You know, I've always found it so hard to be here.'

My sisters bob through the bubbling water, settling on either side of me, each linking an arm. 'We know.' They murmur unanimously.

'I always blamed myself for Mam and Dad's accident.' It's barely more than a whisper, but having said it out loud once to Jayden already, the second time it flows surprisingly easily.

'Why on earth would you blame yourself?' Victoria asks.

'Because I asked them to stop by that stupid takeaway on the coast road on the way home. If they'd have just come straight home, they'd have taken the main road and none of this would have happened.' I disentangle myself from their arms so I can reach my drink.

Victoria tuts in my ear. 'That's utter self-indulgent bollocks, Chloe Sexton, and you know it.'

'Language, Victoria,' Sasha chides, but with not nearly as much enthusiasm as usual.

'What? It's the truth,' Victoria says. 'If Chloe's thinking that way, then maybe I should blame myself, too? After all, it was my school Christmas concert. If it wasn't for me, they'd have never left the house that night. Hell, if you want me to slide right down that slippery slope, straight into your pity party, maybe I should also feel guilty for surviving the crash.'

'Victoria!' My hand flies to her mouth to stop her uttering

another word. 'How can you even dream of saying such a thing? It wasn't your fault! It was an accident.'

Victoria settles back against the mosaic tiles of the jacuzzi, lips pursed but tilted upwards with something that looks suspiciously like victory. 'See? I think I made my point. It was an accident. Enough lives have been wasted. Let's not ruin ours over it as well.'

Holy fuck. When did my kid sister grow into such an intelligent, articulate adult?

My raised eyebrows meet Sasha's. She squeezes my arm and shrugs. 'She should have applied for law, not medicine.'

The three of us burst into shoulder-shaking laughter, huddling into an awkward, but highly gratifying group hug. I laugh and laugh and laugh until I'm crying. Tears of joy. Of release. Of sorrow. And finally, of acceptance.

It wasn't my fault.

It was a tragedy. But my wise little sister's right. If we don't live our lives to the fullest, that will be an even bigger tragedy.

The following night, Victoria's eighteenth birthday party is in full swing. Ryan's on stage performing for her friends, most of whom are sporting dresses short enough to show their back-sides and wearing more badly applied make-up than a clown. The joys of being a teenager. I don't miss those years.

A supple arm flicks round my waist as I stand at the bar, one of the few women not enthralled by Ryan's performance. After not only watching him live five times this year, but planning every leg, I've had my fill, and that's without Slane Castle in a few days' time.

I scan the room and when I see no one's watching, I relax, resisting the urge to swat Jayden's hand away. My heart is so full it's overflowing. I'm surrounded by everyone I love, and it feels so damn good.

Sneaking around the castle is exciting, but also utterly exhausting. I'll be glad when we're out in the open.

I can only imagine the shock Sasha will get when she realises I've gone from hating her future brother-in-law to worshiping the ground he walks on. She might be even more shocked to discover the feeling is mutual.

Chapter Thirty-Four

JAYDEN

Slane Castle has been hosting rock concerts in Ireland for over forty years, starting with Thin Lizzy and U2 in 1981. Set in the middle of a 1500-acre estate in the heart of County Meath, it's one of the country's most sought-after venues. To see my brother headlining tonight after everything we've been through, our mother leaving, Dad dragging us out of the country before abandoning us on the streets, is an almost spiritual experience.

Pride swells in my heart, the heart Chloe Sexton ripped from between my ribcage and has claimed as her own.

This is the biggest concert of the tour. We couldn't give our hometown anything less. Almost a hundred thousand fans coalesce, shrieking, singing and chanting my brother's name. I can only imagine the buzz he's feeling, although however transcendent it may be, the high of being with Sasha Sexton obviously trumps it. Now, I can finally understand why.

The stage production is out of this world, as it has been on every other concert in the *It's Always Been You* tour. Hundreds of thousands of stacked silver records exactly repli-cate the Giant's Causeway. The perfectly sculpted replica of the iconic rocks is complete with a forty-foot accompanying water feature.

Ireland's newest boyband rocks along with Ryan, while Sasha and Victoria watch from backstage, heavily guarded by Ryan's security.

Chloe and I survey our handiwork from a cordoned off VIP area, also heavily manned with burly, radio-clad men sporting blindingly bright high-vis jackets.

'Six down, two to go,' Chloe shouts in my ear to be heard over the noise, her face flush with excitement. In the week she's been here, she's flourished. Exuberant and increasingly light-hearted, she's delegating more of her work, interviewing more staff for new positions to lighten her load. She's really blossoming into her role as the CEO of a global events management company.

I am as proud of her as I am of Ryan.

I've never believed in true love. Probably because I've never witnessed it or experienced it myself. To me, there was only ever lust and sex. Marriage was something people did out of convenience, not because of a burning desire to tie themselves to another person.

My parents separated when I was a toddler, so I don't remember ever having been loved. Now I don't know how I ever lived without it, even if Chloe still hasn't said those three special words to me out loud.

With Chloe, I feel whole. She gets me. She knows my past and understands I'm not perfect. Hell, she more than anyone can relate to that. I feel like I've finally found my home. With her. In her.

We haven't spoken about what happens after the tour yet. It lingers in the air between us like a wisp of smoke neither of us is willing or able to grasp, but I'm pretty sure we're on the same page. She was looking at offices in LA, after all.

Declan came up trumps with Lula and her visa arrangements. If she's willing to put the work in, there is an alternative to us having to get married. When I get back to LA I'll break the news that we don't have to go through with the sham wedding, after all. She was so averse to going back to Mexico, she would have compromised her own happiness tying herself to me, well, on paper at least. Now she won't have to compromise anything. And I'll have fulfilled my promise to Sofia.

Now I've found love, I can't imagine tying myself to someone I don't feel that way about. Lula deserves the chance to tie herself to whomever she pleases, not because she fears deportation.

The urge to confess everything to Chloe is still eating me alive, but I can't. Not yet. Not until the details are finalised. If she finds out I'm technically engaged, she will freak out, especially after what Ethan did to her. I've never touched Lula, nor ever would. She's like a sister to me, but would Chloe see it that way given her past experiences? Highly unlikely.

The only issue outstanding now is this dirty business with my artists. Declan reckons he's close to identifying who's behind it, but I can't truly relax until that's sorted. With any bit of luck, by the time we get to Edinburgh for the seventh concert, I'll have crossed my t's and dotted my i's.

Only then will I be in a position to ask Chloe to move in with me. Because now I have her, I don't want to spend another day apart from her.

My palm presses against her lower spine. Sparks ignite like lit kindling doused in diesel. 'Come on, we have about thirty minutes before our siblings come looking for us, unless you want to listen to another round of how in love my brother is with your sister?' I say.

She doesn't object as I nudge her past the security. 'Where are we going?'

'To wait in the limo.' My palm drops to the curve of her bum and squeezes.

Blue eyes light, sensing an opportunity. 'I see,' she purrs.

With everyone's attention fixed on the stage, we're barely noticed as we thread our way out. Just two more Ryan Cooper fans. Anonymity is a luxury I'm going to miss dearly.

'You must be tired if you want to retire to the limo, I guess?' Chloe teases. She knows damn well the only thing I'm tired of is having to wait to be inside her again.

'I'm tired of having to behave myself in public when all I want to do is devour you. We need to make the most of these opportunities until we come out.'

'And when will that be, Mr Commitment-phobe? Don't think I don't know why you're holding out on me...'

'Because we're smack bang in the middle of the biggest gig of your life and I'm trying to protect your reputation?' And sort my life out in the process, of course. Not that I can tell her. Not yet, at least. A sliver of shame ripples through me.

Tell her.

No. Why risk her grasping the completely wrong idea and flying off the handle when she's finally opening up to me? Allowing me full access to the fragile heart that's been tucked behind the high, cold walls she spent years erecting.

'No.' She slaps my arm gently before grabbing my ass. 'Because I think secretly you thrive on sneaking around. Admit it, it turns you on doing something you shouldn't be doing. Or doing someone, I should say.'

'Well, if you fuck me in the limo, at least we can tick car sex off the bucket list.'

We half walk, half jog towards the car as the sky darkens. Thunder rumbles in the distance, barely audible over the thrumming basslines of Ryan's band. The rain's never far away in Ireland.

I grab Chloe by the hand and up the pace towards the waiting limo, flanked by two SUVs and more security. We've been caught out before by crazed fans. Pierce, Ryan's personal bodyguard, vowed it would never happen again.

The driver spots us approaching and steps out of the vehicle, followed by one of the security detail from the SUV.

I'd recognise that shaggy crop of blond hair anywhere. His stance is all wrong. Too aggressive. His jaw's set hard in a grim line, and there's a coldness in his metallic glare that supersedes any display of emotion he's ever expressed before.

'Colton? What are you doing here? Is everything ok?' Unease stirs in my gut. Something's not right. Colton should be in LA with Lula, protecting her. Not 5,000 miles away here in Ireland.

'I got the first plane over.' He thrusts a thickly padded A4 envelope under my nose. Huge glinting eyes dart between Chloe and me before settling on our joined hands. His lips lift in a cunning smirk, the most emotion I've seen from him in the eight months he's worked for me. 'Your *fiancée* asked me to give you this.'

Like hell she did.

Colton's here for one reason only. To cause trouble, but this second, I don't have time to question who actually sent him.

A gasp slips from Chloe's lips. Her head whips around to face me so quickly, it's a wonder she doesn't get whiplash. She squeezes my hand as if to tell me to correct him. That he's got it wrong. But, of course, I can't.

If looks could kill, I'd have put Colton on the floor with his head decapitated from his tortured body. The smile on his face sets an icy shiver down my spine, and I understand now why Declan wasn't entirely convinced of his innocence.

In fact, it's obvious now. He's the only person who could have had access to me and my artists who were targeted.

Someone in a position of trust. But that's something I'm going to have to ponder later. Right now, I've got bigger problems.

Having delivered the brown envelope, Colton hops back into the SUV. I note the number plate, but it's not one of ours. The driver's window slides down and he pokes his head out. 'The Johnsons send their regards.'

What the actual fuck?

Chloe stands shell-shocked at my side, her trembling fingers still entwined in mine.

I take her other hand and turn her to face me so I can look her in the eyes. 'Chloe, it's not what it seems.'

'Your fiancée?' It's barely a whisper. Fireworks soar and explode in the midnight sky. Fluorescent shooting stars illuminating the shit show that my life has just become.

'It was only ever going to be on paper. It was the only feasible option at the time...'

Adrenaline kicks in with one hell of a surge. Chloe snaps her hands out of mine and takes three steps backwards. I reach out, but she shouts, 'Don't fucking touch me, Jayden. Don't you dare touch me again.'

'Chloe, give me a chance to explain.'

She raises a hand, palm facing my face, cutting me off before I can begin. 'You want a chance to explain that the whole time you've been sleeping with me, you were planning to marry somebody else?'

'It's not how it seems. I should have told you. I was trying to do the right thing by everyone. This was supposed to be a fling. I wasn't supposed to fall in love with you.' From the thunderous look clouding her face, that was possibly the worst thing I could have said.

I try again. 'I'm not in love with her. I barely even know her. Not really.'

A cold, shrill laugh pierces the air. 'And that's supposed to make me feel better, is it? And you had the audacity to say *you* were protecting *my* reputation.'

'I swear to you Chloe, it's not like that. I promised her sister a long time ago that I'd do whatever it takes to — '

'Her sister? Exactly who is this fiancée of yours?' Chloe yells at me with flamed cheeks.

'Can we talk about this in the limo?' Enticing her into a safe place to talk might be the only way to prevent her from running away and executing her favourite party trick - fleeing the country.

'If you think I'm going anywhere with you ever again, you're badly mistaken.' A hissing sound whistles from between her teeth. 'You're engaged. You made me into the other woman, something I swore I'd never be. You cheated on her. You cheated on me. But the one person you really cheated was yourself. I would have loved you for the rest of my life, more fool me. You are an absolute embarrassment, Jayden Cooper.'

Now she says she loves me. Or would have done, at least.

I flinch and hang my head as she rips open the one wound I can't fully seem to close.

I am an embarrassment, running round trying to save the world as if I'm some kind of superhero. What the fuck was I thinking?

'I trusted you. You're the first man I let in after everything. I thought you were different.' Her voice cracks with emotion.

'Chloe, can we at least talk about this? It's not what it seems.'

'I'm done talking. It's not exactly all it's cracked up to be. Have a nice life.' She slips into the back of the limo and slams the door behind her. The tyres screech down the driveway, leaving me shaking next to the one remaining SUV.

The skies open and it's biblical. Huge globules of rain lash from the sky as if a dam has burst from heaven itself. The fireworks subside as Ryan belts out his final song.

I rip open the envelope to find evidence of the latest scandal I accidentally created while I was stupidly trying to do good. Pictures of Lula sunning herself by my pool, a copy of the initial visa application, and the prenup Kim and my lawyer drew up when we embarked on this crazy quest for Lula's green card. There are also images of Chloe and me on the beach in Dubai. Fuck. It will probably be all over tomorrow's papers. Just when Declan found a workaround, I've ruined everything with Chloe.

I toss the paperwork onto the muddy, gravelly ground, and climb into the back of the SUV, watching as the rain soaks through the contract. So powerful, so binding, yet under the first drop of water it wilts.

I can relate.

Archie and Frankie, two of Ryan's most reliable security team, are sitting in the front of the vehicle. There's a small modicum of comfort in that.

'Everything ok, Jayden?' Frankie asks, fingers drumming on the steering wheel.

'It will be.' I'm just not sure when. 'Take me to the airport, please.'

I need to sort my life out, starting with finding out who the fuck the Johnsons are, and pray to fuck that in the meantime, Chloe calms down enough to let me at least explain.

Chapter Thirty-Five

CHLOE

I text Sasha to tell her I've returned to the castle with a migraine and that the limo is on its way back to pick them up. It's not entirely a lie. My head is splitting, but not nearly as much as my heart.

How could I have been so stupid? Expecting the biggest player in LA to change his ways and settle down with me. For being vain enough to think the reason he hadn't been papped with a string of models this year might have anything to do with me.

It's the sneakiness, the underhandedness, I can't get over. He's been lying to me this entire time. None of what we had was real, and yet every single minute with him felt like the most real, the most profound minutes of my life.

Mr Commitment-phobe is getting married. No wonder he was reluctant to commit to me! He was already committed to someone else. It would be hilarious if it wasn't so tragic.

All the time I thought he was sheltering me from the public eye, protecting me, he was protecting himself. I was nothing more than his dirty little secret.

I can't get my head around it.

His words from the first few weeks ring through my head on repeat. *'One last final fling.'* He said it himself. *'Don't worry, I'm not going to fall in love with you.'*

Then he went and said it anyway, and stupidly I believed him.

I didn't mean to fall in love with him. I'd never willingly sign up to be the 'other woman.' I hate that's who he made me, but I hate myself more for letting him. I'm such an idiot. My heart aches, but so does my pride. Thank god no one knows about us. Small blessings.

I pace up and down the thick burgundy carpet of my bedroom with an all-consuming urge to flee. To hop on a plane, like I've done so many times before, and disappear. My finger instinctively goes to my wrist to snap my elastic band, but the bastard even took that from me.

So much for putting on my big girl's pants. I might have forged a new, deeper bond with my sisters, but the need to put a million miles between me and this castle remains the same. It's not my parents I see everywhere now. It's Jayden.

Firing up my laptop, I book myself onto the next flight back to Dubai. It's fifteen hours away, which feels like fifteen years right now, but at least I'll get to see the girls in the morning.

They can never find out about this.

This is exactly why Sasha warned me about getting involved with Jayden. She was right. She knew better. I thought what he and I had transcended everything. Huh, more like transitional. I wish I'd listened.

I brush my teeth, shower, go through the motions, but I'm like a zombie. Dead inside, walking the earth aimlessly. When my head finally hits the pillow, all I can smell is him. Intoxicating aftershave mixed with his heady raw masculinity.

Inhaling the Egyptian cotton, I hate myself for needing to

drink him in one more time. Tears flood my face, drowning the bedding as sobs rack through my body.

I've experienced more pain than most in my short life, but this serendipitous bout is on a different excruciating level. How long will it take me to piece my shredded heart back together this time?

The truth is, I don't think it can be done.

I toss and turn all night, barely sleeping a wink, and in the morning it takes a mountain of concealer and foundation to hide the evidence.

Sasha high fives me over the table, her usual bouncing curls matted in a just-fucked, messy nest. 'Great job on the stage production. The water feature was epic. Seriously, sis, you nailed it. I can't wait for Edinburgh.'

'Thanks.' I sip my coffee, unable to stomach anything more. 'Speaking of Edinburgh, I'm going to have to meet you there.' My gaze drops to the floor. I hate lying to her, but I can't tell her the truth.

This fallout between me and Jayden cannot taint her wedding. On the plus side, everyone thinks I hate him anyway, so that's nothing new.

'What? I thought you were planning on hanging round for the week? What's the point of flying out just to fly back again?' Victoria demands, slathering butter onto thick white toast at the dining table.

'Ruby emailed. There's something that needs my urgent attention.'

'Huh, are you sure it was Ruby and not Pedro who emailed?' Victoria snorts, blissfully unaware of the knife she's twisting into my already crumbling heart.

Jayden hasn't called. Not that I would have picked up. He hasn't even texted. I thought he might at least try. Clearly, he doesn't give a fuck. Oh, unless you count the hundreds of fucks we shared behind his fiancée's back.

I'm so angry with him, but even more so at myself. What I need is to get into my office and work myself into the ground because it's the only thing I'm good at. The only thing that never leaves me.

'Me and Pedro are over.' I didn't intend to say it out loud, but the weight sitting on my chest lifts a fraction simply by sharing.

Perhaps I haven't regressed completely, even if I am jumping the country again.

Victoria's toast slips through her fingers. 'Oh, Chloe, I'm so sorry. I didn't mean to put my foot in it.'

'It's not your fault, petal. Don't worry about it.' It's a battle, but I muster a small, tight smile.

'What happened?' Sasha watches wide-eyed from across the table. 'I thought you were working through things?'

A sigh whooshes out of my chest as I slump forwards, elbows on the table. 'I honestly don't know.'

'But did he call you? Did he end it? Or did you?' Victoria probes.

'It wasn't what I thought it was.' I take another sip of coffee because I don't know what else to do.

'Chloe, I hate to say it, but are you sure you're not just panicking and fleeing at the first sign of trouble?' Sasha's coaxing voice sounds like a police officer pleading with a violent offender to put down a gun.

'If the first sign of trouble is him being in a relationship with someone else the entire time, then yes, I guess I am.' Tears threaten again. The castle walls are closing in on me. I need to get out of here. The chair legs screech against the varnished wooden flooring as I push it back from the table to stand.

'What?' Sasha's tone sounds as incredulous as I feel. 'Are

you sure?' She stands, skirting round the table to reach me. 'You seemed so happy the other day. Pedro, or whatever his real name is, seemed to breathe life into you. Life you've been missing since the accident. I can't believe it.'

'I heard it from the horse's mouth.'

Victoria stretches across the table, taking my hand. 'Please don't go, Chloe.'

It yanks on every single fractured fragment of my broken heart, but I can't stay.

'I really have to work.' Even if it's for personal reasons. 'How about I meet you in Edinburgh a few days early and you can show me the college you applied for? We can look at apartments for you?'

Given Sasha's high-profile status these days, it goes without saying that Victoria can't reside in traditional student digs like most of her peers. She might even require her own personal security, something we've yet to discuss.

'Okay.' Her reluctant acceptance does nothing to ease my guilt, but the need to escape wins.

On the way to the airport, I ring Ruby.

'I'm on my way back.' Familiar landmarks whizz by in my peripheral vision. The Irish Sea to my right. Portmarnock. Velvet Strand. All the places Mam and Dad used to bring us when we were kids. I miss them so much my heart swells at the memories. But now I can finally remember them without the guilt.

Maybe Jayden had his uses after all? What is it they say? The people you meet in life are a lesson or a blessing? When I calm down, maybe I'll see Jayden was both. Or maybe not if the agonising pain pressing against my chest is anything to go by.

'Is everything ok?' Phones ring in the background against a low hum of the office.

'Jayden's engaged.'

'He's what?' Ruby's shriek rings through my ear. I pull the phone away for a moment until I'm certain my hearing is safe.

'I don't really want to talk about it, but if you're free tonight, can we please go for three thousand glasses of wine? I need to get out of my head.'

'Sure. Brad and I are over-over. As Taylor Swift would say, 'we are never, ever getting back together'.'

'You say that every time.' I tut, but at least I know I'll have a drinking buddy for a week or so.

'I took your advice. I've always believed I'll know right away, so why am I wasting time on settling for anything less?'

'Brilliant, let's drink to that.'

'Email me your flight details. I'll pick you up from the airport.'

I'm about to protest, before I remember the new me. The one who gave up carrying guilt and shame. The one who used to risk assess every possible outcome. 'Thank you.'

If Ruby's surprised, she hides it well.

'Chin up, honey. See you tonight.'

I check in to first class and head straight to the lounge area, trying to focus on anything other than the hot mess that's my life right now.

As I wait, I deal with a few emails on my phone, mostly enquiries from Sydney and LA. Ruby's proving her weight in gold, managing the entire Middle East, opening a brand-new office in Abu Dhabi as well as securing new, larger premises in Dubai to incorporate our hugely expanding staff. I don't know what I'd do without her.

Finally, my company's a truly global business. All I need now is to stir up some interest in London, and then I'll have achieved all my ambitions. I should be excited. Instead, I'm deflated.

I can work myself to the bone for the rest of my life, but truly, what's the point in any of it? Do I even want to leave Dubai now?

Before I met Jayden, absolutely. While I was sleeping with him, deluding myself we had any kind of future together, absolutely.

Now?

Now I don't know what I want because nothing else in my life will ever compare to what I thought we had.

'I thought it was you,' a friendly voice rumbles from behind me.

A wince creases my face and my shoulders hunch as I try to place it in the brief few seconds I have before etiquette demands I turn around.

Nope. No idea. Maybe if I wasn't so sleep deprived and twisted with turmoil, my mind would be more focused.

Inching around slowly, it's a relief to see Levi, my travelling companion from all those weeks ago. His light brown hair falls in those same floppy waves. Bright eyes dance with amusement.

'Levi, what are you doing here?' I gesture round the first-class lounge, but what I actually mean is what's he doing in Ireland.

'Same as you, I guess. Waiting for a plane.' He shrugs, flashing that happy-go-lucky smile I remember so well.

He presses a kiss to my cheek and his gaze rakes over my tear-stained face. I can only imagine what kind of state I look after the last twenty-four hours.

Sympathy softens his expression. 'You look like a woman who's been mixing business with pleasure again.'

My phone lights up. Jayden. I swear the man has some

sort of radar when it comes to me moving on. I reject the call and switch the phone off.

Levi winks and pulls up a stool beside me. 'Do you think there's a reason we keep meeting like this?'

'One hundred percent. The universe has conspired, so I have someone to drown my sorrows with.'

Levi shrugs and signals a passing waiter.

Chapter Thirty-Six

JAYDEN

It comes to me on the flight. I know who the Johnsons are. They're the parents of Chardonnay Johnson, the talentless wreck I refused to sign. It has to be.

Unbelievable. Welcome to Hollywood, where the drama is high, plots are poor and the cash to produce is plentiful. If there's a bigger motive than my refusal to sign their darling Chardonnay, I'm still waiting for Declan to uncover it.

I switch the flight mode off on my phone, willing there to be something from Chloe. Anything. I'd take abuse over silence. At least that would mean she's still thinking about me.

Forty-eight work related emails.

A reminder for a check-up at the dentist.

Nothing from Chloe.

The second I've sorted this mess out, I'm going to hop on the next plane to wherever she is, but right now my priority is to confront the Johnsons and put a stop to this madness before they can do anymore damage.

As I stalk purposefully through the airport towards the exit, Declan rings.

'Are you ready for this?' he says.

I step out into the blinding sun where Kim is waiting, as instructed, with my car. 'What did you find? Don't tell me, I shagged the wife? I barely remember the daughter.'

Kim clicks her tongue distastefully against her palate and hops into the passenger seat.

I raise my hand in greeting and mouth Declan's name to her as I slide in behind the wheel. Kim's been updated on everything, including my newfound love for Chloe Sexton. I'm just waiting for the tongue-lashing when Declan gets off the phone.

'You might wish it was that straightforward,' Declan scoffs. 'Not only did you reject their only darling daughter, Chardonnay, spectacularly by all accounts, but they have a journalist quoting you as saying, "Chardonnay Johnson, what talent?"'

'It's ringing a bell alright.' I shake my head at Kim, unable to believe this entire vendetta is based on something so fucking petty. 'I rejected three of her tapes, then somehow she ended up getting a face-to-face audition. Richard Lambert insisted I heard her for myself, but she was shockingly bad. I mean, tone-deaf bad. Her parents had spent hundreds of thousands of dollars on vocal coaches and stage schools, but it was a waste of my time. Chardonnay had zero raw talent.'

Declan clears his throat noisily before continuing. 'Money's not a problem for the Johnsons, as you've gathered. They're also exceptionally well-connected. Kurt Johnson's been implicated in a number of bribery and corruption scandals, but his direct involvement has never been proven in any of them. However, I've found evidence that he gifted Richard Lambert a yacht the week before his daughter's audition. How's that for a bribe?'

'You're kidding? For fuck's sake. I don't believe it.' It's the epitome of everything I despise about this industry. Talent can't be bought and sold. The simple fact is, Chardonnay had less talent than a dog with one leg. 'Are you trying to tell me that's the reason he wanted to bring me and my artists down?'

'After you rejected her, dear, sweet, untalented Chardonnay went on a downward spiral into drugs and drink. And guess what? She even had a stolen sex tape she made with her boyfriend go viral. Sound familiar? The only difference being was the boyfriend was her father's best friend, married, and twenty years her senior. It almost caused a war.'

'And Colton? How does my silent, brooding bodyguard fit into this puzzle?' I ease out onto the slipway. The traffic is terrible as usual.

'Colton is Mrs Johnson's nephew. Colton's her maiden name, which is why it took me a while to make the connection.' Declan coughs. 'I'm sorry about that.'

My bullshit detector didn't pick him out either. Although, technically, he didn't lie to me. It was his brooding silence that kept him under the radar.

'I guess the real question is, what are we going to do about it?' I muse.

'You could go to the cops, but we don't exactly have much hard evidence,' Declan reminds me. 'If it were me, I'd go a different route.'

'Put him on speaker,' Kim interjects. 'I called Gareth last night when we learned the Johnson's were behind this. I asked him to arrange a little video of his own. It's currently streaming a live feed from Johnson's office. I'll get you access to it, Declan. It's a long shot, but a man surrounded by that much scandal has to have a few secrets of his own. Or worst-case scenario, he might say or do something that proves his involvement in what's been going down.'

'You called Gareth?' I ask.

'Eyes on the road, buddy.' I don't miss her smirk.

'You mean you called him on the phone? Or you called his name from the comfort of his bed while he washed the post-coital sex stains from his balls? Did you two finally get it on?'

Cat-like pupils slant across the dashboard. She flicks her honey-coloured bob from her shoulders. 'You ever hear that saying, people in glasshouses shouldn't throw stones? Want to tell us more about you and the Sexton sister?' She offers a salacious wink, playfully thumping my arm.

They might actually be a match made in heaven.

'Can we just get back to that feed?' Declan's voice echoes through the car.

'I'll send you the link now,' Kim says, taking out her phone.

'So, we just have to wait?' I blow out a long, slow breath, squeezing my frustration out on the steering wheel. The Johnsons need to be shut down before they can do any more damage, especially with Ryan's final two concerts coming up - the perfect chance to make another statement.

'For now, yes. We wait,' Kim says. 'You have other matters to attend to, though. Lula, the girl whose heart you're about to smash into smithereens.'

'Oh, fuck off, Kim. This stupid engagement was purely transactional. You know that better than anyone. You drew up the damn prenup contract yourself.'

'I'm going guys. I'll let you know when I have something.' Declan hangs up.

'I'm just saying, if I was her, you know clearly I'm not, but if I was...' Kim says.

'What? Spit it out.' I indicate and take the slip road towards Santa Monica. I'm in desperate need of a shower, an Advil, and three years' worth of sleep, preferably curled around Chloe Sexton, who I'm praying to every god I don't believe in, will miraculously forgive me for not telling her about any of this.

I'm such a douche. She opened up to me about her guilt and shame. I should have done the same.

'How do you think Lula's going to take the rejection?' Kim asks.

'Rejection? You can't be serious? You don't actually think she wants to marry me, do you?'

Kim's violet eyes rake over me. She blinks, slowly, deliberately cocky. 'Well, I suppose you're not entirely awful to look at.'

I pull into my long, winding driveway. 'And this house is just about habitable, I guess,' she continues, shrugging dramatically. 'I've never seen what's in your trousers, but your bank accounts are substantial enough to make up for anything lacking.'

'Lacking?' I take my foot off the pedal and the engine cuts out. 'Thanks, Kim. That's really fucking helpful.'

'You're welcome.' Her sarcastic beam exposes a perfect set of white teeth. 'She's home, by the way. No time like the present.' Kim smiles sweetly, hopping out of the car. 'I'll be in your office.'

Bad enough I broke one heart already. I hope to fuck I don't have to break another. No, that's stupid. I'd have known if she had feelings for me. She doesn't. I was always her older sister's pain-in-the-ass-friend trying to help keep her in line while she took out her teenage frustrations by rebelling on the roughest streets of LA.

I creep past Lula's pastel pink bedroom. The door's closed. I shower, shave, and try to ring Chloe twenty times, with no success.

I'm empty. Filled to the brim with nothingness. So much for trying to be honourable. I've let down the only woman I ever loved in the worst possible way, by trying to save another one. And the really fucked-up thing about the whole scenario is that I'm realising the only person who really needed saving was me.

Chloe did that for me.

She allowed me to be me in all my fucked-up glory. We're the mirror image of each other, driven and ambitious with work, hedonistic out of it, especially in the bedroom. We complemented each other perfectly. It's like she was made for me.

Even our demons are similar. Only she was brave enough to confront hers, admitting to me and her sisters the things she was ashamed of. I might have said I love you, but I hid my other demons, duelling them in private. Trying to save everyone yet helping no one in reality.

I pad down the stairs and take a deep breath.

Lula's hair is even longer than the last time I saw her. It now almost reaches her waist.

I kiss both her cheeks, and she blushes. Oh, god, don't tell me Kim was right about her, that she has feelings for me? That's the last thing I need right now.

I motion Lula to follow me into the kitchen. Her huge brown eyes drink me in.

'Sit. Please.' I pull out a bar stool at the island. 'Can I get you coffee? Tea? Water?'

I'm stalling for time. Where's ruthless Jayden when I need him? What is it about women in need that does something to my ability to say no?

'Water, please.' Lula flicks her long dark hair from her shoulders. She's the image of her sister, another olive-skinned beauty, with the same chocolate-coloured eyes thickly framed by an abundance of long black lashes. Lula is a far cry from the child I once knew, yet when I look at her, that's all I see. A child.

She sits rigidly in the chair, her tanned knuckles white as

she clenches her fists. Is she nervous? Anxious? Frightened of me? I've never given her any reason to be.

'We need to talk.' My eyes finally meet hers as I place a bottle of water and a glass for her on the marble counter.

She nods. She's never been much of a talker. We've barely had ten conversations since she got here. As a teenager, she might have been rebellious, but as an adult, she's quiet, thoughtful and seemingly determined to keep her head down.

'I can't marry you, Lula. I'm sorry.' My head shakes with shame.

Her shoulders sag.

'I've made alternative arrangements for your visa, don't worry. There's absolutely no way I'll allow you to be deported. I'll take care of you, just like I promised your sister.'

Her knuckles relax and she takes a deep breath.

'How do you feel about going to college? It'll buy us four years and I'm certain in that timeframe I could pull some strings to push for a more permanent solution.'

She stares at me for a long beat, an enigmatic expression on her face.

'Say something, Lula, please.' I take a sip of water.

'I'd... I'd like that, I think. Thank you, Mr Cooper.' She flashes me a huge, heartfelt smile, something I've only ever been treated to twice before.

'Please, call me Jayden. You don't mind that we're not...' I motion to the air between us awkwardly with my hands.

Could I make any more of a bollocks of this?

'What I meant to say is the quickest and most effective way to object to your deportation was to claim you were my fiancée. But time has provided an opportunity to explore alternative avenues.' I push a pile of brochures in her direction. A prospectus for every course in California.

'Mr... Jayden, I'm beyond grateful for everything you've done for me this year. You owe me nothing, yet you continue to give.' She motions to the Prius outside the door. I'd have bought her an Audi if that's what she wanted, but no, she's not like other girls.

'It's a relief, to be honest, that there is an alternative option.' A small smile plays on her lips again.

The penny drops. 'Ah, hah. There is a boy...'

She nods. 'Diego, from the restaurant.' There's that smile again. 'And there is a girl, no?'

I clink my glass against hers. 'There is, but it's complicated. She and I have a longer history than you and me.'

'Then you have a good solid foundation, no?'

'We did until she heard I was engaged.' My lighthearted tone isn't fooling anyone.

'Well, in that case, maybe this time I can finally help *you*?'

'No, but thank you. I think it's finally time I helped myself for once.'

Chapter Thirty-Seven

CHLOE

Ruby's at the airport waiting in almost the same spot where I waited for Jayden.

Jayden.

Everywhere I look, I see him. My brain has an uncanny talent of summoning high-quality images of him in a terrifyingly lifelike way.

Red-tipped fingers grip mine and squeeze. 'How are you holding up?'

'I've had better days.' I turn to Levi, who's hovering a foot behind me. 'This is Levi. Levi, this is my friend, Ruby.'

Ruby's pupils double in size as they settle on Levi. Even in his tired, crumpled suit, he's still a sight for sore eyes.

'Do you need a lift somewhere?' Ruby isn't discreet.

'He'll meet us at the bar in an hour, won't you, Levi?'

'I wouldn't miss it for the world.' He winks, his attention focussed entirely on Ruby. Good. I hope they hit it off, because despite my earlier intentions, I can't imagine I'll be much company tonight. A tiredness like I've never felt before weighs me down.

Ruby grabs the handle of my suitcase.

'It's ok, I've got it,' I protest.

'You've got enough baggage, honey. Let me at least carry this one. Tell me, how do you know hot stuff over there?' She nods at Levi's retreating backside.

'We sat next to each other on a flight a few weeks ago and then we were on the same flight again today. He actually seems like a really decent guy. Ha, but then again, with my track record, he's probably a crazed, axe-wielding murderer or something.'

Ruby drapes her arm across my shoulder as she leads me out into the heat.

'Come on. Let's drop your stuff home and get you changed.'

Slumping into the passenger seat of Ruby's Toyota, I crank the air-con to full blast.

My phone vibrates with an incoming call.

Jayden.

I reject it and it rings again.

'What does *he* want?' Ruby snarls.

'He wants to talk. He tried to tell me it's not how it seems, which is exactly what Ethan said.'

'What a douche. TMZ just broke the story about his engagement.' Ruby holds her phone up as she settles into the driver's seat.

'What? Let me see that.' Ruby has an obsession with celebrity gossip sites. She claims it's research for work, but I know it's just her guilty pleasure.

I scroll through the short article with a shaky finger.

Looks like Hollywood has lost another eligible bachelor. Rumour has it Jayden Cooper is set to follow his broth-

er's footsteps straight down the aisle. Twenty-nine-year-old LA Playboy and agent to Ryan Cooper is said to be engaged to twenty-five-year-old Lula Flores, a stunning beauty, originally from Toluca.

Though the two have yet to make an official statement, our inside source says the two are very much in love.

Pictured below is Flores, outside Cooper's Santa Monica mansion, where she's been staying for most of this year. No wonder we haven't been able to get a glimpse of him out in public. He's clearly been very busy in private.

Nausea swells in my stomach as I pour over a picture of Jayden's fiancée standing in the garden of his familiar Santa Monica home.

Lula is absolutely stunning. With waist length hair and huge brown eyes, she's every man's Latino dream.

So much for, "it's not how it seems."

Are they together right now? Does he inhale *her* hair when he holds her, the way he used to do with mine?

Stop it, Chloe. Stop it.

'I can't believe it. I feel like such a complete and utter fool.'

'Neither can I.' Ruby starts the engine, politely pretending not to notice the big, fat salty tears streaming down my face.

'You sure you're up to going out?'

'It's either that or sit and wallow at the villa on my own. I'd work on my emails, but I can't concentrate.'

'Don't worry about work. That's what you have me for.'

. . .

Two hours later, we're in the same bar we were in the first night Jayden spent in Dubai. It was barely three months ago. Everything looks the same. There's only one thing different.

Me.

Levi and Ruby are necking shots, engrossed in conversation, and if their over-familiar touchy gestures are anything to go by, utterly enamoured with each other already. I don't need a fortune cookie to work out their immediate future.

I'm happy for her. I really am, but I should have opted to wallow at home. I'm nauseous, barely able to take three sips from the drink I'd so badly longed for.

'I'm gonna call it a night, guys,' I announce.

'Ah, Chloe, don't go,' Ruby says, but Levi doesn't protest. I don't blame him. Three's a crowd and all that.

'I'm sorry. I shouldn't have come. I'm no company at all. You stay and have fun with Levi.' I lean into her ear. 'He's a great guy. Go for it.'

'Are you sure it's ok? You don't ...like him?'

'No, Rubes, I don't. He's all yours.'

Levi stands and politely pecks my cheek. 'I knew there was a reason I kept bumping into you,' he whisper-shouts over the music into my ear. 'Your friend is AMAZING.'

'I know. Just do me a favour. Don't hurt her.'

'Scouts' honour.' The skin on either side of his eyes creases as his lips lift into a grin.

At least something worked out today.

Naveesha, my housemaid, arrives before eight o'clock the next morning. Normally I'd be on the terrace having my coffee and croissants, but this creature of habit is well and truly rattled.

Jayden, the man who won't commit, is actually engaged.

I can't get my head around it.

I grab my phone from the bedside locker and see another eight missed calls from him. It's well and truly over. There's no coming back from how he's treated me and I don't want to talk to him. And yet I can't bring myself to block his number.

The pitter-patter of approaching feet draws my attention. Naveesha pauses, hovering at the bedroom door, and her familiar features crinkle into the biggest grin.

'Miss Chloe, welcome home.'

I can't return an ounce of enthusiasm.

She crosses the floor, placing the back of her hand against my forehead. 'Are you sick, Miss Chloe? You look terrible. Is it that time of the month?'

My hand falls to my stomach. My periods are few and far between because of the birth control shots.

Oh god, I never got my last one. What with the tour and trying to take over the world, it didn't even cross my mind.

I couldn't be... could I?

'Let me get you something. You look like a ghost floated right in front of your face. Naveesha make you some nice camomile tea.'

'Can you lace it with gin?'

She frowns as she peers at her watch. 'It's eight o'clock.'

'And?' Although alcohol won't help. Nothing will. And there's no way I'll drink a drop of anything until I'm one hundred percent certain I'm not in the club.

I can't be. I just can't be. But the nausea lately...

No, that's just heartbreak, plain and simple. Still, I'll buy a test to rule it out.

Naveesha folds her arms over her gingham shirt and shoots me her disapproving mom look. 'What's wrong, Miss Chloe? Maybe I can help.'

It would be laughable if she didn't sound so earnest.

The truth is, no one can help me.

No one.

Jayden Cooper has ruined me in every possible way. I let him in. Trusted him. And he was lying to me the whole time.

Yet, it didn't feel like he was lying to me. I remember the hazy drunken confession I made in the hall about my shame.

We all have things we are ashamed of.

Those were his exact words. I should have questioned him. Perhaps I would have done if I wasn't so wrapped up in my own self-pity.

Although having a secret fiancée stashed away in god knows where is pretty shameful. There's no coming back from that. And where was she while I was in Vegas?

The contents of the bathroom cabinet, the skin care. It wasn't Jayden's at all.

God, I'm so stupid. The urge to scream into my pillow is overwhelming.

How am I supposed to get through my sister's wedding, paired up with him as the best man, when he's the worst possible man I've ever encountered?

An image of us standing at the altar together pops into my head. He'll obviously be bringing *her*. A fresh wave of nausea surges up my throat. Sasha warned me. I've only got myself to blame.

And now the hole in my chest has become a full-blown crater.

Naveesha draws the floor length curtains. The sweltering summer sun beams in, illuminating every inch of my misery. She opens the door to the terrace and humidity floods the room.

'I know it's hot, but you need some fresh air. I'll make you some tea, then you can tell me all about it.'

When she returns carrying a tray with two cups and an enormous pot of herbal tea, I drag myself into a seated position, patting the bed next to me. She's so much more than my housekeeper. She's my confidant, friend, and the closest thing

I've had to a mother since I got here. She cooks healthy meals for me, even if I don't always eat them. Her heart's in the right place. I know it is, but no one can help me today.

She sits, pats my hand with a sympathetic touch, then pours me a cup of tea.

'Miss Chloe, I only saw you like this once before.'

Ethan.

I shrug. That poor excuse for a heartbreak has nothing on this.

She slurps from her cup before resting it on its saucer. 'It's that man, the American, no? The one with the big...' Vacant eyes close, searching for the right word. It almost makes me smile. Almost.

'Job.' She nudges me. 'He paid me to leave you alone.'

I nod, unable to deny it.

'What happened? He's a good man, Miss Chloe. I saw it with my own eyes. I say to myself, this man loves Miss Chloe. I worry you move to America for him.' Dark eyes well with emotion.

'Oh, Naveesha, I am supposed to go to America, but not for him. For me. I have business there now. But this place,' I gesture round, 'will always be my base.'

'I will miss you.'

'You'll enjoy the peace. No one moping around crying. Unless you want to come with me?' Maybe I could work it.

Naveesha's the closest thing I have to family, other than my sisters, of course.

'Me? In the United States of America. Shish... What would I even do there?'

The same as she's doing here. Like me, she has no family. She has siblings in Sri Lanka but no children of her own. That's probably why she mothers me.

I shrug, taking a sip of tea. Its heat is comforting, but it does absolutely nothing to help my ruptured heart.

'I might not even go yet.'

I honestly don't know what to do with myself.

The urge to flee plagues me, but there isn't a corner of this earth I could escape my misery.

This time, I have no choice but to face it head on.

Chapter Thirty-Eight

JAYDEN

My phone rings incessantly. Congratulations on my 'engagement' pour in from every corner of the globe from what feels like every person I've ever met in my life, bar one, of course.

'Those sneaky bastards. I can't believe they leaked that story, just when Declan had sorted the visa application.' Kim paces the kitchen, furious at the injustice of it all. 'They just seem to be one step ahead. What are they going to do next?'

The buzzer sounds from the front gate and Kim practically runs to the security camera at the front door. 'The reinforcements have arrived,' she announces.

I join her at the door as she pushes the button allowing them access. We watch together as Gareth's Tesla crunches up the driveway. Declan's in the passenger seat. The pair of them crash out of the car and stalk into the house.

My friends' arrival causes an embarrassing lump of emotion to form in my throat.

Gareth slaps my back. 'We'll figure this out. Don't worry. Everybody knows anything in TMZ is only shitty speculation, anyway.'

My teeth worry at the inside of my cheek. 'It's just breathing oxygen into an already flaming fire, though. I'd hate for Chloe to think there was ever more to the situation. I need her to know I only ever had platonic feelings towards Lula. That I was only trying to help a friend.'

'I'm putting copies of the private prenup which states the exact nature of your and Lula's relationship, and the visa application in a OneDrive file for Chloe's eyes only. They prove your intention's are purely to help Lula with the green card,' Declan says. 'The immigration interview's been cancelled and Lula's student visa's being fast-tracked as we speak,'

Kim's tongue clicks against the roof of her mouth. 'Guys, I hate to tell you this, but you know what bomb they're likely to drop next, yeah? They've just told the world you're planning to marry Lula. What's the next worst thing they could do?'

'Drag Chloe into it,' I groan.

'Exactly. Did Colton know you were sleeping with her?' Kim asks.

Clearly, given his arrival at Slane Castle. She was the entire reason he came. To ruin things between us. An image of us laughing and running towards the limo, hand-in-hand, flashes through my brain. 'Yeah, he did.'

'Then prepare yourself for that to be tomorrow's headline, unless we can find some leverage to persuade the Johnsons to stop.'

'I was this fucking close, Kim.' I pinch my finger and thumb an inch apart. 'This close to saving everyone.' Even myself. 'I just couldn't pull it off.' My voice cracks, my throat dry.

'You can still do it, Jayden. We'll help convince Chloe you weren't going to go through with the marriage once you started dating her.'

Declan steps forwards. 'We can make this right, Jayden, but not while the Johnsons are rolling around like a couple of loose grenades. Although, as luck would have it, Senator Johnson has dug his dirty dick in some very tight holes.' Declan smirks.

Gareth steps forwards, thumbing his chest proudly. 'I've got something.' His sandy-coloured eyebrows wiggle like a cartoon character. It's apt seeing as he's one of the biggest characters I know. 'Think Monica Lewinsky and Bill Clinton. Kurt Johnson's daughter isn't the only one with a flair for home videography. He looks pretty good on the big screen, you know, if you're into the silver fox trope,' Gareth chuckles wryly. 'Caught with his trousers down with his secretary.'

'What a cliché. I thought he might have been a little more original.' Kim plants her glossy lips on Gareth's parted mouth with a smack. 'When this gets out, his political career is dead.'

'What about planting a couple of wraps of meth in his car?' Declan suggests. 'What goes around comes around. I'd love to see the LAPD taking a guy like that down in cuffs.'

I shudder. I've seen enough cuffs for a lifetime. 'As entertaining as it would be, I think the tape is probably enough at this stage.'

'Dang it.' Kim's fist drops, but she's grinning.

Finally, we have a plan, thanks to the amazing people around me.

I pull Gareth into a man hug. He slaps my back.

Adrenaline sparks in my veins, reigniting that relentless drive I've had since I was a kid. The one I saw in Chloe. The one that pushes us to succeed, no matter what it takes.

As if I'm going to be defeated by a couple of LA has-beens.

'Arrange a meeting. Immediately.'

· · ·

It's the following evening when I strut into Johnson's downtown office, armed with a USB stick and two brand new security guys, sourced and vetted thoroughly by Declan.

'Wait out here,' I tell them as the evening sun beats down on us.

In the reception area, I see a face I recognise from Senator Johnson's salacious home movie.

'He's expecting you,' his secretary smirks. I can't wait to wipe it from her face.

'Sadie, isn't it?' I shoot her a look. 'I almost didn't recognise you with your clothes on.' Her jaw drops, but I don't stop to gloat, stalking past her to the thick panelled door behind her desk. I shove it open without knocking. We're way past such pleasant niceties.

Kurt Johnson glares at me from his throne-like chair positioned behind a desk that's big enough to comfortably seat two people.

'It's polite to knock,' he barks, straightening himself in his chair. Like every other fool in LA, the man is unnaturally tanned, his face weathered from too much schmoozing on the golf course. I know his type and I detest them. The man's probably never done an honest day's work in his life. Born into money and clawed into power.

The coldness in his eyes matches the silver streaks of his greying temples.

'Yeah, and it's polite to respect someone's professional opinion when they decide their daughter lacks any discernible talent,' I spit.

'You ruined her life.' His arms cross over his chest, animosity oozing from every pore.

'*You* ruined her life by letting her believe there was a hope in hell of getting a record deal. You thought you could throw your money around and magically make your little princess a star.'

'You know nothing about us. My daughter is every bit as good as those girls you've dragged up from the dirt. Mind you, it seems to me you only sign the ones who have some tragic sob story.'

'No, I only sign those who have raw talent and the work ethic to get in front of me.'

'Same thing.' Johnson shrugs. 'And anyway, by the time I've finished with you, you won't be signing anyone else, talented or not.'

'Is that right?' A framed picture of Johnson and his botoxed model wife standing smiling with the President dominates the wall to my right. I wave at it, flashing my fakest smile.

Johnson's bushy eyebrows furrow. 'What are you doing?'

'Waving to the camera.' My index finger twirls and points at the tiny dot in the corner of the frame. 'Say hello to my friend, Gareth Reynolds. You might have heard of him? I'm fairly certain that picture was taken at the premier of the movie Gareth's company shot, and which was partially filmed at the White House.'

The colour drains from Johnson's face quicker than lightning. A spluttering cough takes hold of him. I perch on his desk and wink.

'What have you done?' he finally blurts out.

'The real question is, what have *you* done? They didn't hire me at "Ruthless Records",' I air quote the nickname for Diamond Records, 'for nothing.'

'How long has it been there?'

'Long enough.' I roll my sleeves up, crossing my ankle over my thigh. 'Now, here's what's going to happen.'

Johnson's gaze darts between my face, the desk and the camera.

'The damage you've done to my artists is irreparable. So, besides a substantial financial compensation, you will apologise to them. Otherwise, you and your secretary's gratuitous performance yesterday will go viral.'

He swallows hard. 'You wouldn't dare.'

'Try me. I've got nothing left to lose. Tick tock, Kurt. Your wife will wonder why you're late for supper.'

I strut out of the office, waving my fingers cheerily at Sadie. From the beetroot red shade of her cheeks, I think she must have heard every word.

Not only do I have him on camera, balls deep in his secretary, I also now have him confessing to setting up Mia and sabotaging Naomi's reputation. Not a bad day's work.

Now the only thing left to do is win back the only woman I've ever loved.

Chapter Thirty-Nine

CHLOE

Edinburgh

Victoria links my right arm, while Sasha clasps my left, as we stroll the length of Princes Street, with two of Ryan's security detail discreetly accompanying us from behind. The iconic Edinburgh Castle towers on the horizon, alight with a lilac iridescent glow.

Edinburgh is fast becoming one of my favourite cities. Not only is the Gothic architecture stunning and every street dripping with rich history, but I have no memories of Jayden Cooper here. I'm determined to keep it that way.

With three days before Ryan's concert, which I've already decided I don't need to attend, I get to spend a few leisurely days with my sisters, shopping, sight-seeing and sourcing a suitable apartment for Victoria.

Hopefully, it's enough to reassure them I'm not totally broken. I'll get over my crushed heart in time. A lot of time. I'll have to because there's more than just me to think about now.

After gorging ourselves at a sumptuous Italian restaurant, Victoria suggests finding a cocktail bar. It's a marvellous idea, even if I can't drink anything myself.

The shock's just about wearing off. It's very early days, but I *am* pregnant.

You couldn't make it up.

A memory of the first time Jayden and I slept together flashes across my mind. *The last thing the world needs is a mini-me in it.*

I disagree. The second the doctor confirmed my pregnancy, something burst to life inside of me. A feeling so strong, so powerful that this was fate. Like it was the world's way of giving me someone to love, now I've finally let my barriers down. For a woman who didn't believe in love, I feel it with every ounce of my being. The crater in my chest is not quite as raw. Hope even sparks at the depths of it at times.

I wouldn't choose to be a single mother.

Nor would I choose a man who's engaged to another woman to be the father of my child.

Equally, I wouldn't undo it. We've all learnt the hard way how precious life is and I'm treating this like the gift it is.

For the first time in my life, I can truly comprehend what Sasha lost all those years ago when she miscarried. Because this baby might be barely more than a seed, but already my heart beats purely for the purpose of loving it.

The joy of watching my business expand doesn't even come close to the elation of being pregnant. I've found the missing piece in my life in the most unlikely of places/. That thing I was searching for wasn't validation. It was purpose.

All of my previous professional ambitions fade to nothing. My new ambition is to be the best mother I can be.

I'll have to tell Jayden at some point. It's not as if I can hide it from him, given my sister and his brother are getting married. I'll probably be showing by the wedding. Of course, when I tell him, it's going to be a shock to his fiancée. I assume she has no idea he's been shagging me behind her back, let alone that I'm pregnant. I have about six weeks to come up with a plan, although even if I had six years, it probably still wouldn't be long enough.

Jayden's calls have been relentless. I haven't answered, but I still can't bring myself to block his number. Even though I don't answer, a part of me likes to know he's still thinking of me. That I'm not entirely in this pregnancy alone.

'Here, let's try this one.' Victoria points to a bar nestled on one of the side streets. A pink neon sign lights the windows.

We traipse in in single file, with Sasha leading the way. She's taken to wearing brown contact lenses when she's out in public and styling her hair in elaborate up dos that showcase her long slender neck.

She claims it's so people don't recognise her but secretly, I think she's finally getting the time to explore her own style now she no longer has to care for our little sister twenty-four-seven. Whatever the reason, she looks elegant and sophisticated. If she's hoping to blend in, it's simply not working.

The girls order three sex on the beach cocktails. I don't correct them, even though I know I won't touch mine. When the barman finally finishes mixing the drinks, we take them to a quiet corner with a small table. The two security guards assigned to us hover at the bar.

My phone lights up again. Sasha's quick eyes glance at the screen before I can hide it.

'What does Jayden want?' She places her cocktail on the table.

'Probably something to do with the concert,' I lie.

'Well, shouldn't you answer it then?' Sasha says.

'It can wait.' I press my lips against the frosted cocktail glass and pretend to take a mouthful.

'Apparently it can't.' She nods at the phone, vibrating on the table. Jayden again.

'Believe me, it can.' I reject the call and switch it off. Maybe it's finally time to block his number after all.

'Is everything ok?' Concern is etched into Sasha's tone. 'I know you and him and I took a while to see eye-to-eye, but you know, he's a really decent guy.'

'Huh.' I toy with the stem of my glass for something to do with my hands, the sickly sweet smell turning my stomach.

'Honestly, he is. Believe me, I was dubious myself, but what he's doing for that Mexican girl is utterly admirable,' Sasha continues.

My head snaps up so quickly my neck's in danger of breaking. 'How is marrying a young, beautiful girl admirable?'

'He's not marrying her.' Sasha stares at me, a look of bemusement on her face.

'What?'

Hope twitches in my chest.

'It turns out they lived on the streets together a lifetime ago. He promised her sister that he'd take care of her. They lost touch for a while, but when he found her again, he promised to help her with a visa to live in the States. The whole marriage arrangement was the quickest way to prevent her deportation.'

My jaw drops so fast it nearly hits the table. 'He's not marrying her?'

'No, but he's doing everything else he can to stop her from being sent back to Mexico. Apparently, her father's involved with some unsavoury people over there. Ryan and Jayden couldn't stand the thought of what she might face back home.'

'But what about the papers?'

'You should know better than to believe everything you read,' Sasha says. 'I don't doubt he's filing a lawsuit for that story.'

'Is he sleeping with her?' The words are out of my mouth before I can stop them.

'What kind of question is that? Lula's like a little sister to them, by all accounts. They'd been searching for her for years, but only found her after she was arrested for working illegally in a Mexican restaurant.'

'If she was like a sister to them, why didn't she reach out before? She must have known about Ryan's rise to fame?'

'She thought he'd abandoned her. And she's been alone for so long, I guess she was used to fighting her own battles.'

Such strength from someone who's barely more than a child. She did the pure opposite to me. Instead of running and fleeing at the first sign of trouble, she stuck it out, got a job and cracked on with it.

The waiter brings our change, buying me about ten seconds to compose myself.

Jayden wasn't going to marry Lula after all. It wasn't what it seemed. I should have known better. I should have trusted him. The pink bedroom flashes to the forefront of my mind. Of course, he wasn't sleeping with her. She had her own room.

He still lied to my face, though.

I opened up to him. Let him see my darkest truths, and yet he still couldn't confide in me about the darkest days of his own life.

Sasha stares at me for a long beat, her gaze narrowing. I can almost see the cogs whirring. 'Oh my god, I don't believe it, but it makes perfect sense! Pedro is Jayden, isn't he?'

My hands fall into my face in shame.

'No. Fucking. Way.' Victoria slams her fist on the table.

'Language,' Sasha and I warn in unison.

Sasha stares at me open-mouthed. 'I don't believe it.' Her mouth closes, then parts again. 'You hate him. He thinks you've got a silver spoon stuck up your ass.'

I sigh. 'Believe me, he removed that a long time ago.' Sasha's eyes dart from mine to Victoria's, who shrugs, then back again.

Victoria rubs her hands together in glee. 'Now, I'd love to hear more about that.'

'Oh god, it's such a mess.' My fingers massage my temples.

'Why is it such a mess?'

'Even if he isn't engaged, he lied to me. I trusted him with the ugliest parts of myself and he couldn't trust me to accept his.'

Sasha tuts and waves a hand in front of her face. 'As if he was going to tell you he was engaged to somebody else. I mean, presumably the two of you thought you'd shag and get whatever weird tension thrums between you out of your systems... I guess neither of you dreamed there might actually be something between you.'

'Careful, sis, you're sounding like you're on his side.'

My phone lights up again. Jayden.

'Take it, please,' Sasha says. 'Put us all out of our misery. I bet he's distraught over in LA. Do you know the shit he's been dealing with on top of this Lula business? Someone's been trying to take him down. That business with Mam and Dad being rehashed. It wasn't to hurt Ryan's image, it was to damage Jayden.'

I reject the call, still far from ready to talk. 'What? Why wouldn't he tell me?'

'Because believe it or not, the man's determined to be a goddamn hero in everyone's eyes. He's spent his life looking out for other people, starting with Ryan when he was only three years old and their mother left them.'

I slump back in my chair, taking it all in. Remembering the way he picked up on every single shift in my mood, determined to support me, to lift me, never once complaining about his own troubles, of which it turns out, there were plenty.

Sasha continues, on a roll now. 'Almost every artist Jayden represents has come from nothing. Do you know how many lives he's changed?'

I think back to Aurelia and the bond they clearly share. The fog is slowly lifting from before my eyes.

'When Ryan and Jayden were on the streets, Lula got in with a bad crowd. She'd go days without checking in with the rest of them. Smoking weed and acting out like teenagers do, but unfortunately it was far from the safety of someone's garage or bedroom. Sofia, her older sister, was sick, really sick, with a rare genetic illness that meant her chances of surviving past twenty-five were slim, and that was without medical care. All Sofia wanted in life was for Lula to have a chance. She got her out of Mexico, away from the dangers of her hometown, but she worried she'd brought her somewhere worse, knowing she didn't have much time left to drag them out of the gutter.

'Jayden made a promise to Sofia that he would find her and help her. They were close. Really close. When Ryan was picked up by Diamond Records, the boys searched for the girls for years. It wasn't until recently they finally found Lula.

'She was about to be deported. Jayden made her a promise, and he was determined to make good on it, even if it meant sacrificing his own happiness. Jayden has a hero complex. It's like he's determined to be the polar opposite of his unreliable parents. But the funny thing is, the only person who truly needs saving is himself.'

Wow.

Shock seeps into my bones.

'How did I not know any of this?' I shake my head in utter amazement.

'You weren't here,' Victoria says in a sad tone. 'Ryan's only just started opening up to all of us in the last couple of months.'

'Believe me, I gave Ryan a tough time for leaving me like he did all those years ago. Things were rough after Mam and Dad died, as you know. But the boys were fighting battles of their own. Battles we'll probably never understand. What happened that night, when Mam and Dad died, changed all of our lives, in so many ways. It took me a while to see it, but Jayden's a good man. One of the best. I'm sorry he hurt you, but genuinely, it wouldn't have been intentional.'

I swallow the lump in my throat. So much information. It's hard to process all of it at once.

'So, he's not engaged?' But he still lied. I can't shake it.

'No. Lula has been issued with a student visa today. It will allow her to stay in the country for up to four years, which gives them time to work out something more permanent.'

Jayden's name lights up my phone screen again.

'If you don't answer that now, I will. After all, we're practically family,' Sasha says.

My thumb hovers over the green button as I deliberate. Victoria's thumb lands squarely on top of mine, forcing it to tap the screen.

My neck cranes to glare at her, but she shrugs.

Gingerly, I lift the phone to my ear. 'Hello?'

'Oh, Chloe, thank god. Are you ok?'

The man has literally been through hell and back according to Sasha, and *he's* asking if *I'm* ok.

'I think we need to talk,' I say.

'Finally. But first, I need to tell you something. Chloe Sexton... I love you. I love you so much. If we can get through this, I swear to god I'll never omit to tell you a single thing ever again. The good, the bad or the shameful.'

I swallow the lump in my throat. Old habits die hard. The

words won't come. Especially not with my sisters' eagle eyes glaring at me from across the table.

'Where are you?'

'LA. I can't get a flight until tomorrow.'

I disconnect the call, pushing my chair back with my bum.

'Where are you going?' Sasha and Victoria speak in unison.

'I'm going to do what I should have done last week.'

Typical that the only flight to Scotland today left half an hour ago. Tempting as it is to hire a private jet, I give Chloe the day to reflect, well night, as it is in the UK right now.

Clearly, Sasha told her the truth of the situation. Something I could kick myself a hundred times for not doing myself.

I expected her to open up to me, but I just couldn't do the same.

To try to clear my head, I hit my home gym hard, but no amount of physical pain can work off my internal agony.

Sara makes me one of her famous steak sandwiches, but I can't stomach it, not knowing if Chloe can forgive me. Or if I can ever forgive myself for being so stupid. For risking everything we had, all because I was so determined to be a hero.

Lula's gone to visit two colleges today and meet with the deans. At least that's something. Sofia would be happy, of that I'm sure. I've fulfilled my promise to her, even if it's cost me my own happiness.

I pack a bag, just to pass the time. My Samsonite's got more action than me this year and that's saying something, given it's the same summer I embarked on the most fabulous fling of my life.

As day turns to night, Kim leaves the office in my house. She's been fending off all my calls and emails today.

'TMZ printed an apology for wrongly announcing your engagement, and Mia and Naomi both called to say someone had anonymously deposited a million dollars into each of their bank accounts. Not sure they'll get an apology though...'

'It's something, I suppose. Any word on that snake, Colton?'

'His car's parked at the Johnsons. No surprises there. Do you want to sue him? He broke his NDA, violated your privacy and almost ruined the girls.'

'I think it would be irresponsible not to, or else what's to deter him from doing it again?'

'I'll get on to the legal team first thing in the morning.' She pauses, shooting a sympathetic look my way. 'Want to go for a beer? Me and Gareth are heading for one, anyway.'

I glance up from the couch. 'No thanks, Kim.'

'Wallowing won't help, you know.' She shakes her blonde hair gently.

'I don't know what to do with myself. I've never been in love before, let alone lost it.'

Kim pads across the marble floor to perch on the couch next to me. 'I might not be the best person to give advice considering my track record, but I think the general rule is, when you find it, you fight for it.'

'I just never imagined feeling this way. Especially about her. Everything's changing and I don't know if I'm coming or going. I guess I'll just have to wait and see what tomorrow brings.'

'It's all you can do.' She pats my hand before standing again. 'All jokes aside, Jayden, she'd be lucky to have you. You're a good man.'

She slips out of the front door, leaving me to wallow in misery on the couch.

Just after eleven, the buzzer sounds from the front gate. I thought Lula was staying at Diego's tonight. If it's Kim and Gareth trying to cheer me up, they're wasting their time.

The only person I want to see is five thousand miles away.

I pad across the open plan space towards the front door. The camera shows it's a taxi. I press the intercom, wondering if Lula's been drinking.

'Hello?'

'Jayden, it's me.' Chloe's breathy tone sings across the intercom, sweeter than the best audition I've ever heard.

'Chloe?' I can't believe it.

I push the button to open the gate and the yellow cab crunches up the driveway at what seems like an agonisingly slow pace.

She hops out, clutching a small case, before handing the driver some cash. Finally, she turns her attention to me. Her glossy chestnut hair is loose across her face. Tired eyes dart over me, drinking me in.

'What are you doing here?' My palms itch to touch her but I don't, not until I'm sure it's what she wants because for the first time in forever I can't read her. She's different tonight. Instead of the high walls and the cool confidence, this Chloe looks drained. Broken. I hate that I've done that to her.

'I told you we need to talk.' She opens her arms to me, beckoning me into them. 'I have a few things I need to say to you. Things I should have said earlier.'

'Can I please say something first? I want to explain. I need you to understand.' I run a hand over my chin.

Chloe nods, following me as I drag her small case into the hall.

'There are things about my past I never told you. I was ashamed, although there's nothing shameful about being homeless. Truthfully, it made us who we are, so even though it was rough, it made me ruthless, which is what makes me good at my job. Without those experiences, I might not have had what it takes.'

She nods as if she's finally reached the same conclusion with her own circumstances.

'When we got to the States, Dad left us with his sister. She had no more interest in us than he did. We hitched across the country to LA. Ryan was determined he was going to make it to the big time. Apart from wanting to provide for us, he wanted to make himself worthy of Sasha after running out on her. It was rough. The horrors we saw and endured...'

Chloe squeezes my hand but doesn't interrupt.

'Sofia was the first friend Ryan and I made on the streets of LA. Barely more than kids. We had no idea how to survive. If it wasn't for Sofia's streetwise savvy, we mightn't have made it past the first night.' A shudder rips over my spine.

'She knew which corners were safe. Which to avoid. The soup kitchens that were legit and the ones fronting as cover for scum to exploit the vulnerable.

'Then one day Richard Lambert saw Ryan busking on the street and offered him a contract with Diamond Records. I had nothing to bring to the table. Nothing except my brother's unwavering loyalty, and a drive to succeed that was stronger than steel. Ryan refused to take the deal unless I represented him. Both of us had grown so distrustful after everything.

'Richard and his scout wanted him so badly, they accepted. While Ryan got an education in being a star, I gained one in spotting them.

'When I went back to get Sofia and Lula, they were gone, nowhere to be found. We were only getting started. I didn't have the resources to hunt them down. No matter how many times I cruised the streets we used to sleep on, I couldn't find them.

'Over time, my searches got less frequent. Ryan was going on tour and I was going with him. Taking on other artists. Eventually replacing the scout that brought Richard to us.

'I never forgot Sofia and Lula, but I am ashamed to say I didn't look nearly as hard for them as I should have, eventually passing the buck to Declan, never expecting to actually find them.

'That is my shame. I spent years thinking if I'd have found them earlier, maybe I could have got Sofia the medical attention she needed. Then finally, somehow, I realised what I told you the other day. When your time's up, it's up. Sofia's condition meant she was never going to live a long life. I just wish she could have seen it out in comfort.'

Chloe's eyes well with tears that spill over onto her unusually pale cheeks. 'I'm so sorry, Jayden, for all you went through. Our parents. What happened. It affected all of us more than I ever realised.'

'It did. But we're here to tell the tale at least.' I yank her into me, crushing her against my chest, revelling in the way she nestles against me. Inhaling the scent of her shampoo. Emotion surges through every vein and artery.

If anyone could see me now, they wouldn't believe it. But I'm done with anyone else who's not here. With anyone who's not us. I've paid my debts. I'm done trying to save the world. The only thing I need to salvage is us. I'm willing to take a risk on getting hurt, on being left, or having her taken, because loving her as much as I do, I can't do anything else.

Liquid topaz eyes gaze up at me. She bites her lower lip awkwardly in the way I've grown to love.

'Jayden, I love you.'

My heart swells, tripling in size. A lump lodges in my throat.

'I couldn't say it before, but I felt it. I've known since the last time I stood in this kitchen. From the first time I slept in your bed. Maybe even before that, but that was the first time I admitted it to myself. Admitting love is like pointing out a weak spot to poke or hurt, but trusting the other person not to do precisely that. I'm sorry it took me so long to trust you.

'I hate you didn't tell me about Lula. I hate you couldn't open up to me when I opened up to you, but I get it more than you'll ever know.'

I shake my head. 'I was trying to do right by everyone, when I should have been doing right by you and me first.'

Chloe nods, her full lips millimetres from mine. 'We need to work through this.' Her hand trails across her stomach and she stares at me for a beat. 'Because all joking aside, we're about to become a family.'

My eyes feel like they're going to pop out of my head.

'We're about to be a family...? Like a *family* family?' I place my hand over hers, the two of us clutching her stomach.

'How? I mean... are you sure?'

'Surer than I've ever been of anything in my life. I didn't mean to come and drop this on you, but if we're being open and honest about everything, it's only fair I tell you now. I love you. I love the baby you put in me more than anything else in the world, and I want us to be a family. I know it's a lot to take in. You didn't want a 'mini-me'. Her eyes drop to the floor. 'And if you don't want to be a part of our lives, I fully respect your wishes. Neither of us planned this. It's a tremendous shock for both of us.'

'Princess, it's a shock alright, but the best damn shock in the universe. I didn't want a mini version of me back then, but I'd move heaven and earth to have a mini version of the man you helped mould me into.' I scoop her up into my arms and her legs wrap around my waist.

'We both grew. Changed for each other.' Tears well in her eyes. 'For the better.'

Our lips meet. Her velvet tongue slides against mine and I swing her round my kitchen in a gleeful twirl.

'Careful, I'm already nauseous,' she warns.

I place her down gently, cradling her in my arms. 'Move in with me.'

Earnest eyes gaze up to meet mine, and the tiny nod of her head causes the heart I didn't realise I owned to swell like a balloon in my chest.

EPILOGUE

Chloe

London

Lush, thick crimson carpet lines the magnificent steps of the Royal Albert Hall. I hang on to Jayden's arm, climbing tentatively upwards. Flashing cameras blind us from every direction.

The paparazzi are out in full force. For once, Jayden isn't hiding from them. In fact, he's offering his trademark smirk while cradling me against the strong sculpted planes of his body. He's making a statement. One that I love. We're together.

Sporting a classic black tuxedo, he's obscenely striking. My stomach flips and my hearts soars. Everything is falling into place. Everything I never knew I wanted.

How is he mine?

His head dips in my direction, huge twinkling graphite eyes seek my own. 'Are you okay, Princess?'

I nod, overwhelmed at not only the commotion of attending my first red carpet event instead of organising it, but at the magnitude of feelings I have for the man beside me.

Precariously negotiating my Walter Steiger peep toes, one foot in front of the other, I hang onto my boyfriend for dear life.

Boyfriend. The moniker doesn't do justice to what Jayden is to me, but for now, it'll do. God forbid we steal Sasha and Ryan's thunder by eloping like Jayden suggested. Besides, just because I'm pregnant, I'm in no rush to get married. Liberated is still my middle name, even though pretty much everything else has changed.

Victoria's a couple of steps behind us, flanked by Archie, Ryan's security guard. Dressed in one of Sasha's stunning Evangeline Araceli dresses, she looks every bit the adult tonight.

Ruby and Levi follow closely behind, with Kim and Gareth at their heels. The entire gang's here for Ryan's big finale. A shiver of excitement ripples across my spine. I hope I've done them all justice.

The Royal Albert Hall exudes a class that no other venue can touch. It was the perfect choice for the final *final* farewell, and for the after-party to trump all after-parties. Although the only people I'm trying to impress tonight are my family. I want this to be the best night for them, not because it's going to drum up more clients. I have more clients than I can manage. Although that doesn't mean I'll consider a merger with Ethan Harte, who's apparently called into my office twice in my absence, asking Izzy if he can 'help out.'

He'll be lucky if he's not 'helped out' a different way because if Jayden gets wind of it, he's likely to throttle him.

Izzy doesn't know it yet, but she's about to get a huge promotion, along with four others from the original Liberty Events' office. She practically organised the Edinburgh concert herself. I was in no shape to do anything. She's proven herself time and time again. Proven to me I'm safe handing over control.

For obvious reasons, my priorities have dramatically changed.

While I'm excited about the new branches, I'll be taking a step back from now on. I don't want to go global on a personal level. I never did, really. What I wanted was to fill the global sized crater in my chest and I've succeeded, with the help of my family.

My eyes slant to Jayden. He replaced the elastic band on my wrist with a diamond encrusted platinum bracelet. Even though I insisted we wait, he's determined to get me to wear his diamonds.

The tour is almost over, and I got more from it than I ever dreamed of, just not in the way I imagined. My hand instinctively roams over the small swell of my stomach. I bite back my smile.

I haven't yet told my sisters, not quite at the twelve-week mark yet. It's torture keeping it from them. The urge to blurt it out crests over me ten times every day.

When we finally reach the top step, I breathe a sigh of relief. I made it without falling. Jayden's lips press against my forehead as he guides me through the colossal doorway to take our seats on the front row.

'How long until he comes on?' Victoria demands from my left. She should know the drill. It was only a couple of weeks ago she watched Ryan perform in Edinburgh. Jayden and I missed the flight he originally booked because we were so engrossed in making up. We only made the concert by the skin of our teeth.

'It'll be awhile yet. Don't worry, someone will be around with champagne in a minute or two.'

I lean into Jayden's ear, scanning the lavish décor. 'I like the red.'

'Are you finally thinking about adding some colour to your villa?' His full lips curl into his signature smirk.

'No, I'm thinking about adding it to yours.' My elbow nudges his torso, bouncing from it. 'All those dark greens and greys are so masculine.'

His hot breath brushes my ear. 'Sweetheart, you can do whatever you like to it, as long as you promise to live in it with me forever.'

Laying roots is something I'm finally open to. Big fat solid ones that reach infinitely into the ground. Not just for me, but for our child. For the first time in forever, it doesn't feel daunting. It feels right.

'Ugh. Will you two get a room? You're as bad as the other two.' Victoria rolls her eyes, but her twinkling irises express a genuine happiness for us.

White-gloved waiters transport tray-upon-tray of bubbling crystal flutes as the hall fills behind us. I shake my head to decline, but Victoria swiftly kicks my ankle, shooting me a look which compels me to take one.

'If you don't want it, I'll have it.' It's barely in my hand before it's in hers. 'What's up with you, anyway?' She gazes quizzically at me for a beat, looking so different without the thick-rimmed glasses. Contact lenses showcase her sparkling hazel eyes.

'Nothing's up with me. I'm working, that's all.'

'Ha. You could have fooled me.'

She jokes, but it's true. Backstage, caterers prepare the most extravagant canapés I could source. In place of a chocolate fountain, I arranged a Dom Perignon waterfall. Jayden persuaded the UK's top DJ to perform after Ryan finishes. The row-upon-row of circular seats are set to be transformed into a rotating dancefloor, one that I'll be avoiding. I'm barely over the dreaded morning sickness which I've been battling to hide for the last few weeks.

Under the ebony silk of my full-length dress, my stomach

is already slightly swollen. I love it. I love the new life blooming inside me.

When Ryan finally makes his appearance, Victoria's on her third drink. She shrieks the words along with him. With her head thrown back and laughter in her eyes, she gives me the warm and fuzzies.

Everything is working out the way it's meant to be. I don't need a plan. I don't need to micro-manage every detail. I just need to be me.

I'm finally realising that I am enough. I don't need to make up for the past or forge a successful business to prove I'm worthy of a place on this earth.

The music flows through me as I rest my cheek on Jayden's shoulder, taking in the production.

The stage looks phenomenal. Thousands of shiny records make a thirty-foot Big Ben. A water feature flowing with champagne mimics the river Thames.

When Robbie Williams sneaks out on stage as Ryan's special guest, the crowd goes absolutely wild, Victoria and Archie included. Although he's assigned to Victoria to protect her, from the way his eyes skim over her, it seems more like a pleasure than work.

Jayden pulls me to my feet. 'Where are we going?'

'You'll see.'

Weaving and ducking through security, Jayden leads me backstage.

Ruby shoots us a knowing wink and nudges Levi. This is their fourth date in as many weeks. Ruby has a feeling about this one, apparently.

They both step aside to let us pass.

Taking my hand, Jayden leads me through security to behind the stage. 'There's someone I want you to meet.' Earnest eyes capture mine and my stomach flips.

I follow him trustingly. I'd follow him anywhere now. To

the side of the stage, hovering by a thick crimson curtain, stands a young couple with their backs to us. She's wearing a teal dress. Her hair is almost jet black, skimming the side of her tiny waist. He's almost a whole foot taller than her. His arm rests protectively across her shoulders.

Ryan's duet ends and the applause from the crowd is deafening. The couple turn to each other and notice us behind them.

'Jayden,' the woman says. I recognise her instantly.

'Lula, this is Chloe. Chloe, this is Lula.'

Huge chocolate eyes light and widen and she throws her arms around me in an affectionate embrace. My heart swells.

'It's so lovely to finally meet you,' she gushes, tugging her companion's arm. 'This is Diego, my errr...' She glances down to her left hand where a simple but stunning solitaire sits, nestled on her fourth finger. 'My fiancé.'

Diego gazes at her proudly while Jayden slaps his back and congratulates him.

Lula takes my hands and earnest eyes bore into mine. 'I'm so sorry for the confusion, for the heartache I caused. I never meant to...'

I raise my hands, halting her before she can say another word. 'Do not be sorry. I'm so glad Jayden found you, and I'm so glad he could help. And I'm sure your sister is up there somewhere...' I swallow the tsunami of emotion swirling inside me, these pregnancy hormones no joke, '...with my mother and father looking down on us all tonight.'

Her sweet perfume wafts against my sensitive nose as she envelops me again. I can't even imagine what kind of life she's had, but as hers has entwined with ours, I've been able to see my own truths that bit more clearly.

We can't control everything. So why waste the time and energy trying?

'Will you come to us for dinner in a couple of weeks?' My

eyes dart between her and Diego as he slides an arm around her again, seemingly unable to leave her alone.

'That would be so lovely, thank you. Something to look forward to when I finally finish unpacking my stuff at Diego's.'

'We'll get something in the diary soon,' I promise as Jayden nudges me forwards, closer to the edge of the stage.

'Are you cooking?' Thick dark eyebrows rise in surprise.

'Yes.' My tone's indignant.

'It's just that Naveesha said...' He bites his lip, not quick enough to stop it curling to the side.

'Never mind Naveesha. She'll be busy enough when this baby comes.' Naveesha has agreed to come to the States and be our nanny. She was so excited, she bawled her eyes out for two hours straight. She thinks she's lucky to be asked. Truthfully, we're lucky to have her. Apart from the fact I really do burn everything, she's the only family I've had nearby the last few years. I wouldn't part with her for love nor money.

'Come on, we'll sneak back out the side exit. The atmosphere from the crowd is electric as they scream and chant, demanding one more song.

As we tiptoe behind the stage props, I can't help but stop to admire them up close. The team has done a stellar job.

The hall crashes into darkness, shocking the audience into silence. It's all part of the final encore.

Jayden grabs my waist, twirling me in the blackness, pouncing on me, his lips feverishly scorching mine in a kiss that's deep enough to drown in. 'Sex on stage? One for the bucket list?' I hear his grin, even if I can't see it.

'You never did tell me the fantasy you had on the beach that time in Dubai. You said it was too much for either of us.'

I remember it like it was yesterday. It seemed so far out of reach at the time, but now, I'm hopeful we can pull it off sooner rather than later.

'Tell me,' he urges, peppering kisses across my neck.

'I was fantasising about our wedding night, wondering what it would be like...' I whisper, a coyness creeping into my tone.

'I promised to tick off every one of your fantasies... I promise I won't make you wait too long for that one.'

Wrapping my hands around the back of his neck, I tug him into me. The audience is getting restless.

'Who knocked the power off?' a voice shouts.

'Who's in control here?' another says.

I can barely hear them, drowning in Jayden's intoxicating kiss.

Bright floodlights flash on and the stage spins ready for the final song, but instead of Ryan being at the epicentre, Jayden and I have somehow ended up centre stage, showcasing a moment ten shades too steamy for a Hallmark movie.

Ryan's laughter echoes over the microphone, reverberating around the grand hall. When he applauds us, so does the audience.

With every spotlight in the place beaming down on us, my cheeks blush scarlet.

I'm not embarrassed, though. Not of him. Not even of myself. I'm thrilled. Flushed with the wonder of love. With an apologetic wave, Jayden leads me off the stage, back to our family. The hole in my chest has well and truly healed. I can't wait to see what our next chapter brings.

THE END

Ready for more from the Sexton Sisters? Turn over for Victoria's story, My Big Fat Fabulous First Love.

MY BIG FAT FABULOUS FIRST LOVE BLURB

Victoria and Archie both have a to-do list, but, technically, they shouldn't feature on each other's.

VICTORIA- To Do:

1.   Finish placement on Accident & Emergency Ward without any further complaints re. my bedside manner. (In my defence, that patient definitely didn't need mouth-to-mouth. Sleaze!)

2.   Invite chic new neighbours over for a house party – nobody likes a Sandra Serious -med student or not!

3.   Get laid – ASAP. It's been a while.

4.   Lose the bodyguard my sisters assigned to babysit me, so I can work on point 3.

Note to self: Stop fantasising about aforementioned bodyguard, especially when he struts around half naked most of the time. I'm a professional FFS! Almost, anyway...

ARCHIE- To Do:

1.   Keep Victoria Sexton out of danger *at all costs*.

2.   Keep Victoria Sexton out of trouble *at all costs*.

3.   Stop Victoria Sexton from inviting half the city into her new home for unruly house parties *at all costs*.

4.   Stop Victoria Sexton from shagging the campus creep *at all costs*.

Note to self: Stop fantasising about Victoria Sexton naked *at all costs*. I'm supposed to be watching her back, not imagining her on it.

Not unless I want to lose my job, the first house I ever truly felt at home in, and my life as I know it... Nothing's worth that. Is it?

Click here to learn more... https://mybook.to/MyBigFatFabulousFirstLove

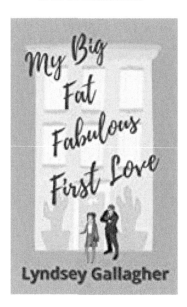

ACKNOWLEDGMENTS

Just like it takes a village to raise a child, it takes something similar to write a book! Without the support of some amazing authors, hours of FaceTime calls with friends I've never met in person (yet!) and a brilliant new editor, this book wouldn't be what it is today, so thank you. You know who you are.

And to you, **Dear Reader**, thank you for choosing My Big Fat Fabulous Fling when there are so many amazing romances on the market! I hope you enjoyed Chloe and Jayden's story as much as I enjoyed writing it. If you did, please consider leaving a quick review on Amazon or Goodreads, they make a huge difference to new authors!

Lastly, to my husband, THANK YOU! For your never ending support and encouragement. For the 3am chats. For loving me on the days I find it hard to love myself. If there's a heaven, you're definitely going!

ALSO BY LYNDSEY GALLAGHER

MY BIG FAT FABULOUS CHRISTMAS

Ten years ago, I, **Sasha Sexton**, inherited our family castle and sole care of my youngest sister. More Cinderella, than Sleeping Beauty, at the mere age of twenty-eight I have a teenager to raise and a hotel to run. If the hotel is to survive past Christmas, I need a lottery win, a miracle, or Prince Charming himself to sweep in with a humongous... wad of cash.

When my super successful middle sister announces she's coming home for the holiday season, I'm determined to put my problems aside and make this the most fabulous Christmas ever. Especially as it might just be the last one in our family home.

I didn't factor in the return of my first love, **Ryan Cooper**. Back then he was the boy next door. Now, he's a world famous singer/song writer. We were supposed to go the States together. He left without me. Now he's back. Rumour is he has writers block. Apparently this is a last-ditch attempt to find inspiration before his record label pulls the plug permanently.

And guess where he wants to stay? You have it in one- the most inspiring castle hotel in Dublin's fair city.

Every woman in the city wants to pull this Hollywood Christmas cracker. Except me. I'm going to avoid him at all costs.

Easier said than done when he's parading around under my roof, with enough heat exuding from his molten eyes to melt every square inch of snow from the peaks of the Dublin mountains...

My Big Fat Fabulous Christmas is a steamy, love conquers all, stand alone romcom, with no cliffhanger- and a guaranteed happy ever after. Click here to learn more...

https://mybook.to/MyBigFatFabulousChristmas

My Big Fat Fabulous Christmas

The coldest holiday of the year
just got blisteringly hot...

Lyndsey Gallagher

THE PROFESSIONAL PLAYERS SERIES

Five Steamy Contemporary Stand Alone Sports Romance Novels. HEA guaranteed. Perfect for fans of Amy Daws, Meghan Quinn and Lucy Score.

BOOK 1: LOVE & OTHER MUSHY STUFF

One sassy radio agony aunt, one swoon-worthy rugby player, and one unlikely but alluring fake dating deal. Abby doesn't need or want a man, except to feature on her show and up her ratings. Callum's not looking for 'the one' merely 'the next one,' but he gets drawn into a bet to date the same woman long enough to bring to his best friends wedding.

Will Abby finally take her own romantic advice? Or will Callum nail his most elusive touchdown yet?

BOOK 2: LOVE & OTHER GAMES

Successful beauty business queen, Emma refuses to think about the rugby player who ghosted her after the best night of her life-much! Exactly one year later he shows up again. His pert backside hogs the seat next to hers on route to a mutual friend's beach wedding. Crossed wires at the hotel result in them reluctantly agreeing to share the honeymoon suite. Will Eddie's practiced tactics win out? Or will Emma stick to her game plan? Is there something else they both want more than each other?

BOOK 3: LOVE & OTHER LIES

Kerry's been sacked from her office job and evicted in the same week and she desperately needs to find a replacement for both, especially because her boyfriends about to be discharged from the military– a fact which she should be delighted about but is frankly terrifying.

Single dad, Nathan, is a successful rugby player at the pinnacle of his career. When he's left sole care of his daughter for the summer he realises he's going to need a nanny. A chance phone call results in Kerry accepting Nathan's job offer, without realising he's the only guy she kissed when her and her boyfriend were on a break.

Will Kerry let her past ruin her future? Or can Nathan convince her he's playing for keeps?

BOOK 4: LOVE & OTHER FORBIDDEN THINGS

When Amy lands her dream job as physiotherapist for the rugby team, she's forced to face the blistering growing chemistry with player number six, Ollie Quinn. Not only is he her patient, therefore utterly forbidden, he's also her brother's best friend. Injuries on the pitch seem minimal to what Eddie might do if he discovers their dalliances.

Is it simply the temptation of tasting the forbidden fruit? Or will forbidden turn into forever?

BOOK 5: LOVE & OTHER VOWS

Recently retired captain of the rugby team, Marcus is struggling to adjust to life away from the club. When his wife of ten years is paired up with his biggest sporting rival on the countries sexiest dance show, he realises he stands to lose a lot more than just his career. Marcus must act if he wants to save their relationship. They vowed to stay together in sickness and health but what about fame and wealth?

Click here to learn more....

https://mybook.to/ProfessionalPlayersSeries

THE SEVEN YEAR ITCH

Twenty-seven-year-old **Lucy O'Connor** has been asked to be her future sister-in-law's bridesmaid despite the fact they don't see eye to eye. The last thing she expected was to fall in love with a complete stranger at the hen weekend. Which wouldn't be a problem, apart from the teeny tiny fact that she's already married to somebody else...

Is it a case of the **Seven-Year-Itch**? Or could it be the real deal?

Lucy needs to decide if she's going to leave the security of her stale marriage in order to find out if the grass is indeed greener on the other side, or whether it's worth having one more go at watering her own garden.

Could this party-loving, city girl really leave the country she loves for a farmer from the west of Ireland?

Is there such a thing as fate?

What about karma?

Is John Kelly all that he seems?

★★★★★ **Raw, relatable and hilarious**

★★★★★ **You'll be hooked from the first page**

★★★★★ **A modern day love story**

★★★★★ *Love can be insane, gut-wrenching, and dizzying*

Lyndsey Gallagher captures the insane, gut-wrenching, dizzying first flush of love when all you can do is think about that other person and can focus on nothing else. Beautifully captured and expertly told. It's also a story of taking risks and proof that if you follow your heart, life usually turns out for the best. Highly Recommend.

Click here to learn more... https://mybook.to/
The_Seven_Year_Itch

ABOUT THE AUTHOR

Lyndsey Gallagher writes spicy romance stories featuring swoon-worthy heroes, sassy heroines and copious amounts of champagne. Her books are filled with heat, heart and guaranteed happy ever afters.

Lyndsey lives in the west of Ireland with her two children, two fur babies, and her endlessly patient husband. When she's not writing, Lyndsey loves long walks, deep talks and more chocolate than is healthy.

For more info, bonus epilogues and freebies sign up to www.lyndseygallagherauthor.com

Printed in Great Britain
by Amazon